UNEARTHED

The past never stays buried...

KATIE S SCOFIELD

Purple Giraffe Print LLC,
Pittsburgh PA

Cover Design by Katie S. Scofield

First Printing, 2026

E Book ISBN: 979-8-950236-00-6

Paperback ISBN: 979-8-950236-01-3

Library of Congress Control Number: 2026912135

Published by Purple Giraffe Print LLC

City of Publication:

Pittsburgh, Pennsylvania, United States of America

This is a work of fiction. Names, characters, businesses, places, events, locales, and incidents are either the products of the author's imagination or used in a fictitious manner. Any resemblance to actual persons, living or dead, or actual events is purely coincidental

Author's Note

Dear reader,

Thank you for taking a chance on my debut novel. I hope that you enjoy it. This is not the story I had planned to tell for my first foray into self-publishing. I had a work in progress that was pretty far along when, unfortunately, my mother passed away. I could not find it in myself to continue that project during that time. For months, I did not pick up a pen but then came this story. Writing this has allowed me the escape I needed to pull myself out of a dark place. I often deal with hard topics through humor, and you will see my characters do the same.

The main characters, Anna and Bobby, both deal with various forms of PTSD and are vocal about their need for therapy and support. If you find yourself in a similar predicament and do not have a support system in place, please know that there are resources out there for you and that you are not alone. If you're in the United States, I have listed some of those resources below. Remember, caring about your mental health is sexy!

Call 988 if you or someone you love need to speak to a trained crisis counselor who can help with mental health related distress. You can also text 988 or chat online with Suicide and Crisis Life Line.

(https://988lifeline.org)

If you are a veteran, or are concerned about one, call 988, then press 1 to speak with a responder qualified to support veterans. You can also text 838255 or chat online with the Veterans Crisis Line.

(https://www.veteranscrisisline.net)

xoxo,

Katie

To my mother, I wish that you were here to see this in print.
And to anyone that needs to hear it:
"Grief and loss have no concept of time."

Content Warning

This work contains adult themes not to be consumed by minors under the age of 18. Potential triggers included but are not limited to:

- Discovering human remains
- Open police investigation
- Mentions of parental death (in the past)
- Mentions of child abuse and neglect (in the past)
- Mentions of abandonment
- Dealing with a parent's alcoholism
- Mentions of characters with PTSD & anxiety
- Talks of therapy
- Violence (not between the main love interests)
- On-page explicit intimate scenes

Prologue

ANNASTASIA

(12 Years ago)

Counting the tiles of the drop ceiling, *the third one from the window is cracked,* I feel the ridges from the engravings of my locket press into my skin, clutched in the vice grip of my palm. I inhale, noting the citrus scent of the freshly mopped hallway floor wafting through my open door. Holding that breath, I focus on the din of voices carrying down the corridor. I exhale, frustrated as I try and fail to pick out a taste to finish this grounding exercise that my therapist urged me to try. It is meant to stave off the growing panic that has become my new normal.

"Adkins, mail," Maude, the Direct Care Staffer on duty, calls as she raps three times on my doorframe. Giving up on the exercise, I rise, a new anxiety washing over my body, leaving chills in its wake. Only two people write to me here; the fact that Caroline's last correspondence lies face open on my desk, just received yesterday, tells me who this letter is from. The thought makes my heart ache.

I hold out my hand, nodding in thanks as she places the envelope in my open palm, her eyes gentling in sympathy. "Still no words, Anna?" I shake my head in response. She places a comforting hand on my shoulder. "It will come in time, Anna. I am confident your voice will find you." I wish I shared her confidence.

I haven't spoken since my father died. I keep a notebook, and they have taught me some basic signs to communicate, but every time I open my mouth to talk, my throat runs dry, and I break out in a cold sweat. It is frustrating, because besides my therapist, who now knows better, people mistake it for a symptom of grief. I don't correct them, but I have not spent a single moment grieving that man. It is illogical, I know that, but it feels like he somehow stole my voice to keep his secrets even from beyond the grave.

I gesture inside my room. Maude, taking the hint, responds, "Alright, Anna, I'll give you some privacy. Don't forget you have a group session in half an hour." I give her a thumbs up to relay my understanding and close the door as she turns down the hall to deliver the rest of the mail.

My palms are sweating as I sit down on my bed. I shouldn't torture myself. I should leave it unopened, throw the letter away, and lock it away in the past. It would be easier to move on that way, but I am desperate to cling to any part of the boy I have spent most of my life half in love with that I can. Maybe I am grieving, but instead of the loss of my father being the center of the storm, it is this. The loss of the potential we had; the loss of what could have been. The loss of Bobby Payne, now that is something worth grieving over. Even if the boy himself is stubborn—holding on to threads so bare, they are bound to snap.

I bring the envelope to my nose, closing my eyes on the inhale, hoping to catch the slightest scent of the cedar and sandalwood cologne he had taken to wearing this past year. I am unfortunately left unsatisfied. *What*

I wouldn't give to be able to inhale his scent. Disappointed, I open the envelope, unfolding the paper inside. I blink back tears—they always come when seeing the sprawling scratch of his familiar handwriting—and I take a breath to fortify myself. Scanning the pages, I slide my pendant on its chain. The rhythmic rasp as it travels over each link grounds me in this room painted in soft blues meant to induce calm, but often missing its mark.

Anna,

I never know how to start these things, though maybe it would be easier if you answered one of them so that I would have an example. Graduation is Friday, you probably know that. It is going to be weird not having you there in the stands to look for. I'll probably still look for you. I am always looking for you.

I am taking an early track and going to boot camp in two weeks. My recruiter said most guys wait 'til the end of summer, give them time to say their goodbyes. I can't stand the thought of hanging around this town if you aren't here, so I will save myself the loneliness.

Loneliness is a concept I never understood in this house full of brothers, but these past eight months, I have become familiar with the idea. God Anna, do you have any idea how much I miss you? I haven't even finished that silly list, because without you, what's the point?

More than anything else, I miss my best friend. I miss the stars reflected in your eyes when you point out the constellations, telling me their stories. You would get so excited. I saw Cygnus last night. I still don't really see how it is a swan, but that's what you told me, so I'll take your word for it. Did you see it? Do they let you out to watch the stars? I hope they do. It makes me feel better thinking we are looking at the same sky.

I wish you'd write me back. I don't even know if you are getting these. I would think that maybe it is against the rules to respond, if it weren't for Caroline getting your letters back to her sometimes. I think she feels bad for me. She stopped telling me when you write. Is it what I said that night? I shouldn't have said it. I wasn't thinking. I was hopped up on adrenaline, and it just came out. I won't lie to you and say I didn't mean it. In the moment I did. But regardless of the circumstances, that's your father, and you were in shock... it was an awful thing to let slip.

If that's not it, you gotta let me know what happened, Anna. Why won't you talk to me? It is driving me crazy here. I can't make it right if I don't know what's wrong. Please, Anna, write back, even if it is just to tell me to fuck off. Anything. Please.

I will write as soon as I am able to at boot camp, so you have an address, but if you send it to my parents, they will make sure I get it. I hope you are okay, Anna. At least let me know you are okay.

Yours,
Bobby Payne

A teardrop lands on the page, obscuring his signature and alerting me to the fact that I am crying at all. Inhaling a shuddering breath, I wipe my eyes on my sleeve. *God, he thinks I am mad at him. For saying that it was good riddance that my dad died.* That is absurd. Even if I didn't agree wholeheartedly with the statement, I would never hold that against him. My dad gave him a black eye, bruised ribs, and broke his arm that night. What Bobby said had never bothered me; it was justified.

My alarm goes off, alerting me that I have five minutes to make it to my group therapy session. My decision to not reply to him wavers as I walk to my vanity. *Can I really let him think that? Hold onto that guilt?* But then I glimpse my reflection in the mirror, my eyes catching the lifeless, dull slate orbs staring back at me through sockets hollowed by nights of restless sleep. Plagued by the terrors that wait for me in the dark. I don't recognize myself. Viewing this sallow, frail, broken version of me only strengthens my resolve. Bobby Payne deserves more than this broken funhouse mirror version of me, and it will be easier for him if I stay the course and let him leave me in the past.

I open the drawer to the right, lifting a dried-out corsage and placing the letter on top of the pile, to join the other pages left unanswered. I meet my gaze in the mirror and narrow my eyes at the me I have become. I know that something has to change, and that change comes now. I close the drawer and leave the room.

Maude is leading group today. As usual, she asks, "Who would like to start us off today?" Surprising her and everyone, I raise my hand. Maude looks around for her clipboard, intent on handing it to me to write out my feelings. I halt her with a gesture, and she stills.

"My—" My voice creaks through tightened vocal cords, raspy with disuse, and I cough to clear my throat. Lindsey, the girl to my left, hands me an unopened bottle of water. I nod to her in thanks as I gulp down the cool liquid, allowing it to lubricate my words. I take a fortifying breath, intent to make sure no one misunderstands this simple truth any longer. On the exhale, I rip it off like a bandage and say, "My name is Annastasia Adkins, and I am glad my dad is dead."

Chapter 1

ANNASTASIA

(Present Day)

This was not the plan. I'm not supposed to be driving the winding back roads of my childhood right now. If I am being honest with myself, I'm not sure I was ever planning to grace these rolling mountains in person again. Sure, Diane, my lawyer, had done a hell of a job for me, proving my right to the land that had in many ways raised me and broken me all the same. It was mine in trust, to be claimed when I reached the age of twenty-five. A fancy trick of my grandparents—who I had never known—to ensure my future.

That milestone has come and gone by three years, and though I couldn't bring myself to go back there at the time, I couldn't bring myself to sell it either. A misplaced girlhood dream that my mother may find her way back to me if I kept this one tether to our shared past. I should have sold it and been done with it. If I could stop grasping to that childish hope the way I grasp the pendant she left me, currently leaving an indent in my palm, I wouldn't be driving a rental SUV up this mountain before the first rays of sun hit its peak. I've put in the work to bury my ghosts in the past through years of intensive therapy, but unfortunately, they keep finding themselves unearthed.

"This road is creepy as fuck." The sharp tone of my passenger cuts through my morose thoughts. "Can you even see anything through this shit? I swear if I get killed by some backwoods ghost or cryptid, I will haunt you 'til the day you die, Tasia."

This mist that clings to these mountains in the early mornings and twilight—disquieting to some—has always been a comfort to me. Mother Nature wraps us in a cozy blanket before we close our eyes and keeps us cocooned until we open them again. I never gave much heed to the tales of what went bump in the night. No, I know the truth of monsters, and they dwell in the bright light of the day all the same. "Reckon I could drive these switchbacks blindfolded from muscle memory alone," I shoot back, and I can feel her laser stare bore holes into the side of my head.

"Reckon? Good God, Tasia, we have been in this state for less than two hours, and you have already gone all West-by-God Virginia on me. And please, for my sake, both hands on the wheel."

Rolling my eyes, I release the necklace and mumble, "You could have stayed in Vegas."

"Right... I could have sent my best friend to the hometown that she left at sixteen, when she was tragically orphaned, by the way, to deal with the literal bodies buried in her backyard—alone. As if this doesn't have the potential to send you spiraling off into another two-year stint in the loony bin." Joanie, my best and probably only non-surface friend, huffs, and I regret ever letting her in enough to know that little fact about me, especially if she is going to throw it in my face when I'm already feeling like jumping out of my skin. This is why I keep most people at surface level in the first place.

"Body," I interject, because I feel like it is important to specify. "They found the remains of one singular body."

"Please do not delude yourself into thinking that makes this whole horror show any less fucked," she deadpans.

Yes, when I said that my ghosts have a way of becoming unearthed —in this instance, I do mean literally. I may have complicated feelings when I think about stepping foot back on the property where my past haunts me like a specter in the West Virginia mists, but as Joanie has so thoughtfully pointed out, I didn't have a choice. Because the contractors I hired to finally do something with my inheritance uncovered more than the skeleton of my fucked-up childhood, they had found an actual body... just as Joanie said.

(5:30 a.m. PST Yesterday, Monday)

The ringing of my phone jars me awake.

Jesus, who is calling me at this God-forsaken hour? With eyes blinded by sleep, I swat for my phone. Overshooting, I send it skidding off the surface, landing between my nightstand and wall, but blessedly, the ringing has stopped. *Good. Must have been a misdial.* No sooner is that thought out of my head than it starts again, but more aggressively as the sound echoes between the wall and the stand.

The now echoing ringtone is followed by furious pounding from the wall I share with my roommate. *Bang! Bang! Bang! Ring. Ring. Ring. Bang! Ring. Bang!*

"For the love of God, Taisia! Answer the fucking phone or throw it out the goddamn window!" Joanie shouts through the wall. And fine, there is no sleeping after this anyway.

Resigned to answer the phone but not yet committing to placing my feet on the floor—to do so would be akin to agreeing to start the day right now—I hang my upper half off the bed, contorting my shoulder and arm, feeling the strain of my ligaments stretched beyond their natural range. Reaching for the wayward phone until the tips of my fingers clasp onto its edge, I throw myself back onto my bed.

"Hello?" I croak out, more in question than greeting. Vegas is the city that never sleeps. Loyal residents that we are, my roommate and I take that to heart—until we close our eyes, then don't bother us 'til noon, at least. Unless you want to endure the grumpiest of welcomes from me and flat-out hostility from Joanie.

"Um... Is Ms. Adkins—Annastasia Adkins, available... sir?" a confused voice intones on the other end of the line as if they were expecting a much different voice to answer the call.

Sending a quick prayer up for patience, because yeah, my sleep-roughened voice may be a little gruff, but not so much as to be mistaken as a man, I clear my throat. "This is she," I state, now two octaves higher with an extra emphasis on the pronoun to overcompensate for the new insecurity his mistaken designation has unlocked.

"Right. Apologies for waking you, ma'am," the speaker states, emphasizing the feminine honorific," This is Joey from Smith and Johnson Contracting, and... well... um, we have run into a little snafu here at the site."

The "site" being my childhood home, back in Boremanton, West Virginia. Now fully awake as a sense of dread swells, I do some time zone math in my head. If it is 5:30 a.m. here in Las Vegas, then back east it is 8:30 a.m. Remembering a conversation I had with the project manager, Paul Smith—not a Joey by the way—town ordinances won't allow any construction to happen before eight in the morning. What could have gone so wrong in the first half hour into a workday that would warrant a call to the property owner? That sense of dread I spoke of now takes root in my stomach, sending a wave of nausea to go with the cold sweat that has taken over my body. Nothing good can come from this conversation, so I rip the bandage off and ask, "What's wrong? Why isn't Paul calling me?"

"Uh... well... that is to say—".

"My God, man—spit it out. What is so disastrous that I have to get up at 5:30 A.M to handle?" I snap because this is getting ridiculous.

"Paul's on the phone with the police—"

"THE POLICE?!" I interrupt with a shout. Which must have been loud enough to get the attention of Joanie, because the only thing she values over her sleep is gossip. She all but Kool-Aid Man burst through my door, sleep mask askew on the top of her crooked bonnet, and mouths, "What the fuck?" Not wanting to recap whatever I am about to learn, I put the phone on speaker and scoot over as she crawls into my bed.

I hear a murmured, "This is above my pay grade..." and a shuffling on the other line until the voice is replaced by the more familiar gruff tone of Paul Smith. "Hello, Ms. Adkins, I am sorry to have to call you so early. I know it's not even six there, but we have run into a problem that is going to shut down the operation for an unknown amount of time."

"Why did you need to call the cops? What is going on out there?"

"We were breaking ground where you want the natural eco pool area to go for the resort, and we found human remains."

"Oh, my God!" I feel sick, and I must have gone pale because Joanie jumps up and runs to the en-suite to grab the trash can, returning to thrust it in front of my face faster than I have ever seen her move. Once she's sure it is secure in my grip, she scoots back next to me, scooping my hair up and braiding it into a messy plait to keep it from my would-be vomit; admonishing me under her breath about how there wouldn't be so many tangles if I would listen to her and sleep in a silk bonnet. She is a good friend.

"The police are on their way to investigate the scene, but the officer I spoke with is going to want to speak with you. In person, preferably. Is there any way you can make it out here?"

The past I have been avoiding for over a decade is calling me home, leaving me no option but to answer in person.

Chapter 2

BOBBY

I haven't set foot on this property since homecoming night my senior year. Coincidentally, there were flashing lights of patrol cars here then too. I shake my head as if that could shake the memories of that night from my subconscious. Now is not the time to revisit ghosts.

Yesterday, a construction crew found a body on this property, which according to the statement of the general contractor, is going to be a mountain retreat of some sort. Strange to think that anyone would pay to stay up the street from my childhood home, but this area is getting new life since that pro hockey team made the neighboring town its home. Even though it's about a forty-five-minute drive to Aberville, I guess rising tides lift all ships.

Bending under the yellow caution tape, I head over to relieve my fellow officer, Deputy Derrick Jones. It seems even the rustle of the breeze has stalled in reverence for the solemn scene. Right there in the middle of the field, overgrown with dandelions and other wildflowers, is the make-shift tent covering the recently upturned soil, revealing the uncovered globe of a skull. It sends a shiver down my spine.

"Late to the party, Payne," Jones boasts, as if this is the most fun he has had in years, oblivious to the respect this scene deserves. I get it, sort of. Beyond the occasional bar brawl down at the Wolf and Whistle—the local dive bar—and the sporadic bouts of teen mischief; Boremanton is pretty boring. But still...

"Come on, man. They found a body. At least pretend to feel a little somber about it," I admonish. I was off duty Monday when the partial remains were discovered early in the morning. The rest of the day was spent securing permits, warrants, and equipment to dig up the surrounding area to find the rest of the remains. We've had one patrol car sitting guard since the coroner set up the tent around the area after claiming it was better to wait for the forensic team to find the whole body than to disturb the scene by removing the bones they have already found.

Unlike Jones here, I am not as unfamiliar with death. He may have more experience on the job than I do but having fulfilled my MSO to the Army with eight years of active duty, I have seen my share of bodies. When I returned home at twenty-six, Sheriff Dobbs recruited me as one of his deputies. Ironic, since he spent most of his deputy years escorting one or more of my brothers to and from the town's holding cell.

"Lighten up. It's not like we are informing the family yet. Gotta figure out who the stiff is first for that." Jones has four years on me and likes to fancy himself the heir apparent when Dobbs decides to give up the goat and stop running for reelection. What Jones failed to realize is that the sheriff is an elected position, and he isn't winning any popularity competitions any time soon.

Not in the mood to engage in this any further; I get down to business. "Anything I need to know before you head out?"

"Fine, fine, suck all the excitement out of it. The forensics team will have the equipment up here in about an hour, and sometime today, the property owner is coming in for questioning. Apparently, they are flying in from Vegas."

Jones didn't grow up here; he moved to town after marrying Jessica Connor, after they met at WVU. She used to go steady with Max, one of my brothers, but that relationship didn't survive the distance of going to two separate colleges. Jessica came home from university with a degree and a ring. Not long after the wedding, Max left town and only visits Ma on Christmas. He has settled in Philadelphia, works in finance, and hasn't had a serious relationship since. So, Jones has never known this property to be occupied; he didn't grow up down the street from a knobby-kneed tomboy who was always following the Payne brothers around.

He didn't see that same tomboy lose some of her pep when her mother ran off, and her father turned to the bottle. Or see her blossom into the beautiful girl I asked to homecoming senior year when I was just a boy, hoping to make her my girl and that she'd be checking her mailbox and returning my letters, giving me something to look forward to coming home to on leave after I joined up. Of course, none of that happened. I did write. She just never bothered to respond.

The last time I stepped on this property is the last time I laid eyes on Annastasia Adkins, and the night a million boyish dreams got crushed. I lost my dream girl and best friend the day she lost her father.

It's common knowledge at this point, though, that this land still belongs to her. Even if it seemed she wanted nothing to do with it. Many developers have been down to City Hall asking about any unused land. Every single one gets the same answer with their offers to buy; it isn't for sale. Until this whole debacle, I didn't think she had any plans for the property except to keep ownership of it for some reason.

It has been vacant for the past twelve years. Why now, after all this time, is she trying to develop it? Is she moving back to run the place? I try not to let any excitement at the idea of seeing Anna again build. A lot can change in a decade. Lord knows I am not the same boy she knew.

Chapter 3

ANNASTASIA

Hands aching from my white-knuckled grip on the steering wheel, which only seems to tighten with every mile closer we creep towards the property, a sense of dread sinks in my stomach. Joanie, in tune to my tells since witnessing the worst of my panic attacks when I was fresh out of residential therapy and sharing a tiny dorm with her in college, must see the warning signs.

Her tone reserved for soothing skittish wildlife, she asks, "Do we need to go to the property? Can't we give a statement at the station?" Probably, and that was my intention: to go straight to the station, answer whatever questions they had for me, make sure I was free to go, and then drive back to the airport. Content to hang out there until the next flight back to Vegas, cancel our just-in-case booking at the inn on the way home. But when I started driving on these familiar roads, it was as if I was on autopilot, drawn straight to my past like a moth to a flame.

Gravel crunches under the tires of our rented SUV as I turn onto the base of my drive. God, images of that night start to rapid fire flash before my eyes, and I can't think to answer Joanie. Slamming on the breaks I throw the gearshift into park. With shaking hands, I struggle with my belt, too far in the grips of panic to feel any relief once I am finally free from the tether. Exploding out of the door, I start pacing to try to expel some of this energy that is pent up inside my body, trying to claw its way out from the inside. *What am I doing here?*

"What are you doing here?" a gruff voice echoes my thoughts. I don't even register that they were spoken out loud by another person until they continue on. "This is a crime scene. You can't be here."

I am on the verge of a panic attack, so I can't respond to the disembodied voice, but for the first time since we got on the plane, I am glad Joanie insisted on tagging along.

"Hello, Officer—"

"Deputy."

I can hear her trying to rein in her annoyance at being interrupted when her response is strained as said through clenched teeth. "Right, well, hello *Deputy.* My friend here is the property owner. We just got in from Vegas. The sheriff said he needed to talk to her."

"Yeah, at the station. Why would she come here? Unless she has something she thought she could cover up." A door creaks and clicks shut—he must be getting out of his car. Oh, my God, am I going to get arrested for being in my own driveway? *I shouldn't have come here.*

"Look here, Barney Fife, we took a red eye and have been driving for two hours to get to this backwater two-bit town. So, she got confused on the details and thought we had to meet the sheriff here—that's no crime. It's been a hell of a day."

Oh, good, at least I won't be alone in my cell. My bestie is determined to earn a cot next to me. At least she came up with some excuse as to why we are here, because I have none. I still can't see straight as images from the past superimpose themselves over the present. Night, day, day, night. Figures silhouetted in headlights are struggling. Joanie's argument with the deputy morphs into the shouts of my father and Bobby fighting. It seems so real, I think I can hear Bobby's voice.

And then there are strong hands cupping my face, thumbs wiping away tears I didn't know had leaked out. A voice that sounds so much like the one of my childhood best friend but can't be—why would he be here at this crime scene—says, "Anna, stay with me. It's okay, you're okay. I'm here."

The voice is so steady that it ebbs the panic, and my blurry vision clears into focus. My gaze locks onto the achingly familiar, kind hazel eyes of the boy who used to be the star of all my teenage dreams. Only now, they belong to the face of a man I no longer know. All I can manage is to squeak out a timid, "Bobby?" Then the world spins and fades to black.

Bobby

"Tasia!" The spitfire, who was giving Jones hell when I got here, yells as her attention turns to us. I've dreamed of having Anna Adkins in my arms many times; in none of those dreams did she pass out after recognizing me.

I heard the commotion at the end of the drive and came to see what the hell was going on. Jones was on his way out, or so I thought, until I heard him and some lady getting into it. The last thing I expected to see was Anna looking like she had seen a ghost, frozen in place at the end of the gravel drive. As I approached, I could see her complexion was pale, her eyes unfocused, and the twin tear trails streaming down her cheeks almost broke me in two.

I could never stand to see her cry. Which is why I took liberties I had no right to and caressed her face; a face that had lost the roundness of adolescent youth I remembered. Her jaw now more angular, her cheekbones more defined, I noticed as I wiped the tears from them and spoke to her like I was soothing a wounded child. The haze lifted from her gaze as her eyes focused on me, and fuck me, even swollen and red, her eyes were still the most haunting glacial blue, fitting because they sure have been haunting me for the past twelve years.

"Jones, do you have any smelling salts in your rig?" I yell out, lowering myself to the ground and laying Anna's head in my lap. Brushing a golden lock of hair from her sweat-soaked forehead, I place the back of my hand to her forehead to see if she is feverish.

"She had a panic attack. Instead of being able to help her ground herself, I was distracted by Columbo over there." Anna's friend says to me as she squats down to our level, taking Anna's wrist in her hand, tapping her watch. "Her heart rate is coming down. She should be okay when she comes too."

"Are you her nurse or something?" I gulp, feeling *my* heart rate pick up at the thought that something is wrong with her. "Is Anna ill?"

She tilts her head to the side, assessing me closer. Now I know what a lab rat being observed by a white coat must feel like. The focus of her attention seems to have stopped time itself; I can't even hear the wind rustling the leaves on the trees. "Tasia," she emphasizes the nickname, "is fine, and you'll forgive me if I refrain from discussing her health status with a stranger while she is unconscious. You are a stranger, aren't you, Deputy...?" She leaves the question open for me to fill in the blank.

So, I do. "Payne. Deputy Bobby Payne."

"The date from the homecoming from hell?" She gasps, wide-eyed and shocked, "Of-fucking-course, because why the fuck not, fucking small bum fuck nowhere towns..." she trails off into more mumbled curses, and I'd be impressed by the way she can interject the word fuck *inside* so many other words if it were not for my own anxiety at having an unconscious Anna, or I guess it's Tasia now—*I don't know that I can bring myself to call her that*—resting in my lap.

I can't help but feel a mix of relief that my name has at least passed her lips in the last decade and annoyance that the whole of our relationship to each other has been reduced down to one, admittedly horrible night. But that night hadn't been all bad. In fact, right up until the end, it had been the culmination of all my high school dreams.

Speaking of annoyance, Jones comes back from his rig with his emergency pack in tow. "No smelling salts, only some ice packs and wound care, but the medics are on their way. What a clusterfuck. Seems super shady to come here before the station, like she has something to hide."

"Are you damaged or something? If you hid a body, would you hire a contractor to dig it up?" Anna's friend snaps at him. She raises a valid point.

"Now you listen here, Miss, you have the right to remain silent. I suggest you use it!" Jones barks back.

"Am I under arrest?" she challenges, eyebrows raised.

"No," I interject before Jones can escalate the situation further. "No one is under arrest. Jones, I can wait for the medics with Ms. Adkins and Ms....?" It was my turn to leave the question open.

"Clarke. Joanie Clarke, and I'm Tasia's roommate, not her nurse," she fills in, using the least hostile tone I've heard from her yet.

"Thank you." I nod to her, then return my attention to Jones. "I got this."

"I'm not about to leave you alone with two unknowns—" I interrupt him before he can get too much steam built up.

"They are not unknowns. At least Anna isn't, she grew up here. Like Ms. Clarke here said, she owns the place." Luckily, I am saved from a lengthy argument by the arrival of the medics. And thank God for that. I am concerned about how long Anna has been out. I know her friend said it was a panic attack, but shouldn't she be stirring by now?

"See, we're all good here. Go on home to Jess. She's going to get worried if you aren't home soon." At the mention of his wife, he softens. As annoying as I find him, there is no arguing that he is a good man to Jess. I think that's part of the reason my brother stays away. If he thought there was a chance, he would have fought for her. But he knows she's happy, and even if he can't watch it, he won't interfere.

Jones nods and heads to his rig, pulling away as the medics, Ryan Murphy and Lorenzo Alvarez, approach. The Alvarez boys may have had even my brothers beat in town mischief as kids, but have all grown up to be respectable men, and Murphy was in Anna's class in school. I brace myself for this reunion.

"Holy shit, is that Anna?" Murph asks, picking up his pace as he approaches.

I swear I hear Joanie mutter another *small fucking towns*, under her breath, but I can't be sure.

"What happened?" he questions. I let Joanie tell the story as Murph settles next to us to check Anna's vitals.

As she is recounting, Alvarez goes back to the bus for the gurney. Murph finishes her vitals and says, "Yeah, that would be enough to send anyone into a panic attack, especially with what happened the last time she was on this property." He winces and shoots me an apologetic look; he must have remembered my role in that horrific night. He turns back to Joanie. "We are going to take her to the hospital for some routine workups, but from what you have told us about her history with anxiety and panic, I'm inclined to believe that is what we are dealing with."

"Shouldn't she have woken up by now?" I can't help but question. "Shouldn't we use smelling salts or something to wake her up?"

This time, Alvarez speaks up. "From what Ms. Clarke here has said, Annastasia has been running on high levels of stress and no sleep. Her body is probably taking the chance to get the rest it needs, and with the volatile reaction being here caused, we don't want to risk her falling into another panic attack so quickly. Best for her to wake naturally in a controlled environment. She is likely at least baseline, dehydrated too, so we are going to start fluids on the way."

The boys get Anna situated on the stretcher and head to the rig. Joanie speaks up. "Can I ride with her? Since you all seem to know Tasia's back-story, I am the closest to family that she has, and I'm not from around here. I'll get lost on the way. The GPS is worth fuck all in these mountains."

They nod, and I am relieved she won't be alone. She turns to me, rooting through her purse and jotting something down. "This is my number. I trust you can inform the sheriff why we will be missing our meeting? He can call me if he needs an update." She looks at the rental and winces.

"Yes, ma'am. And I can get someone to deliver the rental to the hospital for you." Tension melts from her shoulders on an exhale. She nods once in acknowledgment and heads to the bus to accompany Anna to the hospital. She doesn't know it, but by agreeing, she handed me the perfect excuse to see Anna again, hopefully awake this time.

Chapter 4

ANNASTASIA

Blinking my blurry eyes awake, I register that I am in motion. I hear an incessant beeping and feel a tightness around my face. Reaching my hand up to swipe it away, I startle when it is jerked back down. Trying again, I find my arm tethered down to my bed. *What the fuck?* My brain is a little fuzzy, and I am having a hard time remembering what happened before I went to sleep. I move my legs and find they are restrained, too. Thrashing in the limited motion I am allotted, I hear an increase in the beeping.

"Shit, she is coming to. Be prepared to push Lorazepam if her heart rate keeps rising..." comes a deep male voice. *Oh, my God, am I being abducted? Are they going to harvest my organs? Did they find out I'm a universal donor?* The beeping continues to climb.

"Let's try to avoid that if at all possible." I feel a tapping on my cheek, and one of my abductors comes into view with a shock of red hair. *Probably not the brains of the operation if they didn't think to cover such an identifiable feature. Unless they've already decided to kill me.* "Let's take some deep breaths, Anna-banana."

The use of that nickname has interrupted my panicked breathing. It is so rare that anyone calls me Anna these days, let alone Anna-banana. Even when I was young, there was only one kid who called me that, and he also had shocking red hair. I do what my abductor says, drawing in a deep breath of air while I let that clear my head and focus. My vision sharpens, and I notice a pair of familiar green eyes. Only the face that holds them is different, more angular than the baby-faced kid I grew up with. I know in an instant that this is Murph. I try to say as much, but it gets muffled and lost in the intake of air from what I now realize is a breathing mask strapped to my face.

"Ahh ah ah, no talking, just breathing okay. That-a-girl, in... and ... out. Good." With his soothing, the frantic beeping slows, and I can take in my surroundings with my mind at full alert. *I'm in an ambulance, and the redhead down the lane got hot.* "I know you are probably confused, so your friend here is gonna catch you up. Your job is to keep your breathing nice and slow, okay?" I nod. "Good Girl."

I bet Murph is the kinda guy to talk you through it. That is the most unhinged thought I could have about the boy who used to eat paste in kindergarten.

Bet he eats other things now.

Holy shit, can stress and lack of sleep cause random bouts of horniness? At least the oxygen mask keeps me from spilling the mortifying thoughts out loud.

Joanie's hand slips into mine, and I squeeze it like the lifeline it is. She is the first thing to make sense since opening my eyes. "Hey, Tasia sweetie, it's okay. You've been overwhelmed. Instead of heading to the inn or the sheriff's office, I think muscle memory and lack of sleep had you drive straight to the property." I nod because that makes sense. "We were met by a not-so-helpful deputy, and I think the combination of everything got to you, and you panicked and passed out. Luckily, one of the other deputies caught you and the medics came to get you to the hospital to get checked out."

Feeling the ambulance slow to a stop, Murph interjects, "And look at that, we are here. Ms. Clarke, if you don't mind, Lorenzo will help you step down. I have to get the stretcher ready to roll. Don't worry, I'll tell the nurses you're her cousin. They won't give you any trouble."

I am staring at Joanie as Murph is talking, and maybe I'm still hallucinating. There is no way I see a flush on the tawny completion of my badass best friend, and because of Murph of all people. *As if I wasn't contemplating his dirty talk and head game mere moments ago.* She nods and makes her way to the back of the ambulance while Murph gets me situated.

"Sorry for the conditions, but it is good to see you, Anna." Squeezing my shoulder once, he gets back to his task. "We should catch up before you skip town for another decade. Drinks for you and your friend are on me when you're up to it." Wheeling me to the edge, he and the other medic lift me up and out of the ambulance and take me into the emergency department.

I'm looked over and given the okay to remove my breathing mask; they want to keep me for a couple of hours to make sure my heart rate stays normal. The nurse finishes attaching the next round of fluids to my IV. It would seem that living off energy drinks does not promote proper hydration. She gives another doubtful look between Joanie and me, not buying Murph's cousin's declaration for a minute, and then heads out after a tutorial on the call button.

"I don't think she sees the family resemblance." Joanie reads my mind, earning a snort from me.

Joanie and I are a study in opposites—she has this beautiful golden tan complexion, while I am so pale that I reflect the flash in photos, and the sun does nothing but redden my skin. Her eyes are warm mahogany with the most amazing ring of amber haloing the iris. My baby blues, while I will admit are striking, are so cool toned that they have been described as glacial. Her hair is a shock of bronze ringlets that she has learned to embrace over the years and wears naturally more than not.

It wasn't always that way. Joanie is bi-racial but grew up with her white father after her mother died in childbirth. Fathers are hopeless with hair; I know from experience. After my mom left, my father took me to his barber for a bowl cut for a year before the church ladies intervened. Joanie's dad had the added challenge of a hair texture that was different than his own. Mr. Clarke managed messy puff balls through elementary, but his mom, no more versed in styling 3b hair, started taking Joanie for regular chemical relaxers at her salon starting at twelve.

It wasn't until college, around the time we met, that Joanie started to embrace her curls. My hair is golden blonde but can't hold a curl for anything. The best I can get is some beachy waves if I layer it too high hell and put copious amounts of product in it. The nurse is justified in being skeptical of any blood shared between us, but in every way that matters, Joanie is my family.

"We're lucky they took us to Aberville and not the trauma center in Boremanton. Chances are everyone there knows every scraped knee I ever had, not to mention every clipped branch of my family tree." I get the exact reaction I was expecting with that one.

"Damn small east of bum-fuck towns," leaves her lips in a disgusted sigh. Though not a native to Vegas, where we now live, Joanie was not new to big city life like I was when we met freshman year. She grew up in Chicago, so this rural atmosphere, where you have to drive over half an hour to the closest hospital, is not her usual scene.

Thanks to a randomized roommate lottery at the University of Nevada, Las Vegas, two young girls with only their majors in common were paired up to live in tiny quarters together. There isn't anywhere better to earn your chops in the tourism and hospitality industry. The program blended classroom learning with real-world experience like no other could. We were an odd pair. From the outside looking in, I'm sure people wondered how we got so close so fast.

Truth is, we were both coming from trauma and soul-deep hurt that recognizes itself in other people. Mommy issues being at the top of a long list of issues bonded us; though my mom abandoned me, and hers died in childbirth. She was left the only non-white person in her family, since her mother had none of her own, having grown up in the foster system herself. You didn't have to act out to be bothered when your skin tone set you apart. Then, there was our lack of peers. She struggled with being from two worlds, but not feeling accepted by either.

While I had plenty of acquaintances growing up, town gossip and speculation left me with only two close friends. Until one night took that, and so much more, from me in one fell swoop, followed by what she so lovingly refers to as my two-year stint in the loony bin. It was a PTSD recovery center. Being basically orphaned at sixteen is a precarious position; I did not have any family to take me in and did not want to be a ward of the state. I have heard horror stories of the foster system, and I had suffered at the hands of abuse for too long to roll that dice.

My lawyer, Diane, helped me find an alternative and guided me through the process to legally emancipate myself and enroll in the program for PTSD youths for two years. The program allowed me to get my high school diploma and attend some much-needed therapy, but you never make real friends in a place like that. It is always a revolving door.

I graduated from the program, but it doesn't cure you of PTSD. It is always lingering in the background, but it did give me tools to cope. However, I did not anticipate how much stress a new environment would have on me, and it didn't take long for the night terrors to take me. Joanie was a witness to them, and instead of judging, she wanted to understand. So, I let her in, told her the whole of it, things my childhood best friends didn't even know. And she, in turn, told me of all her insecurities, how she tries to be the best in all aspects of her life because she thought if she didn't, she would've been even less accepted. We found that at least we belonged to each other; ride or die as she would put it. As much as I tell her she could have stayed home through all of this, I am glad she didn't.

"I'm glad you're here." It comes out a little watery as if I may be on the verge of tears.

Rolling her eyes, she takes my hand. "You couldn't shake me if you tried."

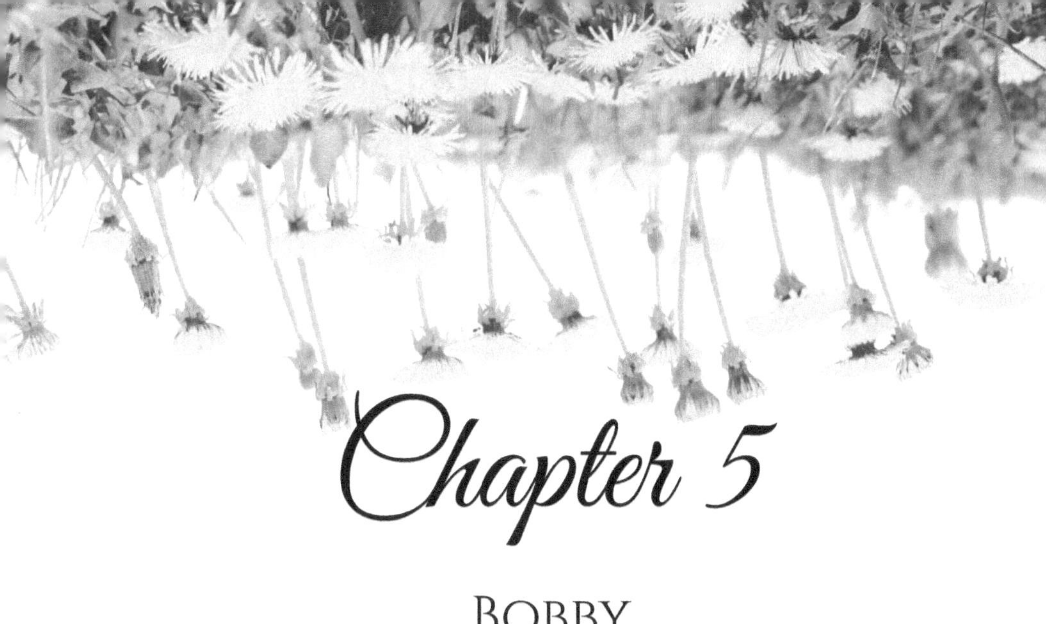

Chapter 5

BOBBY

If you had told me the highlight of my day would be witnessing my childhood crush mid-panic attack and catching her as she fainted into my arms, I would not have believed you. But somehow, the day has gone downhill faster than a boulder in a landslide.

Forensics arrived shortly after the ambulance departed. What we all assumed was going to be a couple of hours spent searching for the missing remains of our Jane Doe—the pelvic bone told them that it was, in fact, a female—turned more complicated when they found a right femur. The thing is that we already had the right femur, and only one can belong to one person, which means we had at least two bodies on our hands. It also meant all the pieces we had assumed belonged to one person might be parts of many. Meaning more warrants for more of Anna's land, and any hopes of this being a one-off, are going up in smoke.

If Anna was planning on a short trip, it just got extended. Since I was the one who volunteered to deliver their SUV, the sheriff had voluntold me I would be delivering the news, as well as an invitation to come to the station for a chat in the morning. Granted, the hospital releases her by then. I want to see her again and make sure she is alright, but I dread being the messenger who delivers her even more stressful news.

She hasn't even been back for a whole day, yet this town is determined to add to her long list of traumas tied to it. Can I even blame her for hightailing it out of here when she had the chance, never looking back? What did she have to come back to? *But did she have to leave me in the dust with the town?*

Eighteen-year-old me was hurt that she left without so much as a good-bye, that she never wrote back to one of my letters. Not that it kept me from writing. I sent her more than I can remember until the day that I received one back, return to sender. By then, twenty-year-old me was pissed and resigned to the idea that the girl he knew was as good as gone. I was too wrapped up in my grief, too focused on what he lost to even consider that she needed to get away. That there was nothing here for her but painful reminders and ghosts. And that maybe I was too much of a reminder of the things she needed to escape.

I can admit now that anger was a cop out; easier than letting myself feel the unending sadness her absence left me with, or the crippling loneliness. *It was easier to hate her than to miss her.*

Climbing into the front of the rental, I spend a moment pairing my cell to the SUV's system and dialing my brother Johnny.

"Hey, Deputy Dip-Wad, what's up?" he answers.

Sighing and debating on whether Tommy would have been the better brother to call, I respond, "Hello, oh magnanimous brother of mine—"

"No," he cuts me off.

"What do you mean, no? I haven't even asked you anything." Older brothers are the worst.

"Yet."

"Okay, fair, but can you at least let me ask it before you outright refuse?"

I hear the long-suffering sigh of a true middle child, honestly, the shittiest position in the sibling hierarchy to be sure. "Fine, ask."

"I need you to meet me at Aberville General—"

"Are you okay?" I hear rustling, and the jingle of keys followed by the slam of a door, "What happened? Do I need to get Mom?" The questions are shot out rapid fire as I hear the click of the seatbelt and the rev of his Chevy roaring to life. The immediacy of action, because he thinks I am hurt, touches me more than I'd ever let him know.

"No, no, nothing like that." I am quick to reassure him. "An old friend fainted and got taken by ambulance. I promised to deliver their car. I'll need a ride back to my cruiser after." I don't know why I don't tell him it is Anna, I just don't. We haven't leaked that we found a body, correction bodies, yet. Without more information, we don't want to stir up the pot and bring a media frenzy to town. The only ones who know are the sheriff's office and forensic team, the construction crew that found the initial remains, and, of course, Anna and her friend. Not that saying it is Anna will lead to talking about the case, but something wants me to keep her return quiet for now.

"And they can't give you a ride back?" Johnny breaks me out of my thoughts.

"I don't know how long they will be there, and I got paperwork to file by end of day. What, since I am not in mortal peril, you can't help your baby brother out?"

"Kinda, yeah," he deadpans.

"Prick. You're already in your truck."

"Fine, fine, I'll meet you there, but you'll owe me."

"Add it to my tab." With that, I disconnect the call and turn up the radio to try to combat the conflicting feelings of dread and excitement that seeing Anna again is causing.

Annastasia

This antiseptic hospital smell is starting to get to me, turning my stomach from the sad hospital lunch they brought. I poke at the electric green gelatin with my plastic fork, concerned by the way the tines bounce off its surface; I decide it is best to leave it. I just convinced Joanie to go find her own lunch when her stomach rumbled so loud it drowned out the TV bolted to the wall. *I hope she brings me back some fries.*

They said if all remains the same, I will be discharged after dinner. I can't wait. I want to go get checked into our rooms and sleep the night away. I hope a good night's sleep will ease the anxiety that has been riding me since that unfortunate phone call yesterday. *Was it only yesterday? It feels like forever ago.*

Deciding to brave the mac and cheese, I pause with the fork half way to my mouth, when there's a rap on my door. *Odd.* Joanie wouldn't knock, and the nurse and doctors come in as needed.

"Come in," I respond, pushing the tray to the side, deciding not to risk the fare after all. I know it's the right choice when the door opens, revealing a sight that makes my stomach swoop. Standing there in the doorway is Bobby Payne, clad in the khaki and brown uniform belonging to the Deputies of the Boremanton Sheriff's office. The sharp pressed lines showcase how well the Army helped him fill out from the boy I remember. *He looks good in uniform.* The unbridled thought runs through my mind, followed by the hazy memory of concerned hazel eyes, before everything faded to black.

It all clicks into place. Bobby is a deputy, Bobby is *The* Deputy, the one who caught me when my panic attack turned to a faint. A thousand memories flash before my eyes in an instant as he takes a tentative step into the hospital room. Scraped knees from falling off bikes, him teaching me how to pick locks, rides home from school, carrying my books, every stolen glance that I thought was on borrowed time before he graduated and left for the military—though our plans ended way before that. A thousand memories before my eyes, a thousand dreams buried long ago resurfacing like the bones found on my property.

This was fine. Everything is fine. It's not like we had a sordid history. I reason, trying to convince myself that seeing him now is a non-issue. *He probably doesn't even remember the last time we saw each other.* It was only one night. One night out of a thousand. One kiss, and I admit some pretty serious heavy petting—you know—before we watched a wolf maul my father to death—and that was after my father yanked me out of his car by my hair. *This won't be awkward at all.* I am lying to myself.

"Hey, Bobby. How's it going?" *Good, that is a totally normal way to greet someone who the last time you saw had his hand up your skirt... and got a black eye and some broken bones from your dad for his efforts.*

"Oh, good. You know, just the average day on the job, catching a childhood friend as she faints at a crime scene; after she skips town for over a decade."

Okay... so we are skipping pleasantries. "Yeah, well, thank you for that. The whole not letting me bust my head open thing."

"Sure thing." His eyes scan me from head to hospital blanket-covered toe; for injury or to be sure I'm here in front of him, I can't be sure. "Where have you been, Anna? Or is it Tasia now?" His tone is clipped, almost frustrated, and I remember another deputy with clipped questions right before I passed out.

Weary, I ask, "Are you asking as a friend or in an official capacity, Deputy Payne?" My tone mirrors his. Just because I once knew everything about Bobby Payne the boy, doesn't mean I know anything about Bobby Payne the man.

"Are we friends?" he retorts. That stings, because once upon a time, he was my everything. *I only have myself to blame.* "My understanding of the term is that friends check in on one another from time to time, maybe respond to a letter or two. Not skip town with no reliable way to contact them and never look back."

Now I am on edge, the frantic beeping from the heart monitor alerting us to my pulse's rising rate. I try my breathing exercises to bring it back down before a nurse comes in with any thoughts to extend my stay.

Bobby's eyes dart to the monitor, and he looks contrite. "Shit, sorry. I am not trying to add to your stress, I'm only here to drop your keys off." He digs the keys out of his pocket, drawing my eyes to the tight fit of his trousers, then drops them onto my tray next to my now warm carton of juice. "And to tell you that the sheriff expects you at the station tomorrow, if you're discharged."

He lifts his hat from his head, running his fingers through his dark chocolate hair—a nervous habit he hasn't kicked since childhood. He would do it when holding back part of a story.

"Don't start holding out on me now, Payne. There is more to it. Go on, rip it off like a bandage." He looks at the monitors and back to me, lifting a skeptical brow.

"I'm not so fragile, and if it causes anxiety, best place for it I reckon." His lip twitches like hearing me slip back into small-town vernacular makes him want to smile. I almost catch a glimpse of the singular dimple indenting his left cheek, *I've missed that dimple.* But he shakes his head, a serious look overtaking his features. I know in an instant that his next words are going to take this situation from fucked up to catastrophe.

"Forensics were at the property not long after you left. They found evidence of multiple bodies, Anna. They are going to get warrants to search the whole property." With those words, I think my plans for the land might be as dead as the poor souls who are being dug up as we speak.

I attempt to swallow, but my dry throat causes my voice to sound ragged as it catches on my next question. "Am I gonna need a lawyer, Bobby?"

"As a friend?" he asks, his tone soft and his eyes kind. I nod. "I reckon that wouldn't be a bad idea, Anna."

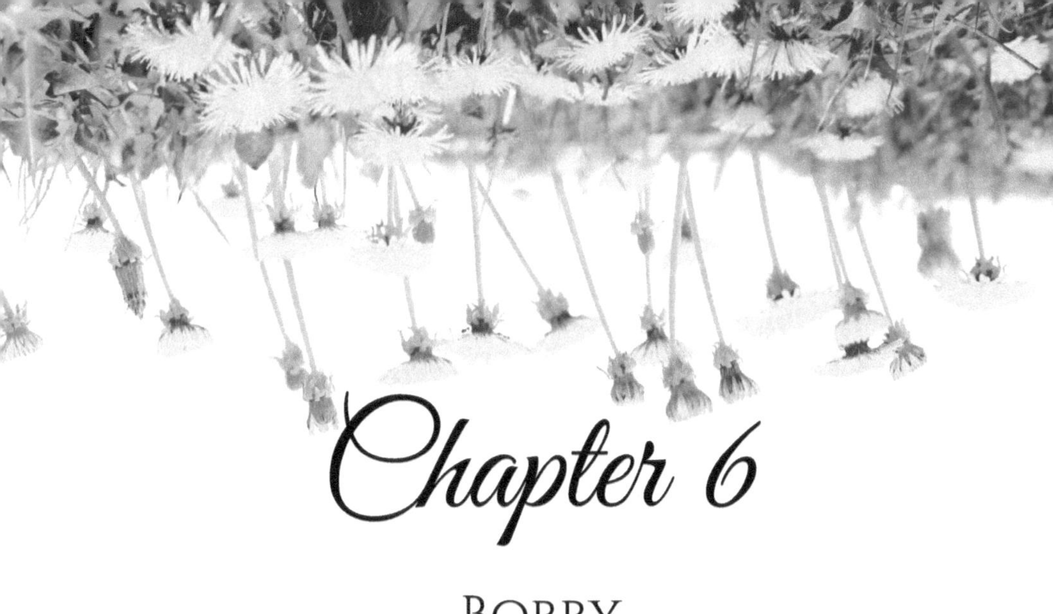

Chapter 6

BOBBY

Slamming my brother's door shut behind me as I buckle myself into his truck, I can feel his stare drilling into the side of my head. "Some way to show your appreciation for this little mid-afternoon detour you have me on."

"Sorry," I mutter, staring out the window. It's late afternoon, but the clouds are blocking out the rays of the sun, the gloom a fitting reflection of my mood. I should not take this out on him or his truck. It's my own fault I let my built-up frustration leak out with Anna, and then by the time I had it in check, I had no choice but to be the messenger of even worse news. She looked so fucking small in that hospital bed, scared in a way that made my skin crawl.

I was helpless, unable to fight her demons for her. All I wanted to do was to scoop her up and tell her it would all be okay, but I couldn't. It is a promise I can't keep; it isn't going to be okay. And professionally, until cleared of all suspicion, it would be a conflict of interest. And I don't even know if she would want that level of comfort from me. It kills me that I can't even tell if the best friend I ever had would welcome a hug from me or not. The years of frustration overtook sense and I became a snarky asshole. *I thought I had gotten past this.*

"Awfully sullen for someone doing a solid for a friend," Johnny states, backing out of the parking space, and I don't like the emphasis he placed on 'friend'. "Don't think I've seen you this out of sorts since you overheard Ryan Murphy in the locker room bragging how he was gonna ask Annastasia Adkins to homecoming and pop her cherry." It's my turn to shoot laser beams into the side of his face as he goes on. "So, tell me, is this 'friend' of the female persuasion?"

It's become an unspoken rule in our house not to bring up Anna, like we don't bring up Jess to Max. There are some spots that even brothers don't poke. What makes him drop the courtesy and remind me of Murph's less-than-honorable intentions back then, I couldn't guess, but it has my hackles up. *Does Johnny know Anna is back?* Following on the back of that thought comes another: *How could I have forgot about that red-haired son of a bitch's infatuation with Anna? Did she wake up in the ambulance? Did they talk?*

Like he has a front row ticket to my mind theater, he continues. "Funny enough, on my way here, I got a call from Tommy. He picked up a shift at the Stop and Go—Lenny's wife went into labor, you see, so they needed a quick cover. So, Tommy went in on his day off." Johnny has always been the most long-winded of my brothers; he has a knack for stretching out stories for dramatic effect. "Imagine his surprise when Lorenzo and Ryan stop in to gas up their rig and pick up some snacks, and he overhears Ryan telling Enzo that he isn't gonna pass up the chance to cross Anna Adkins off his bucket list now that she is back in town." My throat goes dry at the thought. "Enzo, for his part, tries to talk him down, mentioning that we don't know why she's back but knocking boots with an old classmate is most definitely not the reason. For all they know she might be in a relationship already."

This thought does not stop the churning feeling making waves in my stomach. Johnny doesn't notice my discontent or, more likely, he does and revels in it. "Then get this...Tommy says Ryan said, and I quote 'no ring on the finger means the ball is still in play'. As if that is a thing that people say. Tommy agrees with me that it isn't, by the way. Then he tells me he asked Ryan where he ran into Anna. And here is what I find interesting... apparently, he just dropped her off at Aberville General."

"I guess HIPAA doesn't mean much to Ryan Murphy; maybe someone should mention something to Chief Miller 'bout that," I murmur under my breath.

"I fucking knew it!" Johnny shouts, slapping his hand on the steering wheel. "This friend you're bringing their car to is Annastasia Adkins, and you didn't even think to mention she was back. Why is she back?"

A wave of guilt crashes over me. Anna may have been my best friend, and we may have been on the verge of something more, before it all went to hell in a handbasket. But to my brothers, she was the little sister they never had. I shouldn't have kept this from him, but...

"It's part of an ongoing investigation." Which is the truth, but not the reason I didn't tell him. I wanted to keep her to myself as long as possible. *Too bad that went out the window the moment that red-headed weasel responded to the call.*

"Investigation? Is Anna in some sort of trouble?"

"Look, Johnny, I really can't talk about it yet. Not until some things are cleared up."

"Fine." He grits through his teeth, sounding about as frustrated as I feel. "Can you at least tell me if she is okay? You said she passed out?"

"Yeah, she suffers from panic attacks, according to her friend. I think the stress of the situation piled on top of flashbacks from that night triggered it." I don't go into the details for the integrity of the case and for Anna's privacy, which, it is clear, has never been a concern of a certain redhead.

"Shit. Yeah, that would do it. How are you?" This concerned tone is not one I hear from my brothers often.

"I'm fine. Why wouldn't I be?" I won't lie to Anna, but lying to my brothers is my favorite pastime.

"Oh, I don't know, only the love of your life, the one that got away, the girl you've been pinning over practically since your balls dropped, finally returns home. And it seems like she is involved in something that you, her knight in shining armor, can't immediately fix for her. Sounds like something that could put a man out of sorts."

"I don't pine—"

He cuts me off, "Right, and Max wouldn't be on a red-eye tonight if Jess called him and told him she and Jones were through. Apparently, we Payne boys are like penguins; we give our shiny rocks to one girl in our lives and hope she returns our feelings, or we remain alone and sad forever. Thank fuck my rock is still in my chest where it belongs."

"Been watching nature documentaries again, I see. You do know I haven't been celibate for the last twelve years, right? Neither has Max, since you've lumped us both into this depressing scenario," I say, incredulous.

"Anonymous one-night stands and casual fucks hardly equate to giving your heart to someone—that is the rock in the metaphor, in case you didn't catch that you numbskull."

"Since when are you so sappy?"

"Since forty percent of my brothers are walking around like their beating hearts exist outside of their chests and are forever out of reach. Max is a lost cause, but you, baby brother, still have a shot. And fuck me for caring, I guess."

"And if she is seeing someone else?" I whisper, trying not to think about how my chest hurts at the thought.

"Well, I hear as long as there's no ring, the ball is still in play." He seems proud of himself for that one.

"You're an asshole, you know that?"

"Nah, I'm just a hopeless romantic. It runs in the family."

Chapter 7

ANNASTASIA

(Wednesday)

Make a left at the stop sign," I say from the passenger seat, and Joanie follows my direction. "Now, two more blocks, then make a right. There should be parking right in front of the building."

"Okay, are you still giving me the silent treatment outside of directions?" I blink at her in response. *I wouldn't even be giving you directions if the doctor didn't advise me to avoid driving until it's been twenty-four hours since I passed out.*

"Alright, I admit I could have told you that it was Bobby Payne who caught you, and that he would be returning the car, but in my defense, I gave him *my* number. I thought he would text *me*, I would slip out for the keys, run interference, and you could have one day's reprieve before you saw him. I would've broken the news after you had a nap and some fries and could handle it better. I didn't want to stress you out."

"It's that white building on the right," is my only reply.

"Come ooonnnnn, Tasia," she whines. "It was for your own good—you scared me." Her voice softens on that confession, and so does my resolve.

"Fine," I sigh. "I forgive you... this time." She pulls into the parking space, then throws her arms around me, jerking me halfway over the console. She is little, but she is strong.

"Thank you, and I'm sorry. Next time you swoon into the love of your life's arms, I will not withhold the information from you for a second." My eye twitches, and I can feel a headache coming. I don't even have the energy to argue the statement.

Opening the car door, I check my watch. I wished I had time to call ahead and set up an appointment, but by the time I was discharged, the office of Jenkins and Montgomery Attorneys at Law was closed. I smile again, thinking about how twelve years ago it was Jenkins and Son, but Diane definitely deserved the promotion to partner. I hope she has time to squeeze me in, or else I fear I will be completely unprepared for my meeting, which I assume will be more of an interrogation, at 12:30.pm.

I open the sleek, modern steel door, the handle smooth and cool under my palm, and once again it feels like stepping back in time. To the left is a man on the phone who I recognize as the assistant to the younger Jenkins, but the girl to the right has me freezing. Where the receptionist desk used to sit, there is a girl behind it who looks very similar to the lady I remember—only if she had aged backwards this past decade. Having stopped short, Joanie slams into my back. Her shoes squeaking to a halt on the marble floor, gaining the attention of the girl.

"May I help you?" she inquires in a practiced professional tone.

"Katherine?" I blurt like someone who has no idea how to function in polite society; as if communication isn't part of my job. Joanie has her head on a swivel, taking in our interaction. The girl's face falls, and I know that look of grief. I see it too often in my own reflection.

"No, I am Leah. Katherine was my mother." I don't miss the use of *was* instead of *is,* and my heart breaks a little. Katherine was the receptionist when I was last here, as a scared, lonely teenager with no one to comfort me. She sat with me and held me while I cried into her shoulder. It had been the most maternal affection I had received in six years at that point, and it remains so to this day. That she isn't in this world to give that to her own daughter anymore is tragic.

"Oh, I am sorry, Leah. I haven't been to town in many years, but last time I was, Katherine was very kind to me. You must hear it a lot, but you look like her." I wince. Having the face of someone you can no longer embrace is its own mix of torture and blessing.

"Yes, often, but my mother was beautiful in so many ways, so I take that as a compliment. Thank you. So, what brings you in today?" Leah handles this awkward conversation with grace, and it reminds me even more of her mother. This time, however, I keep it to myself.

"I was wondering if Diane—sorry, if Ms. Montgomery is available. She did some work for me last time I was in town, and currently I find myself needing some urgent legal advice." I skirt around the subject. I feel like outright shouting that they have found bodies on my property, and I'm the main suspect—might be something best said behind closed doors.

"Oh! Well, Ms. Montgomery, as a partner, only takes meetings by appointment." Of course, a partner of a law firm wouldn't take walk-ins. My disappointment must show on my face. "However," she says, typing, "we have a few associates available."

I can feel my stomach knot and anxiety rise. Joanie takes the opportunity to step up behind me and interject. "Leah, was it?" She waits for Leah to nod. "We appreciate that Ms. Montgomery's time is very valuable, and we would normally not hesitate to call ahead for an appointment. Annastasia and I only arrived yesterday and spent most of the day in the hospital.

By the time we were made aware of the need for legal services, your office was already closed. Which is why we endeavored to be the very first people through the door." Joanie is leaning hard on her prep school upbringing, and I am glad for it in this moment.

"Annastasia? Oh—" Recognition lights in Leah's honeyed eyes as they shift to me. "You're Annastasia Adkins?" At my nod, she continues." Oh my. My mother spoke of you. I am very sorry for your loss."

It is my turn to fall back on the pleasantries of polite conversation, "Yes, well... it was a very long time ago."

"Grief and loss have no concept of time," she says as only someone who walks with both daily can understand.

However, I do not mourn my father in the way she mourns her mother, but that is more than I am willing to share, so instead I say, "Ms. Montgomery was very helpful to me back then, and I trust her implicitly. You could see why I would seek her out now."

She scans her screen for a moment and stands. "Hang on a moment, okay?" With that, she disappears behind a door marked with an 'M' monogrammed in gold. Less than a minute later, she reemerges and settles behind her desk. "Ms. Montgomery will see you now."

Relief ripples down my spine, which had gone ridged with anticipation. We step through the threshold, nodding in thanks to Leah as we pass. There, behind a mahogany desk, sits Diane, still the most put-together woman I have ever met. I recall at sixteen thinking I wanted to be her someday; a force, someone people respect and take seriously. Twelve years later, and I am still missing the mark.

She rises from behind her desk and approaches me, her stoic face melting into genuine affection. "Anna, my dear, it has been too long," she states, pulling me into a hug and then holding me at arm's length to assess me. "Leah tells me you were in the hospital?"

"Only a little fatigue mixed with stress, the cause of which brings me here," I inform her. It is then that she notices Joanie. "This is my friend and roommate, Joanie. She made the trip with me so I wouldn't have to face everything alone."

"Yes, I can understand the overwhelm you may be experiencing returning home. Come in, both of you. Have a seat. Tell me all about it."

Taking a seat in one of the plush chairs in front of the desk, I tell her what's been going on. Joanie fills in the blanks from when I was in the tightest grips of my anxiety. Then I finish with the message Bobby gave me last night about the additional bodies and the summons this afternoon.

"Well, that certainly is a lot to wrap your head around. I am glad you came to me. It is most likely a meeting to remove you from the suspect pool, but you should never go into a situation like this unprepared." She taps a button on her phone and summons Leah to her office.

The door creaks open, and Leah walks in, tablet in hand. She pulls a stylist from behind her ear, causing a mocha ringlet to fall loose. The door closes with a click behind her, and I notice how well it blocks the background office noise. If only I could have one installed in my mind to make a quiet room to retreat to.

"Leah, I need you to make room in my schedule. Move anything that is not time sensitive, and delegate anything that is to one of the associates. If there is anything that absolutely needs my attention today, shift it to after 2:00 pm." Leah nods and then dives into her tablet.

"I can move the research for the McCalls case to Levi, and your meeting with Mr. Davis should be fine to reschedule. I'll arrange for his favorite bourbon to be sent to him to soften any rough edges the short notice should cause. There doesn't seem to be anything I can't reasonably rearrange." I am impressed with the speed and attention to detail she displays in the face of such a daunting task.

"Thank you, Leah. That should be all for now." Dismissed for now, she nods back and slips outside the office, set on her task. Focusing back on me, Diane says, "Now, my dear, we have three hours to prepare and get you ready for an interrogation."

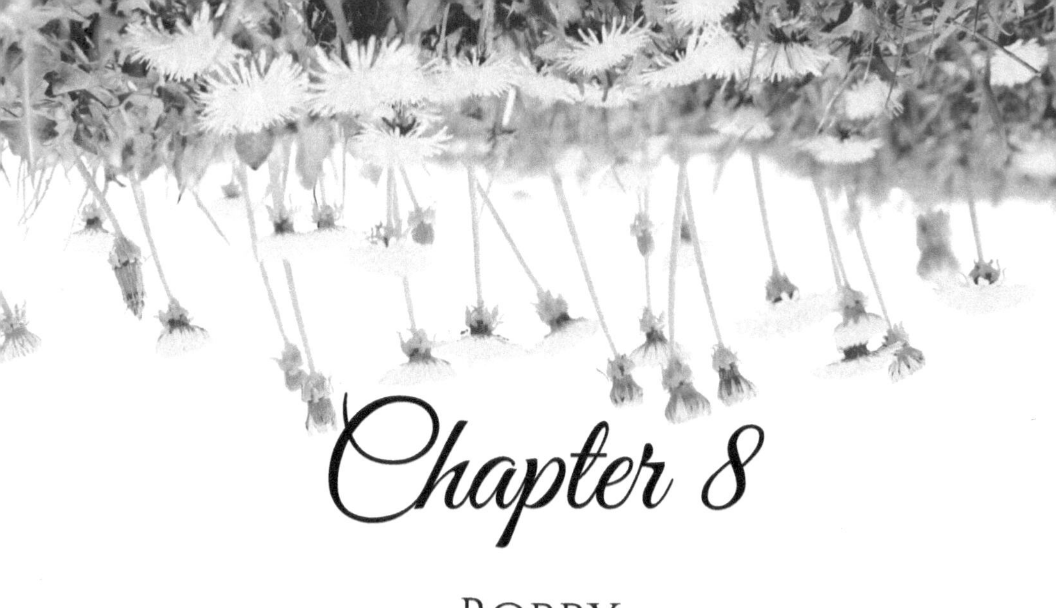

Chapter 8

BOBBY

I had to bribe Johnny to keep his fat trap shut about Anna's reappearance in Boremanton. I will pick up his tab for a month at the Wolf and Whistle. The glint in his eye as we shook on it already has my wallet crying, but if it keeps Anna out of the Payne family newsletter, then it will be worth it. But to be sure I have the funds liquid, I am checking my online bank statement as I push the door open to the sheriff's office.

Stepping over the threshold, I feel a prickle of unease. Sensing eyes on me, I look up to see Leanne Baily giving me a pitying look. Brushing it off as my overactive imagination, I greet our receptionist with a tip of my hat. The stares do not stop with her, though. Making my way into the bull pen, I can't help but notice all the other deputies look like they have stopped talking mid-conversation. Their eyes trail me as I sit at my desk, each of them mirroring Leanne's pity. *What's going on?*

Jarred Wojack, the only deputy to graduate in my class, strolls over to my desk, concern plastered on his face. It's beyond pity, but it's a look I know well. It's the look people give you when you're the sole survivor of a mission gone wrong, like one misstep or wrong word is gonna set you off like an unspent round of artillery. Ask me how I know that look.

Hands up, placating like he was approaching some wounded animal, Jarred breaks the silence. "Hey man, I'm just the messenger here. Remember that, okay?"

Brow raised, I nod, really fucking confused at what's got everyone acting so strange. "Go on then, rip it off quick like a bandage." One day seeing Anna again and I am already borrowing her sayings.

"Well, man, we all know your history with the Adkins girl, but we are from around here, so we all have our own history with her, too. No one thinks it's gonna interfere with your job."

"Wojack, I said, quick, not pull each stuck hair individually."

"Ahh shit, okay." Jarred takes a breath like he is fortifying himself, and then on the exhale, he lets it rip. "We all knew you were close, and there may be some lingering... uh... feelings about how everything went down. I mean, it was an awful thing—tragic really, and you were there, so I don't have to tell you that. Never crossed our minds that it would affect this case for you. But Jones ain't from round here. He didn't know. Must have went home and got talking to Jess and mentioned the case, or at least the part about Anna being back."

I don't like where this is going. *Am I the only one round these parts that can keep anything confidential?*

"And seeing as she knows ya better than most, she must have filled him in on some details. He came in here spewing nonsense on how you're too close to investigate thoroughly and went to the sheriff to get you off the case," he finishes.

A myriad of feelings wash over me at once; anger that Jones thinks I can't do my job; especially since he is the one giving case details to a civilian—a little betrayed that Jess would gossip about me—she was the one that held me when I cried and my brothers were too out of their emotional depth to comfort me when everything went down—and last, a bit of relief. If I am off the case, I could go to Anna, offer her comfort, bask in her nearness for as long as I can, and be her support. *If she lets me.*

"I mean, we know that's bullshit. It's been twelve years. You are a professional. You can separate your past from the case. It's a small town, we all know everyone. There would be no one to run any case if we were excused every time we have a relationship with someone."

That part is true enough. I've run my own brothers into the drunk tank a time or two, but I don't get time to settle on how this newest revelation makes me feel before I am being summoned.

"Payne, my office," cracks the whip-sharp tone of Sheriff Dobbs. I am on my feet and across the room in an instant. Stepping through the threshold, I see Jones sitting in one of the chairs in front of the desk and have to clench my jaw to keep it shut. Despite my complicated feelings about this case, he shouldn't involve himself in my business.

"Have a seat, son." The desire to snap back that I'm not his son is strong, but I tramp it down. Sheriff Dobbs is my superior and deserves my respect. I take the seat by Jones and wait to hear that I am being pulled from the case.

"I'll cut right to the chase." One thing to admire about Sheriff Dobbs is that he doesn't beat around the bush. "Deputy Jones here has brought up some concerns about your ability to remain objective in this case due to your history with Ms. Adkins."

Glancing over to Jones, I don't miss the self-satisfaction written all over his face. I am not sure what his motivation is here, but I want to slap that smug smirk off his face.

I almost get lost in the fantasy of doing that when Sheriff Dobbs' next words shock me back into attention. "However, I disagree. I think that your history with that property and Ms. Adkins can only provide much-needed insight and perspective. That's why I am going to have you be second to me on this case."

Before I can respond, Jones pipes in. "Sir, do you think that's wise? Jess says that there was something of a romantic nature between them, how can—"

"Yes, Jones, believe me, we are all well aware that Payne took Anna to homecoming. I myself was first on the scene when they put her father in a body bag after that unfortunate business with the wolf. If you were around back then, you wouldn't need to be hearing it second hand from your wife. The whole town is aware." His eyes narrow in focus on Jones. "On that note, Deputy Jones, I recall issuing a gag order on the specifics of this case, and last I checked, wives were not included in that confidence, so for that reason, you are off this case as of right now."

Standing so fast, the chair is sent screeching back on the linoleum floor, Jones seethes. "You cannot be serious!"

"Oh, I am very serious. When I ask for confidentiality, I expect it to be honored. And if you don't calm down, you will bluster your way to a suspension. Why don't you take the day to cool off, son? I don't want to see you back until tomorrow." Sheriff Dobbs doesn't raise his voice, but the command is there all the same. Jones must hear it for what it is, a clear and concise dismissal, and with a frustrated grunt, he storms out of the office slamming the door in his wake.

Sheriff Dobbs turns back to me. "I meant what I said, Bobby. I think you can bring some valuable insight to the case, especially with your knowledge of the property. However, if you feel like it's too much, no one would blame you for stepping back."

No one would blame me, but they would pity me, and that's worse. "No, sir. Shouldn't be a problem."

"Good to hear. Ms. Adkins is coming in at 12:30 today for her interview. I want you in the room with me." He must read the surprise on my face because he continues, "For one, your presence should put her at ease, and second, people have tells. As you know, unless they've trained against them, they don't easily fade with time. I'd bet no one knows Anna Adkins tells better than you. If you think she is lying, you'll let me know when the interview is done."

"Yes, sir, but is this an interview or an interrogation?"

"They are one and the same, Payne. Now go on and do your interview prep. I need you up to date on the preliminary findings before we go in."

Understanding I am dismissed, I go to do as instructed, but before I make it through the door, the sheriff adds, "Once Ms. Adkins is clear of suspicion, any... fraternization would be above board." Reading the confusion on my face, he says, "Life doesn't often give us second chances. Don't miss an opportunity when it's given to you."

Chapter 9

ANNASTASIA

After spending the last hours being prepped and prepared for my meeting with the sheriff, I am less nervous. Leah was an absolute godsend, while Diane grilled me with all manner of invasive questions that might be asked. So I wouldn't have an emotional reaction out of surprise, Leah, with input from Joanie, put together a detailed timeline of my life and whereabouts from the time I left Boremanton when I was sixteen.

If those bodies had been placed there within the last twelve years, there was a detailed account with witness references that proved I could not have been the one to put them there. She even had photo references picked from the internet profiles of college and work acquaintances throughout the years. She is definitely worth whatever Diane is paying her.

If the bodies are from before I left town, well, I guess that murderer might be another bullet point I can add to my father's list of shining titles: drunk, abuser, poacher, hypocrite. It wouldn't even be that far of a stretch.

"You need to get that look off your face, dear. We need you to be neutral, not nauseous," Diane's voice rings out in the car, bringing me back to the present.

The thought that my father could be even more of a monster than the man in my memories does make me want to vomit, but Diane is right. I need to calm down.

"Now, I know you haven't been to the sheriff's office since the night of the attack, but try not to let it put you in an emotional state," she says as if I have control of what triggers me or not.

"I will focus on the present. Or at least try to."

"Remember, Anna, you have nothing to worry about. Stick to the facts. This is all a formality. Something they have to check off before they concentrate their efforts elsewhere."

"Do you really think they will call my coworkers? I don't want this to follow me back home." Because I have worked hard to separate my life there from the one I lived here. Boremanton has not been home for many years, and now any thoughts of a potential return were fading fast. Small towns have long memories, and even if I could find a way to live with the constant reminders of the past, I'm not sure I could live with the addition of this stain as well.

"It would be their due diligence to fully investigate all the information, so yes, I do believe they will," she says.

Joanie stayed back with Leah to contact some of our coworkers to let them know they are listed as references, and they may be contacted to confirm dates and times. The Las Vegas day is just starting, and many in our industry don't work typical nine-to-five hours. Calling them any earlier would be rude but not giving them the heads up would result in them screening the calls and dismissing them as a scam. I mean, who would believe the sheriff of a town you've never heard of would be calling you?

Diane pulls up in front of the station, letting her engine idle for a moment while I collect myself. "Anna, it is going to be okay. I promise not to let them steam roll in you in there. You were right to have come to me." Patting my hand, she turns off the engine and exits the car.

I take the moment alone to ground myself in the present.

Five things I can see: the black front door of the sheriff's office. The blue border of the West Virginia state flag. The statue of Arthur Boreman in front of the courthouse. The white rhododendrons. The woman walking a Pomeranian in matching Steelers shirts. The starlings on the telephone wire.

Four things I can feel: the supple leather of the car seat. The smooth silk of my blouse. The textured weave of my tweed skirt. The cool ridges of the engraving on my locket as my thumb rubs over it for comfort.

Three things I can hear: the hum of small-town traffic, the click of a car door shutting, the lilting laughter of the children playing at Sally's daycare two doors down.

Two things I can smell: the jasmine car freshener clipped to the vanity mirror, the light coconut scent of my sunscreen.

And one thing I can taste: the winter fresh flavor of my chewing gum clenched between my teeth.

I take a deep breath, exhale, and then I am out of the car and following Diane into the station.

The building hasn't changed over the last twelve years, though I guess these utilitarian buildings have no need to change with the times. One notable difference is the person sitting at the receptionist's desk. Last time I was here, that seat was occupied by Mrs. O'Reilly, a kind older woman. But now I am face-to-face with Leanne Bailey. I try to stay in the present, but the memory comes to me unbridled.

(Twelve years ago, homecoming)

"Did you see Anna Adkins in Caroline Stone's hand-me-down dress? How embarrassing." The nasal tone of Maggie Baker echoes off the stalls of the restroom.

"Oh my God, I know, and it doesn't even fit her. Her boobs are spilling out of it," Collette Swanson chimes in. "She looks like a hooker."

"It's the only reason Bobby would ask her over you, Leanne. She is easy, just like her mother," Sarah Harkins adds her two cents. "The way she follows him and his brothers around is pathetic. She'd probably let them all run a train on her."

"Well, let's hope he gets his slumming out of his system and that she doesn't trap him like her mother did her pa. Getting knocked up in high school and leaving the poor guy with the brat when the next dick to ride out of town came along, can you imagine? It's no wonder he is a drunk," Leanne Bailey, the group's ringleader, contributes. I have had enough. I flush the toilet, announcing to the group of gossips that they are not alone. I walk behind them as they fuss with their hair and powder their noses to the sink to the right of them to wash my hands. Maintaining eye contact through the mirror while I lather, I smile.

"As much as I am honored to be taking up prime real estate in y'all's minds, I need to be getting back to *my* date. Did you know Bobby told me that my dress made my eyes sparkle like sapphires, and he's never seen a prettier sight? Ain't he sweet?" Their silence is almost as loud as their jabbering. "Well, I'll let you get back to speculating about my life while I go out there and live it." The outraged gasp that follows my departure is satisfying.

I am remiss to note that Leanne has not let herself go; she looks much the same as she did the last time I saw her in that bathroom on homecoming. Sure, her face has lost the roundness of youth, but the now pronounced set to her cheekbones suits her fine. *Would it be too much to ask that she'd have leathered under all those tanning bed lights?*

"Hello, welcome to the Boremanton Sheriff's office. How can I help you?" Her pleasantries are as fake as her veneered smile. Before I can suss out if she doesn't recognize me or if this is her posturing to get under my skin, she notices that I am not alone. Her eyes bulge at the sight of Diane plucking a nonexistent piece of lint from the lapel of her Prada jacket. "Oh, Ms. Montgomery." She sounds flustered, clicking away at her keyboard." Did we have you on schedule today? I don't know how I missed that." With the rapid way she is clicking her mouse, you would think she was sending out Morse code. "This system is such a sieve. We really need more funding."

"Calm yourself, Leanne. I am accompanying Ms. Adkins here for her interview with Sheriff Dobbs." Diane manages a tone that rings of boredom and condescension—not for the first time I think I want to be her when I grow up.

Sitting up straighter, her gaze falls back on me. "Oh my, Anna. I hardly recognized you." Her gaze does a scrutinizing scan from head to toe."

It's no wonder. It has been ages, and you always were an unkempt little tomboy back then. I would have walked right past you in your fancy new clothes and been none the wiser." The barbed compliment delivered in that saccharine tone rolls off my back like molasses on a hot day, but I will be goddamned if I let her know she has any effect on me.

"Oh well, Leanne, I can't say the same. You look just like you did in high school—almost like you never stepped foot out of this town. Good for you." The jab lands as intended, to make her feel small, like this town. Her smile tightens, and there is a barely noticeable tick to her right eye. I have the advantage of not being on the clock, and my customer service voice clocked out two days ago.

"Well, anywho, why don't you and Ms. Montgomery take a seat right there? I will go see if the sheriff is ready to see you. Won't be but a moment." She pushes against her desk, the motion sending her office chair wheeling back even after her lithe frame has left it. It hits the filing cabinet with a thud as she disappears behind a corridor.

"Can you believe that insipid little twit thought she could waltz into my office and be handed a job, not even one day after she heard of Kathy's accident on the police scanner? Her death wasn't even made public, and she comes walking in like she just won the golden ticket. Mind you, I had not even been notified, and that is how I found out."

"Oh no! That is awful! From what I remember, you two were close."

"Yes, she had become somewhat of a sister to me. And her kids—like the nieces and nephews I never had. You can bet Miss Bailey was fit to be tied to hear that I gave Leah the job right out of high school."

"Tragedy aside, I would have paid to see the look on her face."

Smiling like the cat that got the cream, she goes on. "Yes, that was satisfying. However, she then made it her mission to make trouble for Leah when she was fighting to keep custody of the kids. Nothing I couldn't counter, mind you, but still watch out for that one. She is a snake."

"Oh, don't I know it."

Leanne slithers around the corner and says, "All ready for you, Ms. Adkins." *So much for Anna.* "You and Ms. Montgomery can head on down to interview room number one. Go down this hall, and make a left, and then it's the first door on the right. Sitting back at her desk, her back ramrod straight, she doesn't spare us another glance—a clear dismissal. *Fine by me. You are one of the last people I would want to make small talk with.*

Diane leads the way, back straight and head held high as her red bottoms make a satisfying click. I do my best imitation in my Steve Maddens, but the sound is nowhere near as intimidating, I am sure. We follow the corridor and find the room where Leanne said we would. It isn't like it is a labyrinth of halls. As if sensing our approach, the door swings inward and is held open by Sheriff Dobbs.

"Diane, it is always a pleasure, but you didn't have to concern yourself with this. It is just a routine interview."

"That is sweet of you, Dwight, but if it was so simple, why did Ms. Adkins fly across the country? Would a phone interview or hell even a Zoom meeting not suffice?" I am standing behind her still in the threshold, but I swear I can hear her perfectly manicured brow rise with that upward inflection in her tone. "If it is all the same to you, Ms. Adkins has asked me to sit in, and that is what I intend to do. There won't be a problem with that, will there, Sheriff Dobbs?"

"No, don't s'pose there will be, ma'am." Sheriff Dobbs steps aside to let Diane pass and his gaze falls on me. "Afternoon, Anna. Sorry to call you back for such unfortunate circumstances. If you would have a seat, we will get this done as fast as possible."

Nodding my agreement, I step into the room and sit next to Diane. It is at that moment that I realize there is someone else seated across from me as my gaze meets the hazel gaze of Deputy Bobby Payne.

"Afternoon, Anna, Ms. Montgomery. " He nods to each of us in kind.

I run my thumb over the textured surface of my ring, and only when I am sure I am grounded enough in the here and now for my voice to come out calm, I reply. "Deputy Payne, a pleasure as always."

"Is it?"

Bobby

After Leanne rushed back here fit to be tied—huffing like a show horse that had just run its paces—to alert us that Anna had brought legal counsel by way of one Ms. Diane Montgomery, I would have thought Sheriff Dobbs had swallowed his tongue. We all have a betting pool that there is some sort of history between the two, but the sheriff is too stoic to entertain locker room talk of past exploits, and no one would dare ask Ms. Montgomery. *That lady scares the piss out of me.*

Anyone with common sense knows that's a nest of bees best left un-kicked. I had almost forgotten that she represented Anna in that court case about the land all those years ago. Makes sense that when she asked if she should talk to a lawyer, she called up Ms. Montgomery, even though it is not like her to take as many pro bono cases these days. I guess having your name on the building lets you delegate those tasks. Though I seem to recall she took up for the Willson girl after that unfortunate accident that took the girl's parents and left her guardian of a couple of kids when she was a kid herself.

That wreck had been brutal. I was one of the first responders. It is amazing that the little girl made it out alive. I shake my head. That one was tough. I had to call my therapist as soon as I made it back to the station. It stirred up too many memories that still haunt me. Maybe Anna had the right of it to leave and stay gone, before becoming another specter in these mountains.

Now called back to deal with more ghosts herself, she looks like she wants to be anywhere else. Her general shock at seeing me contrasts with her pleasant greeting. I find there is nothing I hate more than witnessing the force of nature of the girl in my memories falling back on polite necessities with me now. Shuffling the papers in the file to keep from reaching across the table to take her hand, I am questioning the sheriff's logic in having me in here. I am out of sorts and uncomfortable in my skin.

The grating noise of metal against linoleum breaks me out of my anxious thoughts as Sheriff Dobbs occupies the seat next to me.

"Alright, Anna, let's get right into it," Dobbs states in a stern but kind manner. "As you have been made aware, human remains have been found on your property. What we first believed was one body, has turned out to be multiple." He pauses to wait for her acknowledgement of this information and continues once she nods. "This is a warrant to expand our search." He slides the document to Anna and then turns to look at Ms. Montgomery. "I wasn't aware we would have you joining us, Diane, so I didn't prepare you a copy, but once Leanne told me that you were here, I had her start the process of getting it sent over to your office. It should be there before you return."

"Thank you, Sheriff Dobbs. I am sure Leah will let me know of its arrival," is Ms. Montgomery's curt reply. I watch as Anna sifts through the paper, posture straight as an arrow, a mask of collected calm sits upon her features, and I can't read her. *How can someone I once knew like the back of my hand feel like such a stranger to me now?* Once satisfied with her perusal, she hands the stack to Diane, who pulls out a pair of readers that I am sure cost more than my car, and places them at the end of her sharp nose as she reviews the warrant for herself.

Anna turns to address the sheriff. "From what I can tell, you want to excavate a twenty-foot radius of the initial site, have cadaver dogs search the rest of the property and the buildings. Is that correct?"

"That is about the sum of it, yes. It is court-ordered and signed by a judge, so presenting this is only a formality, but are there any objections that you have to these actions?" If I hadn't been so trained on her, I might have missed the unsure shift of her eyes to Diane and her barely perceptible nod in return. *Ah, so not non-paused. Just well coached.*

"No objections. I am not going to interfere with your investigation, Sheriff. The faster you get to the bottom of this, the faster we can get back to the plans for the land. Remember, it was a crew that I hired that found this mess after all. I have nothing to hide."

"What are your plans with the land?" The words are out of my mouth before I even register that I was speaking. I was meant to be a silent observer; so much for that. *It's a valid question for the investigation. It's not like I am asking because I want to know if she is moving back,* I almost convince myself. Dobbs nods his head, backing up my question, but I feel like we are going to talk about my breach of protocol once this is over.

"The plan was to have it be a retreat of sorts. A place to get away from the stress of constantly being plugged in, but still respecting the nature and wildlife of the land. They were breaking ground for a natural swimming pool—they rely on aquatic plants and biological filters for a chemical-free filtration process." She reaches into a briefcase and hands some papers to the sheriff, even though I asked the question, effectively ignoring me. *Nothing new there.* "Here are the construction plans and a copy of my business plan. It is a rough outline, but you can get a gist of the scope of the project."

"So, you were moving back to run a resort?" Why do I sound so hopeful? Does she pick up on the tone? *I hope not.*

"I was planning to hire staff and run it remotely at first. If it proved to be successful, I would reevaluate the need to maintain my current position in Vegas. It's to be a retirement plan of sorts. Vegas is great for the industry, but it wears on you for long-term living. I was planning on a quieter option in the long run."

"Why now?" Dobbs interjects. "The land has been vacant for over a decade. What made you decide to develop now?"

"Well, I don't know if you know this, Sheriff, but until I turned 25, the land was held for me in trust. I could not make any move to sell or develop it until then."

"Still, that was three years ago."

"Yes, and three years ago I was still green in the industry and was not confident enough in my experience to take on such an endeavor, nor did I have the liquid capital." *I can't figure out if she was coached to speak like this, or if this is who she has molded herself into. Where is my Anna?* It is at this point that Diane chimes in, pulling out a portfolio from her own case.

"Let's cut to the quick of it, shall we, gentlemen? Annastasia has spent the last decade in Las Vegas, and the two years between the passing of her father and freshman year at LVU were spent at a residential boarding school while she worked towards graduating and dealing with PTSD.

That folder details her whereabouts for the last twelve years in chronological order, with references to signed affidavits and time-stamped social media posts. Dwight, Leah should have an electronic version of this with hyperlinks and an Excel sheet prepared and sitting in your inbox by now.

Annastasia hasn't stepped one foot into Boremanton since she entered the halls of Westly Hall in Morgantown twelve years ago. So, unless your forensics comes back that any of those bodies predate her being sixteen years old, there is no way that she is involved. If that is the case, well, I hardly think her to be capable of mass murder at such a tender age. She is here as a sign of good faith and is willing to cooperate with you and your investigation, but she does have a life, job, and plans to attend to. How long do you think she needs to stay in town for? She needs to make accommodations if it is beyond this week."

"Well, this is certainly... uh, thorough, and does cover most of the questions that we had for Miss Adkins at this time. We will need time, of course, to verify this information—"

"Of course, so we will get out of your hair to allow you to do just that." Standing, Ms. Montgomery interrupts. Anna rises from her chair as well, but hesitates.

"In the spirit of cooperation and full disclosure, sir," pausing to chew on her lip, a nervous tick she has had long as I can remember, "well, the dogs, if they are only trained to find, uh, human remains, it may not even matter. But a couple of years before my pa, well, passed," Her polished tone falters, and she falls back onto more familiar speech patterns, "I found some evidence that he may have been poachin' in that old shed out back. I can't be sure that there ain't animal remains. It's been a long time, and as we've said, I haven't been back to check on the state of things."

Before they can take one step to the door, I blurt out, "Why not sell the land?" And then, quieter, I continue, "When you first had the chance? Why hold on to something that has obviously caused you so much pain?"

Her answer is unrehearsed, real, and raw. "If she came back, how else would she find me?" And the timid crack in her voice at the end is what breaks my heart. After all this time, she is still holding out hope that her mother will come back for her. It takes all my willpower to stay rooted to my spot as she follows Ms. Montgomery out the door.

Chapter 10

ANNASTASIA

So how long do we have to stay?" Joanie asks from her place on the fluffy paisley duvet that covers the king-size mattress that we are sharing for the foreseeable future, as I pace the floor. Once we got out of the hospital, it was hours past our check-in at the bed and breakfast off Coal Avenue, and they gave away our suite with two double beds. The only room they had left was the honeymoon suite. Seems there is an orientation happening at the local college, and all the rooms in town are booked. So, we find ourselves in our very own one-bed trope, with no chance of either of us getting lucky but a one hundred percent chance of Joanie hogging all the covers.

At least it is warm in West Virginia in early June. Had this visit been in winter, we would have had a fight on our hands. However, had this been winter, I wouldn't have had anyone digging up all this trouble in the first place—so there is that.

"I don't know. Depends on what they find and how long it takes them to realize I had nothing to do with it. Hopefully, all the data you and Leah collected will go a long way to help in that respect."

"They can't expect you to hold up here indefinitely, though. You have a life to get back to. A job, rent to pay," she mumbles that last bit as she pops the second of the heart-shaped chocolates left on our pillows into her mouth.

"I have PTO banked, and I can probably take a personal leave, but I know it isn't ideal." I stop my pacing, take a deep breath, and on the exhale, I spin to lock my gaze on hers. The abrupt movement has her stopping in mid-chew; cheeks puffed out like a hamster storing snacks for a later time. "You should go back. I am okay. I can handle this."

Deep brown eyes roll so hard I imagine I could hear them rattle like dice in her head. "Yes, autopilot driving to a crime scene to almost get arrested and then passing out screams 'I got this' energy."

"I hadn't slept well, and I admit I was not in the best frame of mind, but now I'm rested and hydrated, thanks to IV fluids. I have been using my breathing techniques, and I will be okay. I promise. I can't ask you to stay."

"Good thing you didn't ask, then." She is so stubborn; usually a quality I admire, but I find it irritating when directed at me.

"Look, I am not leaving you to wallow in this shit alone. Not when you don't have anyone on your side." She holds up a hand as my mouth opens. "As lovely as Diane is, she is on your payroll, and she isn't going to keep you out of the paths of Billie Jo Jean, the homecoming queen—"

"Leanne," I interrupt

"—and her cohorts," she continues as if I hadn't spoken. "And your only actual friend here is actively investigating you, if you can even call someone you haven't spoken with in twelve years a friend."

"That's not fair, Jo. He was serving in the military."

"Until yesterday?" she questions. I don't mention the stack of unanswered letters from my time at Westly Hall; they have a special place tucked inside a locked box beneath my bed.

"No, but it isn't like I left a map of where to find me, or a forwarding address. All of my socials are Tasia Finley for a reason. I didn't necessarily want to be found. You don't understand what it was like at first. That was the most salacious thing to happen in these parts. Up until now, I suppose, once word gets out. It didn't matter that I was a minor—the reporters were relentless and tracked me all the way to Westly Hall to get a statement. Once I could get away, I did. I couldn't stay."

Her eyes soften, and she scoots to the end of the bed to take my hands. "I know, and that's why I don't want to leave you here with no one in your corner."

"I could call Caroline, we still talk. Granted not as much as I should, but she can be in my corner."

She tilts her head to the side. "I thought you didn't talk to anyone from here anymore."

"Caroline wrote to me in the boarding house." I leave out that she wasn't the only one. "Before I left, I made sure she had my email. She had moved to Pennsylvania to go to school and stayed with a boy she was seeing after she graduated, but she moved back to town last year when her mom got diagnosed with MS. We don't talk like we used to in school, but we do catch up here and there."

"You have been keeping secret friendships from me?" Her voice gets quiet, and she looks down as if she is unable to keep eye contact.

"You have friends besides me, Jo."

"I don't keep them from you. You have apparently been talking to her for years. Why keep it a secret?"

"It isn't like that, Jo. It's just she still had ties here, and if I severed this one last ribbon home, what if Mom came back? How would I know? And now that I have said it out loud, it sounds ridiculous and selfish to only keep in contact with someone for the information they can supply."

"You don't use people, Tasia. Even if that is why you say you kept talking to her, even if it is part of it—it isn't the only reason. If you take the time to keep up with someone, it is because you care about them. I'm not upset that I have to share you, but that you didn't think you could tell me."

"I will bring it up with Jenn next session. I am not sure why I wanted to keep it so separate."

"Well, I want to meet this friend. I have to make sure you're in good hands before I leave you with them. I have a vested interest."

I know it is a turn of phrase, but it makes my stomach sink. I am reminded that I'm not the only one with stakes tied into this resort plan, and that thought makes me queasy. What if I can't build? What if I lose the money Joanie invested because she believed in me?

"Hey, where did you go just now? What is with the face?"

"Joanie, if we can't continue with our plans, if this mess makes it impossible, I promise to sell the land so I can pay you back. I don't want you to worry about your investment."

"Tasia... God, that's not what I meant. I wasn't even thinking about that. My interest is in you. You are my best friend. I know what this land means to you. I know it is the last tie you feel you have to your mom. I would never ask you to sell it, unless that is something you want to do. I invested in your business idea because I believe in you, and would a return on that investment be great? Yeah it would. But we live in Vegas, babe, No one understands the concept of 'you win some, you lose some' more than us. It is fine. Whatever happens, it isn't going to break me. Don't even worry about that right now. One thing at a time, remember?"

"You're right, sorry, I am catastrophizing." Breathing out, I fall back onto the mattress next to her. Staring at the ceiling fan blades as they go round, I try to calm down by breathing. All this stress cannot be good for me.

"Have you talked to Jennifer at all since this all started happening?"

"Jo, you have been at my side this whole time besides just now at the station, so you know damn well I have not contacted my therapist." The unimpressed look that she gives me would make a weaker person recant whatever it was they said that caused it, but after a decade, I am immune to her laser gaze.

"Well, now that you have nothing to do but sit around and wait, don't you think that it may be a good time?"

"We don't have a scheduled session for two more days."

"You passed out due to a panic attack and landed in the hospital, you have quite literally driven into the physical embodiment of all your past traumas, and there are bodies, plural, now that it has been confirmed, involved. I think now is the perfect time to pull the emergency lever and contact your therapist who specializes in Post Traumatic Stress Disorder. Seeing as there are triggers around every corner here."

"There hasn't been any time."

"Well, there is time now. Unless you have committed the rest of the evening to counting the rotations of the ceiling fan?"

"I hate you." That comment is met with a fluffy down pillow to the face.

"You don't. I will even take a walk around town to give you some privacy and see what this little town has to offer."

"Okay, fine!"

"Message this mysterious other friend while you are at it. I want un-hinged childhood stories, at least, as penance for you never mentioning them."

"I've told you childhood stories," I say in offense.

"I want them from other people's point of view. You are an unreliable narrator." Slipping on her shoes, she turns, heading for the door to leave me to my tasks. Before she can turn the knob, she gives me a sly look over her shoulder and says, "Though I guess I could always seek them out of the friendly neighborhood deputy, or that ginger paramedic that clearly has the hots for you. You didn't tell me you left behind a harem when you left this sleepy little town, you ho." Ducking before the pillow smacks her in the back of the head, she gives me a dubious look as it thuds against the wall and falls to the floor, purpose unfulfilled. Shaking her head, she slips through the door with the echoes of her laughter bouncing off the halls.

Left alone to my own devices, I decide not to set myself a lecture upon her return and shoot off a message to Caroline.

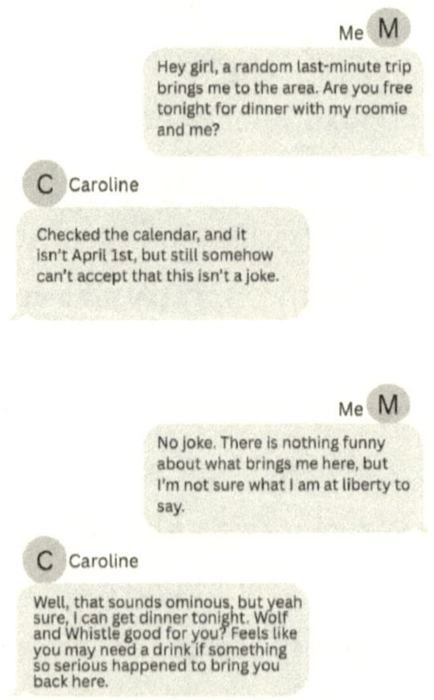

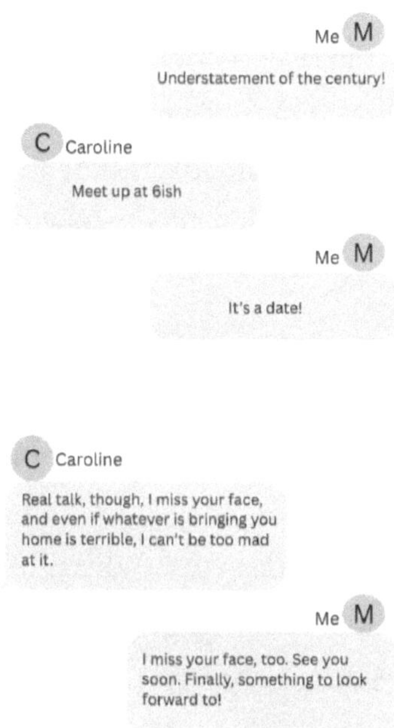

Exiting my messaging app and pulling up an email, I type out the cliff notes version of the past few days to my therapist to give her some background and ask when she has time to talk to let me know. As annoying as it is to admit, Joanie is right; I am drowning here. I need a life raft. I hit send and resume my former state of tracking the ceiling fan. It takes five minutes for my phone to alert me to an incoming video call, *two hundred rotations,* I click accept and hold the phone aloft so I don't have to pull myself into a seated position.

"Annastasia Finley Adkins, what do you mean you are in your hometown for a police investigation involving literal bodies buried in your backyard and have not bothered to call me yet?" Jennifer scolds, which tells me I've really done it now. I've riled up my unflappable, even-keeled therapist enough to use her 'mom tone' on me.

Sighing, I sit up, scooting back to feel the cool press of the wrought iron headboard through the thin layer of my blouse. This needs to be an upright conversation. "Hey Jenn, I didn't want to be a bother." She has a way of conveying her skepticism with a singular lift of an eyebrow that translates even to the tiny screen of my phone. *Okay, clearly, she is in no mood for my diversions today.*

"Tasia, I am your therapist, and you are in a field full of land mines set to trigger you at any moment. This is the exact time that you need to call me. You can't raw-dog your mental health and hope to make it to session. Not with PTSD."

"Okay, okay, I hear you, I understand. Where do you want me to start?"

"From Monday morning when you got the phone call, and none of this abridged bullshit. I need the nitty gritty."

On an exaggerated exhale, I mutter, "Fine."

Chapter 11

ANNASTASIA

(15 years ago)

Duct tape tears off between my teeth with an echoing rip, the roll falling to the ground as I loop the tail around one more time, securing the flashlight to my handlebars. I asked for a fancy combination radio/headlight for my bike for Christmas, but Dad thought it was a ridiculous request and instead got me a set of gardening tools and a couple of packs of seeds. I can see the tools collecting dust in the corner of the garage. I tried to grow something, but I do not have a green thumb; the seeds barely sprouted before they withered and died.

I only wanted the light for occasions like this, when I get a call from the barkeep down at the Whistle telling me Pa had too many and they took his keys. It is saying something that he trusts a thirteen-year-old to drive over a drunk, but Pa doesn't keep many friends who could fill in for the job. So, I'll ride my bike down the switchbacks and load it in the bed of the truck while Mr. Wolfson loads my incoherent father into the passenger seat. I hope he was drinking beer tonight; whiskey makes him mean.

(Present day)

Pulling up to the Wolf and Whistle, I was worried that I may be subject to more rapid flashbacks. Lord knows I spent enough time here hauling my drunkard father back up the mountain long before I had a license. But unlike most of this sleepy little town, the Wolf and Whistle has not stayed stuck as a static image in my memory. It has undergone some changes over the last decade. The once gravel parking lot has been paved, and the old sagging shingle roof is gone. In its place is what appears to be a brand-new metal one. The neon glow of the sign is, however, the same incandescent yellow reminiscent of the golden gaze of the wolves it is named for. I don't have much worry that walking inside will trigger my fight, flight, or freeze response. I did not spend as much time inside as I did in the parking lot.

"This place looks like it could be straight out of a hillbilly movie set, Like the backdrop to a Hatfield and McCoy feud," Joanie says as we walk toward the door, which I open and hold for her to make her way ahead of me.

"You should have seen it before the updates," I mention as she passes me.

"Updates? There is no way anything in this town has been updated this century, let alone decade."

"The paved parking lot and aluminum roof say otherwise."

She gives a skeptical look over her shoulder, then back to me. "Where did they park before they put in a lot?" The question is so genuine, I feel bad for the laugh that bursts out of me.

"There was a lot, but it wasn't paved."

"So, what? Like, just dirt?"

I snort at her confusion and say, "Close, but no. It was a gravel lot. Not sure when they laid asphalt down."

"That would be when Roman took over," a familiar voice interjects with the answer. Both Joanie and I are struck speechless for a beat.

"What the fuck are you wearing? Do you moonlight as a Furry?" Joanie cranes her neck to look around, as do I; we both find similarly dressed women carrying trays of drinks to tables. "Is this a fetish bar? Do they have those in the sticks?"

Leah, who was wearing a pristine business professional pant suit when we saw her this afternoon at the law firm, rolls her eyes. "No, it is a gimmick, like Hooters or Dixie Stampede."

"Okay, that explains the short shorts and tied-up plaid shirt. But what's with the fuzzy ears... and is that a tail?" I know for a fact that this was not the uniform the last time I was here. Not that there was one. There wasn't a wait staff at all, only a bartender, since they didn't serve food, but he did not wear fuzzy ears of any sort.

"Leaning into the name of the bar, one of the owners, Ken, thought it was a good idea to have a distinct theme." The reappearance of her eyeroll tells me all I have to know about her thoughts on that addition to the uniform.

"What are you doing moonlighting at a bar? Is Diane not paying you enough?" Joanie, ever so tactful, asks what I'm thinking myself.

"She pays well, but I have mouths to feed and dreams to fund, so I work as much as I can. However, I don't usually work Wednesday nights. I'm filling in for someone. Do you guys want to sit at the bar or a table? The hostess is on her break, but I have a table in my section if you want it."

"You can't poach all the tables, Leah! You are not even supposed to be here tonight. I told Ken I can take care of it. It is just a Wednesday." A redhead approaches from Leah's left.

"Uh, well, we're actually meeting someone here. Caroline Stone. She texted that she was already here." The other waitress loses her steam after hearing this, and in a huff, walks away.

"You can follow me. She is already in my section." She grabs some menus as she leads us off to the right, past the bar. I glance around as we weave in and out between the throng of bar patrons, and I notice that though there have been updates. The bar maintains a lot of the same rustic charm that I remember, with all the natural wood accents and decor.

Following Leah through an archway, I notice that the biggest change of all. Wolf and Whistle is a lot bigger than I remember. I did not notice it from the front façade; all the additions must have been added to the back. Passing a set of pool tables and some other electronic games, we are shown to a corner booth, where Caroline sees us coming and stands. Before I can even speak, she has her arms thrown around me in a bear hug that I swear could break a rib if I were a little less sturdy.

"Can't breathe." I huff out a laugh, patting her back awkwardly. If I am being honest, I wasn't sure how this reunion was going to go. Caroline has as much reason to strangle me as she does to hug me. She tightens her anaconda grip for a moment longer before she releases me from her hold, only for her to get her coils around Joanie a moment later.

"Oomph... uhh hello, I'm—"

"Joanie. Of course you are. I have heard all about you," Caroline interrupts before Joanie can introduce herself. Caroline whispers something into her ear, and I watch Joanie's eyes soften. I watch as any leftover annoyance at me for never mentioning Caroline to her melts away. *As if she has any reason to be concerned about her place in my life.*

Bemused, Leah takes in this odd reunion. "Well, I'll leave these here," she says, setting the menus down. "Can I get you something to drink before I go check on my other tables?"

"Thanks, Leah, I'll have whatever cider you have on tap." Scooting into the booth, I expect Joanie to slide in after me, but she is all but shoved into the other side, boxed in by Caroline. Suspicion sends tingles down my spine as this starts feeling like another form of interrogation that I am about to face.

"I'll have a Jack and Coke… actually make it a double." I swear I hear her mumble under her breath that she is going to need it, and now I am regretting not ordering something stronger myself.

Caroline takes whatever concoction is in her glass and throws it back. I can feel the vibrations through the wood table as she slams it back down in her enthusiasm. "I'll take a refill, Leah love, and we need a round of shots—Washington Apple to start."

Smirking at her antics, Leah gives Caroline a salute with the tip of her pen before securing it into the mess of curls on top of her head and leaves us to whatever fresh hell we have wandered into.

"Care, what are we celebrating here? I am not exactly here on a joyous occasion."

"Circumstances smirkumstances. I am celebrating seeing you in the flesh for the first time in over a decade, and to new friends," she says the last part, pulling Joanie into a side hug that looks no less crushing than the full-body one she had just escaped. Joanie's eyes scream for me to help her, but with a wince of remembrance, I decide it is better her than me and find a new appreciation for my solitary side of the booth.

Caroline may appear petite, but she is solid. Having grown up as an athlete, she has a strength that you would not guess upon first glance. A strength that I had begun to forget in its daily absence, and I regret that too. A bit defensive, I reply, "You knew where I was, Care. You could have come to me."

"To Las Vegas? I suppose I could have, but you were building a new life, and I didn't want you to be forced to entertain your past. No, that is your sanctuary, and without an invite from you, I was not going to be invading your safe space for my own whims." Her response takes on a more serious tone than her effervescent greeting from a few moments ago. Somehow, I feel worse, though I know she meant it to soothe. There is obvious mending that needs to be done here, and I guess this is where we start.

"Ladies," a deep voice interrupts whatever response I had, "here are the shots you ordered. A Hurricane for Caroline. Now, who gets the cider and who gets the double Jack and Coke?"

The man standing at the end of the table sets my teeth on edge. Something in his smile seems a little too put on, a little too slick. Nothing in his outfit stands out; it is your typical blue-collar uniform: work boots, cargo pants, flannel over a t-shirt. Except that the boots are unmarred, the pants are a little too pristine, no show of wear and tear, and even his undershirt looks to be pressed. It is as if he is wearing a costume of how he assumes a blue-collar man should dress.

Joanie points me and says, "Cider," then to herself, "Double Jack and Coke."

Placing her drink in front of her first, and as he sets my cider in front of me, he says, "It's good to have you back, Anna. Are you planning on sticking around?"

The question takes me back because I am positive I have never met this man before. I hesitate before I answer, "Just a visit this time." Trusting my instincts to keep things vague.

"Not planning on moving back into the old house? I mean, I can't blame you there. Has to be hard after everything that went down."

"Great talk, Ken. Way to bring up morbid shit no one wants to rehash. Really makes your patrons feel warm and cozy," Caroline interjects before Joanie can jump over her and smack the guy upside his head. "It is always so pleasant to be graced with your company." Hearing his name sparks a memory of a lanky, rich kid that I went to school with. If I squint and tilt my head, I think I can see the resemblance. He at least has the decency to look ashamed for a moment.

"Sorry, Anna, she is right. Shouldn't have brought it up. You ladies have a good night. Leah will be around if you need anything." He turns and leaves before I can answer, not even looking back.

Turning to Caroline, I ask. "There is no way that that was Kenny Sinclair, right?"

"Yup," she says, popping the 'p' as she takes a swig of her cocktail. "In all his smarmy glory. He may have bulked up since high school, but I assure you he has not been exercising his social skills. He is the general manager—runs the place under Roman."

I stare at his back until he disappears beyond the archway, contemplating the odd exchange. I shake my head, clearing the thought away, and say, "Well, let's not let the awkward encounter dampen the celebration." Looking at my two friends, in the same place for the first time, I grab my shot raising it in the air. "To good friends new and old." Caroline whoops and Joanie cheers as they tap their shots to mine. I let the glass bottom tap the wooden surface of the table once before raising it to my lips and tossing it back, feeling the tart liquid warm me from within.

I lost count of the rounds of shots we've consumed as I caught Caroline up on the real reason for my sudden reappearance in the town of my birth. Early into the tale, she declared that we would need something stronger and we switched from Washington Apples to straight shots of Fireball. I *do* know that I have had enough of the cinnamon-flavored burn that is known to accompany the libation, that my face is feeling warm and tingly.

"If this is a normal Wednesday night for you, Caroline, I have to say, you would fit right in if you did come to Vegas," Joanie states, followed by a hiccup that causes me to snort. "Though you may need considerably deeper pockets. How is everything so cheap here?"

"No one would be here if they hiked the prices. I am not sure if you noticed, but we are not exactly a booming metropolis full of opportunities," she responds with a roll of her blue grey eyes. "They'd just go back to their stills and homemade whisky and shine."

"Oh, and Mrs. Bianchi's dandelion wine! Remember, Care how she'd pay us to collect baskets full of them? Did you ever get a chance to try it?" I ask, as I recall one of the better memories I have from my youth.

"Of course I remember. Damn near paid the heap of junk I called my first car with pennies saved up from dandelions of all things. But sadly, no. The old bat kicked it before I moved back. I never did get to try some out for myself. Consider it a bucket list item forever left unchecked."

"I am sure you can find someone else who makes it," Joanie interjects. "From what I hear, it is a popular enough Italian tradition."

"Not the same," both Caroline and I state at the same time, leaving no room for further argument on the subject, but I continue the thread anyway. "The list specifically states, 'Drink a bottle of Mrs. Bianchi's dandelion wine', and the list allows for no substitutions."

"Oh, so this is a literal list? Not a metaphorical bucket list?" Joanie seems amused by the idea. She is looking at me funny as if she is seeing me through a new lens; a side of her friend she doesn't recognize. I am dying to know if it adds or subtracts from her estimation of me, but at the same time, I am afraid of the answer.

A new voice steals the answer before Caroline or I can voice it. "Oh, it is definitely a real list—signed at the bottom in blood, if I recall correctly. Isn't that right, Tom?"

"Yeah Pat, our baby brother was always a stickler for the rules. If the list says Mrs. Bianchi's dandelion wine, no other's will do, I am afraid. You'd be going against a blood pact, you see." The last bit was directed to Joanie in particular. "He and his friends here have a whole, actual scribbled-down list of things they wanted to do before they put this sleepy little town in their rearview."

I am up and out of the booth, with one arm around each man, before either of them can share more of our childhood secrets. Engulfing them in an embrace with a strength granted by alcohol—one that even Caroline would envy—I let out the most undignified screech that has ever passed my lips. "Oh. My. God!" I emphasize every word. "I can't believe you are here. I can't believe what I'm seeing."

Disengaging from my death grip, Thomas Payne holds me out at arm's length, one calloused hand on each of my shoulders, taking inventory to make sure I am here and whole. "It is far more surprising that you are here, Anna, though I had heard through the grapevine that it was true. I was having a hard time believing it myself. How have you been?"

The change in tone on the last bit, the little softening in his eyes—eyes the same hazel hue as his youngest brother but somehow wiser in their depths—is what breaks me. I cannot stop the tears that streak down my face or the broken sob that bubbles out of my throat. I can't even get my answer out in a coherent statement before Patrick has me engulfed in his arms and safely tucked under his chin against his barrel chest.

In a scathing tone that can only really be dismissed by brothers, Patrick says, "Good job, asshole. You went and made her cry."

"I didn't do anything. I just asked a question," Tommy shoots back, exasperated.

"I think maybe she has had a little too much to drink." This rather astute observation comes from another new voice, but one I recognize all the same.

"Hi, Johnny," I say, though muffled up against Patrick's chest, I am not sure if it came out as clear as I intended. I am wrestled free by none other than the true middle of the Payne brothers. I am suddenly concerned if a scolding from Max, the oldest, is awaiting me next.

"Hi, Squirt, been a while." His crooked smirk loosens another tear from my eye, but he catches it with his thumb and soothes, "None of that. No need to cry. We've got you, Anna... we always have." Hearing sniffles that are not my own, I turn to see Joanie and Caroline have devolved into sobbing puddles of goo at the scene that they witnessed. Letting go of a long-suffering sigh, Johnny addresses the table. "ow much have you girls had to drink tonight?"

"It's just so cute seeing men be so emotionally intelligent," Caroline stutters out, ignoring the question while blowing her nose in a cocktail napkin.

"Why didn't you ever tell me you had a harem of mountain men waiting for you back home, you bitch, and will you share? It's not fair to hoard them all, you hussy." I should have expected that from Joanie, but it causes the brothers to laugh.

"Okay, girls, I am going to settle your tab, and by that I mean I'm going to transfer it to Bobby's tab—he owes me one anyway. Tom and Pat are going to help you out to your cars. I'll meet you in the parking lot."

We must have drank more than I thought because even Joanie nods her consent without so much as a sassy remark and loops her arm through Tommy's right arm as Caroline mimics the action on his left. Patrick offers me his elbow, and I follow suit as we are escorted to the lot on the arms of the Payne brothers. Though I can't help but think of a different brother I would like to have my arms around tonight. *That's the liquor talking,* I try to convince myself, but there is that saying that drunk lips tell no lies. Good thing I didn't say it out loud.

Chapter 12

BOBBY

(Thursday)

S haking my head as I walk down the hall to the forensics lab, I re-read the text I got from Roman.

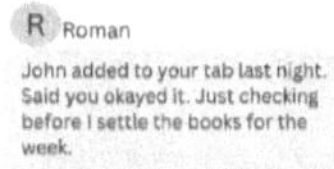

I scan the attached balance, trying to wrap my head around the sum.

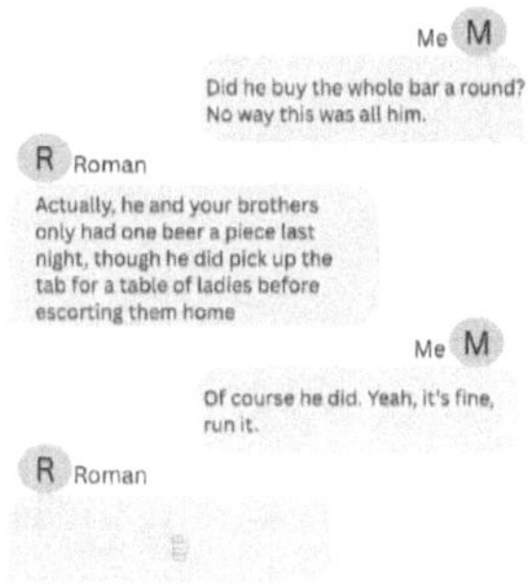

I pocket my phone as the door to the lab opens; I see my efforts to beat the sheriff to this meeting were futile. He is already in the room talking to one of the techs.

Nodding me over, he says, "Caitlyn was telling me something interesting that she found when going over the evidence from the Adkins place. Go on dear, fill Deputy Payne in."

"Well, our full report will take some time. We aren't high on the list of priorities, given the decomp rates of the remains. Since we have found no indication that any victim has died within the last year, we may be looking at solving some cold cases. Nothing so dire as to bump us up on the schedule for DNA results, but I think we can conclusively say that for the remains already discovered, they were definitely moved there."

"So, we are looking for another murder scene, is that what you are saying?"

"Not exactly. I am actually not certain they were all murdered at all. What I *am* saying is that they were moved. Though I guess that it would still be another crime scene that we are looking for, but one for theft, not murder." She must see the confusion in my stare as she explains. "These remains..." She gestures to the exam table. "...and all the ones that I have reviewed from the initial findings so far all have trace elements of soil inconsistent with that of the site. Furthermore, we can tell that the site had recently been disturbed when compared to the surrounding soil."

"So, you are saying we have a grave robber? Who what, dumped a bunch of bodies at the site?" Something in my tone must irritate her as she rolls her eyes before she can continue.

"If you would please save any incredulous questions to the end, you may find that you won't need to ask them." She always has been a sassy one. Caitie didn't grow up in Boremanton, but she landed an internship in our lab when she went to the local university and has stuck around since. I mimic zipping my lip, earning a chuckle from the sheriff and a satisfied nod from Caitie.

"Now, as I was saying. The bodies have been moved, but not from a grave. Well, not from a traditional grave. I believe that they were moved from a body farm." She says it as if I have any idea what the hell that means, "And not just any body farm but the one at St. Brigid University. There is something in the pattern of the soil that is similar to a signature I'm familiar with. I can't be one hundred percent certain until I hear back from them, but I believe that the remains we have in our possession belong to their forensics program. Which is good news for us, because they keep immaculate DNA records, and if I am right, we can have these bodies identified in a fraction of the time."

"So, what you are saying is that these aren't murder victims so much as stolen university property?"

"That is my working theory, yes," she confirms, lifting a weight from my chest in the process. I have no doubt of Anna's innocence, but thoughts that her father could be that kind of psycho have been kicking up dust in my mind. He did pull Anna through the window of my truck on homecoming night before knocking me around after all, so I know firsthand he had a violent streak. *Question is whether that was a one-time occurrence caused by alcohol, or if he was more than just the town drunk, but a murderer to boot.*

"Problem is the semester just ended, and summer sessions don't start for a month—there is no one at the University right now to confirm my suspicions. I have inquiries out, but they will need to be signed off by the head of the department. Dr. Cedric has a long-standing tradition of taking a cruise this time of year. It is the only time I have known him to not respond to correspondence. So, we may be a week or two out from any confirmation."

"Which means this likely clears Annastasia from our suspect pool, as we have her whereabouts meticulously accounted for in the time span Caitlyn thinks the remains were planted. But we can't let her off the hook until confirmation, so she is going to have to see if she can extend her stay for a little while yet," the sheriff interjects.

"And of course, we still have the dogs covering the land in case they find any more remains which I will run through analysis for the same patterns. Though they were coming up with increasingly fewer finds as the radius from ground zero grew," Caitie agrees.

"That will have to wait as well. The team got called for a search and rescue out in Babcock State Park, and finding live survivors takes precedence over our operation here. They may not be back until sometime late next week to finish searching the land marked in the warrant."

"Okay, so to be clear, we are no longer treating this as a murder investigation but as a theft and dump situation?" With their nods of accent, I proceed. "So, what now? We focus on why the hell someone would do this, and who?"

"Pretty much. We need a motive and suspect pool—business as usual. Which means I've got to call Miss. Adkins council and see if we can arrange another interview to see if she has any insight into who may have a reason to do something like this." He says it as if he would rather drink sand than bother Ms. Montgomery with this. "But seeing as we have some time, I may hold off till next week. In the meantime, we should update the case notes and see if anyone has any working theories on who could be responsible for this, and why."

Turning to Caitie, I say, "Good work, kiddo." Smirking when she takes the bait.

"Eww. I am like, three years younger than you. Gross." I laugh, seeing the way her nose scrunches up with disgust. If I ever had a little sister, I could do worse than our sassy lab tech. I go to ruffle her hair but stop short at the look of impending doom that crosses her face.

"Don't torment the forensic tech, Payne. She is likely to put all your cases to the bottom of the backlog," the sheriff calls over his shoulder as he exits the lab. For her part, Caitie looks smug. Shaking my head, I give her a tip of my hat in farewell as I follow the sheriff to the bull pen. Hopefully having some new extra eyes on this fresh theory will get us closer to some new leads. *It will be nice to have a suspect pool I've never kissed in the back seat of my truck.*

By lunch, we haven't added any names to our suspect poll, but are floating a number of theories that lead to motives. Pouring over the files, the thing that I keep coming back to is the timeline Caitie laid out. It fits too closely with the filing of the building permits with the clerk's office. These filings are public record, same as land sales and transfers.

"Wojack?" I call out, and he perks his head up from the case file in front of him. "Do you still talk to that receptionist in the clerk's office?" He blushes like a schoolgirl at the mention, and if it were any other time, any other case, I would rib him about it. But I need answers.

"Penny? Yeah, we, um—talk sometimes still."

"Think you can casually ask her if anyone has made any inquiries on Anna's land in the last six months, focusing more on the last two? And if you can get a bead on their interest levels without tipping her off that the information is for an ongoing case?"

Tilting his head to the side like an inquisitive pet dog I once had, he asks, "You think that a developer is involved?"

"I think that the timelines between that permit being filed and the remains being placed are too close to be a coincidence. If anyone knows of anyone who would have an interest in that land, it would be the receptionist at the clerk's office, who you just so happen to be friendly with."

He glances at the clock and says, "She takes her lunch soon. Usually at the café down on Arthur Ave. I could bump into her. Coincidentally, of course."

"Good thinking. Let me know what you find out." Thinking about lunch, my stomach rumbles.

I send a text out to my brothers to see who was free to grab a bite at the diner. I need to see what the excessive tab rang up at the bar last night was all about. It's good it didn't end with a call to the station to break up a bar fight, but it all seems a little too suspicious to me. While they are good guys, brothers are not the white knights riding in to save the damsels in distress types. They would all tell you that it is my role in our dynamic. I am shocked that they all reply within minutes that they are free and will meet me there. Somehow, I feel as though it is going to be me in the hot seat, but I still haven't a clue as to how they will turn it around on me.

Leanne stops me on my way to the door, calling out, "Deputy Payne, can you hold on a sec? I have a favor to ask."

"Come on, Leanne, I think that we've known each other long enough. Bobby is fine." I am not sure why, but that seems to please her.

"Okay, Bobby, are you going to the gala next weekend?" She is referring to the county's annual Civil Service Gala, where most of our funding is raised. The sheriff told us in not so many words that it is mandatory for anyone who has been on the force for over a year. The rookies will stay back to man the station for the evening. She knows this, so the question is bizarre.

"You know that I am. Leanne, is there a point to this? I have to meet my brothers for lunch."

She flinches a little at my abruptness but says, "Yes, sorry, I'll get right to it. My car is in the shop. It needs a lot of work. The part they need is on back order or something. Can you give me a ride? Most everyone else is married, and I would feel like a kid in the back seat, and it would be awkward to ask the sheriff. Unless you have a date, that is."

"I don't have a date." I say, wishing I could ask Anna, it could be a redemption of homecoming night, but without officially clearing her from the suspect pool, that would be inappropriate. "I can give you a ride." Checking my watch, I know my brothers are going to give me hell if I keep them waiting. Walking to the door, I call out, "Be ready by four-thirty, Sheriff Dobbs will have my hide if I am late."

I hear a shout of, "Thanks, Bobby," before the door closes behind me.

The metallic ding of the bell attached to the diner door makes a stealthy entrance impossible. I can feel the intense focus of my brothers' attention all the way from the back corner booth. That little scene with Leanne upon my leaving has cost me the advantage of arriving first. Sighing, I accept my fate and head back to the table.

Patrick is the first to greet me, standing and punching me in the shoulder before pulling me in for a quick embrace with three pats on the back, same as he has done since we were kids. "Hey, bro, I didn't even know you were home."

"We finished the job a week early. I got back last night." Patrick works in concrete, pouring foundations for commercial jobs. It takes him all over the state, often for weeks at a time. The last two years have increased the demand, and he has been home less and less. Sometimes I wonder how long he can survive this nomadic lifestyle. I'm one to talk with my eight years spent in the military, moving from place to place, so I don't voice my concerns.

He allows me to slip into the booth first, and I can't help but think it is to block a quick escape if I go to make one, but I am grateful at least to have my back to the wall and facing the entrance—some habits from training are hard to break.

I nod in greeting to my other brothers as the server comes for our orders. "The usual, boys?"

"When are you going to let me take you out, Deb?" Johnny flirts, batting his eyelashes for extra drama.

"Honey, I used to change your diapers. I think I'll pass on that offer—indefinitely. 'Sides, Mr. Deb isn't into sharing, and you better be careful, or else he will burn your order."

"Fine, fine, but you're missing out," he laments, glancing around for our nods, "But yes, four Payne brothers' specials please."

"Ernie, four 'Payne in the Butts', for here," Deb shouts with a smirk and winks toward her husband on the grill.

"Ruthless!" Johnny states, clutching his heart as if she dealt him a killing blow.

Used to his antics, I ignore him and address the brother closest in age to me. "Why the hell did you let him ring up my tab so high last night, and what's this I hear about y'all taking some drunk girls home? What the hell were you thinking?"

Tommy is not the one to answer; instead, the only brother not in attendance's voice echoes from a phone's speaker. I turn to my right and see that Patrick has set up his phone on a mini tripod, and I am staring at a miniature version of Max on the screen. "Would you rather let Anna and her friends drive back to their rooms drunk, Bobby? And while we are on the subject, when were you going to share with the class that she was back in Boremanton?"

"She isn't back. She is here as part of an ongoing investigation, one I am not at liberty to talk about, by the way. As soon as it is cleared up, I am sure she will set this town in her rearview mirror and never think of it, or us, again. Kind of like a grumpy older brother, I know." Am I being defensive because this intervention turned on me somehow? Yes. Do I give a damn? No.

"I've been back, and you can come see me here. Nothing is chaining anyone to that town, and you of all people should know it." What is it about oldest brothers that makes them think they can scold you like a parent even once you are grown?

"Max, you aren't even here, and you weren't there last night. Remind me again how any of this involves you." Crossing my arms over my chest, I slump down into the booth, feeling every bit the youngest child that I am. It is like all the years spent in the military and as a responsible officer of the law melt away when I am at the receiving end of the disappointed look on my eldest brother's face. *Ridiculous!* I think as I sit up straighter and try to will the petulance from my voice as I say, "If you want to know what's happening here so badly, come home. Mom would be happy to see you more than once a year."

"Ohhh, he brought Mom into it," Patrick singsongs, and it is hard to believe he is the second-oldest brother. I resist the urge to elbow his ribcage.

"Careful, baby brother," Max says, I am sure to piss me off. "I am the only reason she isn't sitting at the table with you. Tommy thought she would have loved to sit in on this intervention." I shoot Tommy a betrayed look. *Traitor.* The two of us—on the younger side of the birth order—are meant to be allies. Everyone knows that. It's the eldest versus the youngest with Johnny as Switzerland. When did allegiances shift? How is it that I am caught unawares?

For his part, he only shrugs. "You are going to fuck this up. I thought you could use all the help you could get."

"Fuck what up exactly?" I am debating crawling under the table to escape this situation. Only the fact that I am in my uniform gives me pause. Well, that and my brothers are not above kicking me in the face.

Deb shows up right then with four plates to set in front of us, so I have to wait for his response. If I am going to put up with my brother's particular brand of lunacy, at least I can do it while I enjoy a quarter-pound mushroom Swiss burger and fresh-cut fries. She doesn't stick around for small talk as the diner has filled in since I arrived. As one of the few places open for lunch in town, they turn a pretty good business.

Johnny goes to speak, but I delay him, holding up a finger. I don't want whatever comes out of his mouth to sour the first savory bite of my lunch. Rolling his eyes as if I am the dramatic one here, he clears his throat, annoyed at being stalled. I enjoy the explosion of flavors on my tongue, taking my time to savor this before I swallow. Setting my burger down and waving at him to go on, I drag a couple of fries through the ketchup set off to the side of my plate in a little metal ramakin.

"Operation Penguin."

I choke. *What the fuck did he say?* I gulp down my drink, trying to dislodge the fry that is lodged in my throat.

"Excuse me?" I am unsure if I heard him right because that makes no sense.

"Operation Penguin," he repeats. So I did hear him right. "It is what we are calling getting you together with the love of your life. You know, the one you gave your rock to?" He is looking at me like I am truly dense and bordering on lost cause territory. Then it clicks, and I recall the conversation we had in his truck on the way back from the hospital.

"Why is Max here then? He gave his rock away, too. Hell, why not work an intervention on him?"

"Who the fuck did I give my rock to?" Max asks as if he is genuinely curious.

All four of us chorus, "Jessica," at the same time as if it was even a question.

"I did not. I don't even think about her."

We all give him our best 'sure Jan' expressions and don't even dignify that comment with a response.

"Anyway," Patrick interjects. "Johnny came up with the name, after a full recap of a documentary he watched. We were all bored to an inch of our lives and too annoyed to argue, but we did agree, especially after last night, that you won't be able to do this without help. You're in over your head."

"Who said I even still have feelings for her like that?" *I am so full of shit. Good thing my eyes are already brown-ish.* They all turn that same skeptical expression on me now, even Max through the screen of the phone. "Okay, counterpoint. Who says she even wants this?"

"Good job, little bro. You are already completing step one to Operation Penguin naturally," Johnny states, like he is proud of me.

"What is step one again?" Tommy questions.

"Do I have to send you a pitch deck?" Johnny asks, and in answer Tommy throws a fry at his face.

"Thomas Payne, do not throw your food. Do I have to call your Ma?" Deb's voice rings across the diner.

"No, ma'am. I'm sorry," he replies, properly scolded. Under his breath, he whispers to us, "How did she even notice that?" We all shrug our response because, short of magic, we have no explanation to offer.

"Anyway, step one is to get subject B." Turning to me, he says, "That is you, by the way, to admit his fears about pursuing subject A. That is Anna, in case you couldn't put it together. And you just admitted that you fear she may not be interested, so that is step one underway."

"Oh, right, I remember now." Tommy perks up, recovered from his recent reprimand. "We learned tons from drunk Anna, and most importantly, being that she is single—"

"'Depressingly single' is how her roommate put it," interrupts Patrick with a mouth full of fries.

"Chew first, you caveman," Tommy admonishes, face scrunched up in disgust; he hates open-mouth chewers. "But yes, she is confirmed single, so there is no guy we have to get rid of."

"Get rid of? How would you even do that?" My brothers, unlike me, are not above breaking a few minor laws. It is a definite cause of concern.

"Moot point since there is no one to get rid of," Max chimes in. "But that wasn't exactly the fear he stated anyway. You are not paying attention. He is afraid she doesn't want him. He won't try because he is scared he will be rejected." *I hate that he is right.*

"Well, until you try, you'll never know. You have to ask yourself what is worse: having given it your all and being rejected or being a fucking coward and wondering what could have been for the rest of your life." Patrick's unusual seriousness drops like a stone in my stomach, and with it, I have lost my appetite.

"Well, none of it matters anyway as long as I am the lead on this investigation, I can't go there whether I want to or not." I nudge Patrick to let me out. "You can finish that." I gesture to the half-eaten burger and almost full order of fries sitting abandoned on my plate. "I have to get back to work." I don't stay long enough to hear if any of my brothers call me a coward out loud. They don't need to. I already know that I am.

Chapter 13

ANNASTASIA

"**S**on of a bitch!" I hear the muffled shout through the door of our connected ensuite. Groggily, I swat my hand out, reaching for my phone on the nightstand, peering at the time through one eye cracked open. It is eleven-eleven a.m. *I wish we had laid off the shots. Do wishes work retroactively? God, I hope so.* I debate pretending I didn't hear Joanie and burrow back under the covers in an attempt to sleep it off, but right as the thought crosses my mind, she bursts through the door. "How could you let me go to sleep without my bonnet? It is going to take forever to get these tangles loose, and wash day isn't supposed to be until Saturday! We left in such a hurry, I didn't even think to pack my full hair care regimen, and I doubt I can get the products I need in this podunk little town."

"Good thing we are looking for flights for you to go home today," I croak out, attempting to block the light with my pillow. It's of no use as she rips it from my grasp and tosses it away.

"Are we now? When did I agree to that?" Her voice hits a level of incredulity that I cannot handle while everything is still spinning. I place one foot on the floor, trying to ground myself. It works—kind of.

"Between the third and fourth rounds of Fireball, you told Caroline that you, and I quote, 'You should be honored I find you worthy to care for my favorite person.'"

"I did not. That sounds nothing like me."

"Then you kissed her on both cheeks and claimed that she had been initiated into the family." She is staring off into space as if she can visibly search through her memories to see if I am bullshitting her or not. I see the exact moment that she finds it.

"Well, shit, I did say that. But that was drunk Joanie. That bitch can't be trusted."

"Come on, Joanie, you need to go back. I am sure your assistant is losing her shit by now." Though we both work in hospitality, Joanie went into event planning, while I went the hotel management route. My position is far easier to find someone to fill in for. Joanie has spent months, sometimes years, building a relationship with her clients, and many of them are so exacting that it is difficult to delegate to someone else.

As if thinking of her assistant for the first time since we left the strip, she grabs her phone—I assume to check her email—and winces. "It is kind of a shit show. If you're sure you are going to be okay, like you have to pinky promise me," she says, holding out the aforementioned finger, "Then I will look for a flight, *after* I have had a whole pot of coffee. Oh, and we need some ibuprofen."

I wrap my pinky around hers, and we both lean in to kiss our thumbs, cementing the pinky promise into an unbreakable oath. "I will go get the ibuprofen and do you one better and bring you back a mocha latte," I say as I walk over to my suitcase, pulling out a sealed bag. I hand it to her. "Go do your full routine—there should be enough to get you through all the steps." She takes the bag with a look of confusion on her face.

"You packed my products?" she questions as she pulls back the zipper and opens the flap.

"I bought the sample size of everything you use and kept them packed in my suitcase. I was going to surprise you with a trip to the beach for your birthday and didn't want you to have to overthink packing. I will replace them before we go... Surprise!"

Her arms are around me quicker than I can react, and we tumble onto the bed with the momentum of the moment. I swear her voice cracks when she says, "You really are my best friend."

I squeeze her back and take a moment to collect myself. I do not want my true anxiety at her leaving to reveal itself in my voice. For some reason, I feel like I need to face this obstacle—this town—on my own, and if I show weakness now, she won't leave my side. She is that loyal, and I am beyond grateful to have found her.

"You're my best friend too, Jo. Now get off of me, you sap. I have coffee to get."

A messy bun and oversized sunglasses do wonders to hide the visual side effects from my hangover. I am hoping some donuts and coffee from The Mountainside Cafe will work some magic on the lingering physical effects. The robust scent of the beans percolating is already doing wonders in waking up my senses. The din of the grinders is soothing instead of grating to my nervous system, and the added aroma of dough and sugar permeating through the air makes my stomach growl, a reminder of how little we ate at 'dinner' last night, having traded food for liquid calories.

Standing off to the side waiting for my order to be called, I scroll through my emails, seeing if there is anything essential I am missing at work. Nothing of consequence. There are enough hotel managers on staff that when one of us takes time off, the operations still run smoothly. Joanie doesn't have the same luxury. While she does have an assistant and there are other on-staff event planners; some clients are demanding and attached to her way of doing things. It isn't fair that I keep her here as my emotional crutch, and I am glad that she is agreeing to heading back home. Despite my initial reaction to being back, I am doing better now, thanks in part to that session with Jennifer.

"Tasia?" The barista's voice carries over the intercom, indicating that my order is ready. Thank God. We slept past the complimentary breakfast and I am starving. I'm not sure if I am going to make it back before breaking into the pastry box. Stepping up toward the pickup counter, I am stalled by a familiar voice.

"Tasia. Wow, I don't know if I can get used to that." Turning, I see Ryan Murphy standing right next to me. *Where the hell did he come from? Am I that unaware of my surroundings?*

"Hey Murph, or... um... I guess I should probably call you Ryan now, huh?" I greet my former classmate. He isn't wearing his uniform, so I assume he is off duty.

"You can call me whatever you want, but what about you? Do you prefer Tasia now?"

It is an interesting question. Professionally, I am Annastasia, and to anyone who knows me from the last twelve years, it is Tasia. At one point in time, I wanted to leave Anna Adkins so far in the past that she was like the mist on the mountains—forever out of your grasp. But do I really want people who have known me since kindergarten or even earlier to address me this way? I think back to my interactions this week. *Do I want Bobby to call me Tasia?* The thought comes out of nowhere. I shake my head to clear it and focus back on the conversation at hand. "No, you don't have to call me Tasia, but do you think you can refrain from calling me Anna-banana? I am not a kid anymore."

Ryan chuckles as he gives me a full body scan. "No, you certainly are all grown up, Anna." The look paired with the deep gravel tone that line was delivered in should have made a shiver of anticipation run down my spine. Would have, if anyone who is as hot as Ryan Murphy has become would have said it to me bar-side in Vegas. But even though the boy has grown into a fine version of a man, the fact that I know he ate paste in the back of Miss Long's first-grade classroom leaves me rolling my eyes at the attempt. *Is it fair to hold him to childhood memories when I just asked him to drop the nickname he gave me in pre-school?*

"Smooth, Ryan," I chuckle, turning to my forgotten items on the counter. "But I'd better get these back to Joanie before she dies of caffeine withdrawal."

"We wouldn't want that," he states, grabbing the carrier and bag from my hands before I can head for the door. "Let me get these to your car for you." Not one to turn down a chivalrous act, I nod and go to grab the door for him.

"I am parked right around the block. Arthur Ave is busier than I remember."

"Yeah. Since that hockey team made Aberville their home, all the surrounding areas are seeing a boost in foot traffic and development. Trickledown effect, I guess." He shrugs his well-defined shoulders.

"I know. I have been getting an increase in offers for my land since they broke ground. It is so weird to me that they even contact me, since I have never listed the property."

"Not to be nosey, but why didn't you sell it? Don't get me wrong, I am glad to see your beautiful face. I never thought it would be around these parts again."

"Were you always such a flatterer?" I nudge him in the side as I dig my key fob from my purse and disengage the lock on the SUV, opening the passenger side door for him to settle the carrier and bag on the floorboard for optimum stability.

"Always," he answers, standing back up. "Maybe you were too distracted to notice."

Trying to avoid the obvious flirting that I suspect isn't quite the joke I thought it was at first, I answer his initial question. "I have a complicated history with that land, that much is true, but it doesn't mean I want it to be turned into a strip mall or developed into McMansions. Or worse still, some resort that the folks around here have no means to make use of and caters to outsiders that will end up pricing locals out of their homes." We have migrated to the driver's side, and before I can open my door, his arms land on the top of the vehicle, penning me in. I turn to see what the hell he is doing.

"So you *do* care about us then? We didn't leave your mind completely." For a moment, he looks vulnerable, like my answer matters.

"Of course I care about this place." I refrain from saying 'you' because even if I mean it in the plural, I don't want him to mistake it for the singular.

He takes a step back, restoring my much-needed personal bubble. "Come to Wolf and Whistle tomorrow. Let me buy you that round I promised." He must see the color as it drains out of my face. "Or just a meal, if you are still nursing this hangover, though I thought living in Vegas you would have built up a tolerance."

"I don't think any tolerance can stand up to Caroline." That earns a true laugh from him, and I see more of my friend in the unbridled emotion than I have in whatever Playboy act he had been running moments ago.

"She is a whirlwind, that is for sure. Invite her out too, and your roommate, Joanie, right?" At the suggestion, I get the feeling that this is a group thing and not a date, and my hesitation dissipates altogether.

"That's right, and sure, I'll see what they say." I am not sure why I don't tell him Joanie is likely going to be on a plane home tonight, but some part of me doesn't want him to know I will be on my own.

"Here." He hands me his phone. "Put your number in, and I'll text you the time everyone is heading over." Moment of truth. By giving him my number, I am allowing another part of my past to gain access to me in the present, even once I head back to Las Vegas. Besides Caroline, no one has had any way to contact me—until last night, but after the reunion with the Payne brothers last night, I can't deny that my heart has had a hole the size of this town since I left, and it is about time I stop burying my head in the sand. I type my number and hand it back.

"You saved it under, 'Anna with a banana emoji?" I can hear the smile in his voice.

Climbing into the SUV, I shoot him a wink and say, "For old times' sake." Closing the door, I push start pulling out onto the street as Ryan steps back onto the curb. Glancing in my mirror, I see him give his phone a half smile as he finishes typing, replacing it in his pocket as he turns to walk back the way we came.

My phone buzzes, activating the vehicle's hands-free text messaging assistant, causing a robotic voice to speak. "Text message from 3-0-4-5-5-5-0-1-8-6. This is Ryan call-me-what-you-want-to Murphy.

Looking forward to catching up tomorrow." Shaking my head at his antics, I think, *well, at least I can tell Joanie I have another friend in my corner before she leaves.*

Chapter 14

ANNASTASIA

Caroline is sitting on the bed rummaging through my suitcase as I curl my hair in the ensuite with the door open. "I can't believe you convinced Joanie to go home. She is like your personal guard dog—not that it's a bad thing."

"She saw reason once she checked with her assistant and found them on the verge of taking a long walk off a short cliff. Her clients are exhausting—to put it mildly. I am glad I steered clear of event planning in school."

"I bet. Good thing she could find a same-day flight. That was lucky."

"Luck has little to do with it. There are always flights to Vegas because it has a steady commercial draw. Harry Reid International keeps contracts with so many airlines, making it basically a day trip from anywhere in the country. You can usually find multiple direct flights into the city a day."

"Hmmm, maybe I will have to look into that once you go back."

Peaking my head around the corner, I catch her eye. "You coming for a visit?"

"If I am invited?" Her voice sounds small and has a little quiver at the end. It guts me. Setting down my curling iron, I walk, sit on the bed next to her, and grab her hands.

"No invitation required—you are always welcome in my life, no matter where I am. I'm sorry if I made you feel any other way." She crushes me to her in one of her signature hugs, but I am prepared, so I remember to brace for it this time.

Releasing me, she gestures to my bag. "You don't have anything appropriate to wear."

"What do you mean? I think I fit in fine two nights ago?"

"That was a Wednesday. This is a Friday night semi da—"

"It is *not* a date."

"Sure. Regardless, you need to step it up. Business-casual is not the vibe."

"Well, gee Care, I don't know if you noticed, but that is not *Mary Poppins'* bag that you are rooting through. My options are limited."

"Good thing I anticipated this exact problem and planned accordingly." She walks over to where she left her tote and pulls out what I guess can be considered shorts, but I think may be better described as a denim belt with a crotch. She glances at me and then back to the cursed garment. "Too much?"

"Too little."

"Fine, wear the dark wash jeans I saw in there, but you are wearing this top with it."

What she is holding up is a deep V halter top that clasps around the neck with a rhinestone choker. When she turns it around, I can see that it will low back with a band that hits right under my ribcage. Several strands of runestone fringe hang from the choker. The color is a deep midnight blue, and the fabric appears to be some sort of satin. It is beautiful and sexy, and I absolutely cannot wear it. My palms sweat, and my throat goes dry thinking of exposing my back to the world in that.

"The support is built in, I promise. I wouldn't lead you astray. I even brought some fashion tape to avoid any nip slips on the dance floor." She misunderstands my reason for protest. "Please just try it. I promise I wouldn't let you look stupid."

I know she wouldn't, but that isn't the point. I try to reason with her. "Don't you think this is too much for a dive bar?

"Do you see what the wait staff wears? Believe me, this is fine. Besides..." She pauses as she pulls out another garment. "I will be right there with you." Holding out what is essentially a bodysuit, I can see where we would both be showing similar amounts of skin; only the back of that bodysuit appears to cover much higher on the back. *That may even be high enough to cover my issue entirely.* I could tell her what's wrong. If she knew my hesitation, she would not want me to be uncomfortable, but she might also look at me differently. I can't stand to see her look at me with pity in her eyes. *This is supposed to be a fun night. Bringing that up will only bring the mood down.*

"Oh, that is really cute. Do you think maybe I could try that one on instead?" She looks at it and back to me and to the blue sparkly top sitting on the bed.

"Sure, I just thought the blue would make your eyes pop, but if you are feeling this more, it works for me. Though if you are going to wear the bodysuit, you have to wear the skirt and boots too." Good thing we were always the same shoe size in high school. I gulp at the scrap of fabric she is calling a skirt, but I would rather show my legs all day than have to expose my back.

Okay, I am going to step into the bathroom and put this on. Once the door clicks, I lean back against it and exhale the tension building in my gut.

I catch my reflection and make a promise to myself to work on letting these people who mean so much to me in a little more—but not tonight.

I shimmy into the outfit and check over my shoulder to see that the fabric does in fact cover my back. Melting with relief, I turn, my eyes widening in the mirror at what I see. I take in the painted-on maroon pleather body suit with opaque lace covering my bust that's pushed up to high heaven, putting the girls on full display. The micro mini skirt hugs my thighs but blissfully has built-in shorts. If I thought this was the more modest option, I was wrong. The cowboy boots are comfortable at least. I feel a little better knowing they won't blisters.

Caroline knocks and then slips into the ensuite. Her top sparkles with every step, and I am amazed that she isn't spilling over the top of the cups. She has chosen the short cut-offs and they hang low on her hip, creating a gap between them and the top, leaving her toned stomach exposed.

She slides next to me in the mirror and holds her phone up to snap a shot, which she promptly sends off to what I am gathering is a group chat, as my phone pings a moment later, followed by several rapid-fire ping notifications. Opening the app, I see that Joanie is the other recipient in a group chat titled 'Bad Bitches', and that she has sent several flame emojis and one *Roger Rabbit* GIF—the one where the cartoon rabbit's eyes are popping out of its head. "See, Joanie approves. I bet Ryan will too."

"This is not a date, and I don't care what he thinks. I am not in the habit of bringing my friends on dates." *Though dates is a strong word for random hook-ups and regular booty calls. People want to get to know you on dates, and I am a fucking nightmare. Men tend to ask fewer questions when they are buried deep inside of you.*

"I'm just saying. Maybe we should come up with a code if you want me to get lost."

"Gee, would that work right now?" I snark as I intentionally spray the hairspray pointed in her direction, causing her to sputter a cough.

"Okay, okay I'll stop, but we should finish up. The Uber should be here in ten." It still amazes me that Uber had reached my sleepy little hometown, but Caroline pointed out that we still had the university, so it was a pretty lucrative side gig for some, depending on the time of year. I can't help but think how much easier that would have made my life, when my dad would get wasted on any given day, to summon a ride share to bring his drunk ass home. *Would have less wear and tear on my bike, that's for sure.* Two short honks bring me out of my thoughts as Caroline checks her app. "That's them. Let's get this show on the road."

Leah greets us again, and I am starting to wonder when this girl sleeps. She leads us to the back room, but this time to a semicircle booth closer to the pool tables. Looking around, I feel more at ease in my attire as I see similar outfits worn by other patrons. I shouldn't have doubted Caroline. Ryan is already seated with some other familiar faces. Lorenzo and one of his brothers, Roberto, are seated at one end, and a woman whose face I recognize but whose name I cannot place is towards the middle.

The moment Ryan sees us, he stands pulling me into a hug that I am not ready for, causing me to stumble into his chest. "Don't fall for me too easily, Anna. I like a challenge." Before I can decide if he was joking or actually flirting with me, he pulls Caroline in for an embrace as well. *Maybe he's just a hugger.*

Ryan gestures us into the booth where Caroline gives the woman seated there a side hug, obviously familiar with her. She waves at me as I scoot next to Caroline, allowing Ryan to take the seat on the end. Leah gets our drink orders before scurrying away, tail swishing with the movement. It is far too busy for her to stay for small talk, and I wonder where she draws the energy from.

"Hi, I am Miranda. We've never been formally introduced, but I remember seeing you in high school." She extends her hand past Caroline for me to shake.

"I knew you looked familiar. Were you ahead of us in school?"

"Yeah, graduated when you and Murph were freshmen. Now I work with him and Lorenzo at the station. You look like you recovered from your ordeal the other day."

Wiping my clammy hands on my jeans, I try to ignore the sudden warmth spreading across my face. *Well, this is embarrassing.* "Yeah, apparently energy drinks don't replace the need for water. Nothing a few bags of fluids couldn't fix up." I play off my panic attack as a bout of dehydration, which isn't a lie per se, just not the whole truth of it.

"I think it's something like seventy-five percent of Americans are walking around severely dehydrated every day, so at least you're in good company." Miranda rattles off the statistic with an easy smile, and I feel my tension melting away.

"You wouldn't believe the amount of dehydration calls we get when hiking season is in full swing," Lorenzo adds

"I keep telling the kids they need to really up their water intake during practice, but do you think they listen to me? No. What do I know?" Roberto chimes in on the conversation.

Reading my confusion, Lorenzo explains. "Roberto is a high school baseball coach, as well as a teacher now."

"At Boremanton High?" I ask. When he nods, I can't help the laugh that bubbles up from deep inside and erupts out of my mouth. "I'm sure—" I try to catch my breath and compose myself. "I'm sure if any of our old teachers are there, they must love that. Between the Alavezes and the Paynes, I am positive you pushed at least some of them into early retirement." I think I hear Ryan murmur something under his breath, but I am still too busy reining in my laughter to confirm.

"At least!" Caroline agrees. "If not the loony bin." Hearing that puts an abrupt stop to my giggles, and I try to hide the physical flinch her words cause. I know she didn't mean it toward me or my situation, but knowing something rationally and how it makes you react emotionally are not always aligned. It is something I have talked to my therapist about at length.

She must feel me still beside her because her head whips towards me, face ashen, eyes wide with regret, apology at the ready on her lips. But I don't want to put a damper on the easy-going nature of this night or talk about where I spent the two years after I left town. And I don't want my friend to think she needs to walk on eggshells around me. So, I squeeze her thigh under the table to let her know that I'm fine. *That it's fine.* Her eyes soften as she exhales, taking my palm in hers, squeezing it back in apology anyway—a silent sign that she will let it go, and I am grateful.

The rest of the table, for their part, miss the interaction entirely, continuing with the conversation. "Oh, there are still some around, and they delight in seeing me get served a heaping dose of my own medicine," Roberto laments. "But kids these days are relentless. You give them an inch and they run a mile."

"You're sounding like an old man, Roberto. Better watch out or you'll be the one looking for early retirement," Ryan ribs his friend, sending a crumpled napkin flying across the table. It would have hit him smack dab in the center of the forehead had it not been for his fast reflexes.

"Don't worry about me, Murph. I still got it," Roberto responds

Amused by their banter, I am not paying attention to our surroundings. It comes as an utter shock when a mess of curly hair carrying a tray full of drinks comes crashing toward us. It takes a moment to realize that it is Leah and another to see half the drinks cascading over Ryan. I jump into Caroline's lap to avoid the tidal wave of alcohol he has been doused with, with barely a second to spare.

Three different voices cry out simultaneously.

"Fuck." That one is Ryan now, dripping in mixed drinks and beer.

"Oh my God, I am so sorry." That is Leah followed by "Ow!" Looks like her knees took the brunt of the fall.

And the third voice sends a chill down my spine with its saccharine quality that screams of false concern. "Oh my, I didn't see you there, Leah. I didn't mean to make you fall." Looking over, I see the table behind Lorenzo seats none other than Leanne and her cronies. How I missed them, I will never know. Head swiveling between her and Leah, something clicks into place, and I recall Diane's words from the other day, about how Leanne had it out for Leah. I know soul deep that this was no accident. It was a petty act from a vindictive bitch who has never grown beyond her mean girl era. I am seething on Leah's behalf. Lorenzo jumps into medic mode, turning Leah until she is sitting with her ass on the floor.

"Are you alright?" he asks as he pokes and prods at her knee. "Any pain?"

"It doesn't feel great, but I'll live. Doesn't look like it broke the skin, but it is hard to tell with these tights on," Leah replies and then looks over at Ryan and winces. " I am so sorry, Murph. I'll cover your tab tonight."

"It's fine, doll, no use crying over spilt—well, whatever was on that tray. Can you walk?"

He holds out a hand while Lorenzo supports her with his hands on her waist. With very little effort between the two of them, they have her standing.

Testing her stability, she declares, "Seems like I can stand alright. Just sore is all."

Miranda nudges Roberto to let her out so she can join in with this impromptu assessment. "Why don't we go back to the breakroom and see if they have any first aid supplies? You can take the tights off and I can assess the damage without the whole bar looking on."

"Yeah, okay. Thank God it is Roman's weekend. Kenneth would bitch an entire fit," Leah agrees, letting Miranda support her as a human crutch. I look over to see Ryan pull off his shirt in a swift motion and use it to mop up the liquid on his chest and stomach. *I can't believe the kid who used to be the class clown now has a six-pack.* A really nice six-pack with a constellation of freckles underneath a patch of auburn hair centered between a pair of Ken doll lines that would have Joanie drooling if she were here to witness them.

Someone yells, "Take it all off."

At the same time, I see someone who can only be Roman Wolfsen walk up and say, "Please spare us and keep it on."

I remember Roman from picking my dad up on benders. His grandfather put him to work as a busboy and dishwasher. He would occasionally help me haul my father into the truck when he was too gone for me to manage on my own. Though only his prominent brow bones and no-nonsense stare share any resemblance to the serious but lanky kid I remember. No, that kid has grown into a bearded, tattooed, muscled Adonis, and I am really starting to wonder what they feed the boys in this town to grow them into men like this. Even the Alverez and Payne brothers have grown into fine specimens.

And yet none of them hold a candle to Bobby. I am going to have to talk to Jennifer about my unhealthy attraction to men who may have the authority to lock me up. *Though I wouldn't object to some play with handcuffs.* I pull out my phone, setting an alarm to call Jennifer in the morning. I need to ask if high-stress situations can cause an increase in libido. Is this a symptom of my PTSD, or am I ovulating?

"Come on, Magic Mike, I think I have a spare set of clothes in my car," Roberto says, turning his half-naked friend towards a side exit. "Roman, do you mind if we go out the side, or would you rather us take this show through the front?

"Side's fine. Let me turn off the alarm. The last thing we need is the rest of the station here to make a bigger spectacle." He hands a broom and a dustpan to Alverez, which I must have missed him carrying over while I was too busy noticing how his shirt stretched over his chest. *When was the last time I got laid?* Maybe I was overdue for an orgasm. *Joanie is right—I am depressingly single.* "Make yourself useful. I'll be right back."

Lorenzo nods taking up the chore, no questions asked. In moments, he has the glass cleared and is on his way to a trash bin on the other side. Now our party has been reduced to two.

"Well, that was something," Caroline states. All I can do is nod my head in agreement because that definitely was *something* from start to finish.

"I can't prove it, but she did it on purpose. I just know it." Confused as to who I mean, Caroline looks around until she sees Leanne at the table next to us, feigning innocence. Caroline's lips as she scoots closer to their side. I follow suit. If I can hear them say something to prove my theory—well, I am not sure what I will do, but I eavesdrop all the same.

"I can't believe how clumsy the wait staff is here," Collette's shrill voice rings out.

"I guess you can't expect quality when they have to agree to such tacky uniforms." Sarah says, adding her coals to the fire.

"Honestly, the fact that she even works here makes her day job look bad. How clients can take her seriously when she practically moonlights as a stripper is beyond me." It takes everything in me not to stand up for Leah right now, but they haven't said anything close to admitting they tripped her on purpose. Not that I know what I would or could do with that information if she did. "Let's not dwell on unfortunate creatures tonight. We are celebrating, after all," Leann states in the haughty tone I remember her best for.

"What are we celebrating again?" Sarah asks.

"God, Sarah, keep up. Leanne finally landed Bobby Payne!" Collette admonishes as if she were talking to a child. *She did what now?* My spine goes ramrod straight, as if I had been electrocuted and all my nerves fired at the same time. Caroline stills beside me, and that is all the confirmation I need to know she heard the same thing.

"Oh, right! To the gala next week. God, Leanne, you are so lucky. That man is so fine."

"Don't I know it. It was only a matter of time, really. He just needed to come to his senses about what he's been missing, and I intend to show him exactly that after the gala," Leanne boasts.

My stomach rolls, and I feel ill. I can't even tell you why. It isn't like I have a claim on Bobby. Hell, from the interactions we have had since I got back, I can't be certain he isn't royally pissed at me. Either way, I cannot sit here and listen to this because out of all the people in the world, *why her?*

Nudging Caroline out of the booth, I say, "Come on, let's go get some shots."

Assessing me for a second, she nods, and we make our way to the bar. So much for taking it easy tonight.

Chapter 15

ANNASTASIA

Our group reconvenes at the bar when Caroline and I are already three shots deep. I can almost hear my therapist's voice inside my head scolding me about using alcohol to cope with stress as the liquid pours down my throat and warms my belly. To be fair, Jennifer doesn't scold so much as she asks if that was the most productive choice. Right now, it seems like it absolutely is. *I'm not upset because Bobby is with someone; it's that he is with someone awful. That's what this feeling is. I am totally not caught up on the first boy I ever kissed.* I wave down the bartender for another one because with each shot, maybe my lies will become closer to the truth.

Ryan is now in a set of gym shorts and a muscle tee, but he makes it look like a choice rather than an afterthought with how he fills it out, so I doubt anyone would fault him. "Whoa, we leave you alone for a few minutes, and you get the party started without us," he teases, grabbing the shot from my hand before I can press it to my lips. He smirks at my cross expression and says, "What? Looks like I have some catching up to do."

It is probably for the best. I am starting to feel the effects with a slight tingle in my cheeks and a giddiness setting in, so I switch to tonic water to dissipate the alcohol's effects and ride out my buzz for a bit. *Don't want another trip to the ER for fluids after all.* I skim the conversations of our group, not listening fully as they talk about work and other small talk. I feel myself sway as the music starts to turn up in volume.

Jarring me out of my own little world, Caroline and Miranda pull me toward the makeshift dance floor as Ed Sheeran's *Shivers* pumps through the sound system, bass reverberating in the floorboards. I try to protest. "No, come on, guys, I don't know the steps." To no avail.

"Bullshit! I saw that video you were tagged in at someone's wedding. You know it," Caroline insists as we join the throng of people already in the throes of the popular line dance.

"Busted," Miranda laughs, aiding and abetting in this little abduction.

"Fine! You win."

If you had told fourteen-year-old me that in a little over a decade I would be drinking and dancing in the same bar I used to have to drag my father out of, I wouldn't have believed it. *But here I am.* It doesn't take me long before the turns and stomps have elevated the dour mood that I had gotten myself in, and I am outright laughing as Caroline and Miranda spin into each other, having gotten turned around.

Soon, the tune slips into something leaning more country, meant for a pair, and Caroline and I fumble who is leading who until Roberto swoops in and dances away with her; Miranda having already paired off with the other Alverez brother.

For a moment, I am left alone and think I can escape back to the bar, but before I take two steps, I am pulled into a two-step with Ryan. "Don't think you are getting out of here that easily," he jokes, spinning me around and into a grapevine, and suddenly I recall every line dance step drilled into us during middle school PE.

"Mrs. Jacobs would be proud. You have stepped up your game since seventh grade," I say before a squeal leaves my lips as he dips me unexpectedly.

"A lot has changed since seventh grade, Anna, but you are still the prettiest girl on the floor."

"You are full of it, Murph. In seventh grade, I still had braces, knobby knees, and two left feet."

"And you were still the girl all the guys wanted to be around."

"To play in the mud with and go four-wheeling, sure. It wasn't like I was beating them off with a stick."

"To be fair, it was kind of hard to get to you through your bodyguards."

"What are you talking about?"

"Those damn Payne brothers would have wrapped you in bubble wrap and set you on a shelf if you had let them."

Aghast and incredulous, I say, "That is a gross exaggeration."

"Is it? Even now, they haven't taken their eyes off you." His declaration confuses me, so I look around trying to see if Bobby came to meet up with Leanne and I missed it. *I don't know if I can handle seeing them together.* But from what I can tell, he isn't here. However, three of the four remaining Payne brothers are. Murph is right; they are all looking at us, well, me. And is that disappointment, I see reflecting in their gazes, or worse, disapproval?

What do they have to be disappointed about? I'm not the one who asked them a bunch of leading questions that made them think that maybe their brother still felt something for me. No, that was all them. Even through my hangover yesterday, I remembered the third degree I got when they took us back to the inn. Why would they do that if they knew Bobby was going to ask Leanne out? Unless they didn't know.

"Ugh, it doesn't matter anyway!" My internal voice apparently didn't get the memo that it is supposed to stay inside, as I shout that for all to hear.

"Good," is Ryan's cryptic reply as he twirls me through the crowd to the less occupied corner of the dance floor and out of their direct line of sight.

After a few more line dances where partners are swapped back and forth, the music takes a turn for a slower, more seductive beat. I am between Caroline and Miranda now as our bodies become conduits of the bass rhythm flowing from the floorboards through our bones. For a while, the guys stand at the perimeter to let us have our fun, but it isn't long before they join in as well, and I find myself with my back to Ryan's front and his hands bracing my hips as I sway.

To start, there is a respectable inch of space between us, but he soon consumes that bit by bit with every beat until we are swaying as one. It is fine at first, nothing I haven't done a million times—with strangers at that—but soon his hands begin to wander. They start to slither away from what I would consider safe zones to more forbidden territory, and I am starting to get uncomfortable. Now I am not so sure if all his flirting was for flirting's sake, and I start to think he may want more from me than I am willing to give. Sure, I admired his physique and noticed how he grew into an attractive man—*I do have eyes*—but I have never wanted to cross this line with him. Not when we were children and not now as adults.

One hand snakes low on my abdomen, and I decide it is time to disengage, but my attempt at distance is countered by him jerking me back, palm almost on my pelvic ridge, grinding his hard length into me as his tongue caresses my ear.

"Where are you going, sweetheart? You can't leave me like this," he says, alcohol heavy on his breath.

Chills run down my spine, raising goose pimples across my flesh, and bile rolls in a torrent in my belly. I try to torque my body to get away from the evidence of his arousal. He misreads my intention and turns me to face him as he leans in for a kiss. Fight, flight, or freeze instincts are warning inside my head but my body at least works enough to turn my head at the last second, so he is met with my cheek instead. However, he is undeterred as he continues to pepper sloppy kisses that smell of bottom-shelf vodka across my jaw to my neck.

He isn't reading my physical cues, so I am going to have to use my words. Placing a hand to his chest, I push as I say, "Ryan, stop. I think you have the wrong idea."

"Oh, come on, Anna, aren't we too old for the hard-to-get games?" he questions, tugging me closer by the hips even as I lean my upper body further away. "You can't tell me you don't want this. Your body is saying that you do." *My body is saying no such thing; I would know it is mine after all.*

Before the words can form on my lips to tell him how wrong he is, I am no longer grappling for space as he is torn away from me by one Payne brother, and I am swiftly shifted behind the back of another.

"I believe the lady told you to stop." It is the thunderous rumble of Patrick Payne's growl as he has Ryan pinned to the wall with a forearm across his chest.

"And what? Did you hear that from across the bar?" Ryan spits with more vitriol than I have ever heard him speak to any other person with.

"You aren't too keen on your surroundings, are you, kid?" I hear Johnny chime in, even if I can't see him over Tommy's frame. I stretch on my tiptoes and lean to the side to get a better view, but Tommy side steps to block me again. "No, if you were, you would have seen that Anna was pulling away."

"What, is your whole family stalking her? What's next—is Max going to video call in from Philadelphia?"

Sick of this backwards two-step we have going on, I try another tactic by stepping backwards entirely so Tommy cannot feel my movements, but this only causes him to turn to me head-on.

"Anna, don't even think about putting yourself in the middle of what's about to go down. Do the one thing I know is not easy for you—stay put." He sounds exasperated, as if speaking to a finicky toddler, and that puts my hackles up.

"What do you guys think you are doing? You can't manhandle people."

Tommy rolls his eyes. "Oh, like he was manhandling you? If you ask me, we let it go on way longer than we should have."

Now I am fighting mad. All those freeze or flight instincts dissipate, and I am left a fuming live wire ready to strike even a man of this stature down—with words at least. "Thomas Edward Payne, I know you did not just infer that you are in a position to *let* me do anything. I am a grown-ass woman. I don't need a group of goons following me around deciding what I can do."

I see the flinch when the dreaded three-name call hits its intended target, and he shakes his head as if he has to physically shake off the blow. "If you are so grown, then start acting like it."

"What the actual fuck is that supposed to mean?"

"It means maybe don't dance with men that have had hard-ons for you since they could get them unless you intend to do something about it."

"Are you implying I lead him on, or that I instigated this? I was dancing with what I thought was a friend. Are women not allowed to have male friends anymore?"

"That is not what I meant, and you know it. I am your friend, Anna. Johnny and Patrick are your friends. Hell, even Max is your friend, if he would show up, like ever, but you and him have running in common. And we would never touch you like that, dancing or no. This asshole—" He thumbs over where his brothers and Ryan look to be getting into an even more heated argument, one that some of Ryan's buddies from the station, that he introduced me to earlier, are now joining in on, "—is not your friend. He has been talking a big game about fucking you since high school."

I notice that he leaves Bobby off his list of my friends, and it hurts that I'm not even considered to him anymore. I know better, but that is the bit I hang on to and I can't stop the words before they leave my mouth. "You're missing a brother there, Tommy, or am I not even ranked among his friends anymore?"

"Don't be stupid, it doesn't suit you. I don't know what you are now, but you left the friend zone in the back seat of his truck on homecoming night, and there is no going back once the cat is out of the bag."

"I don't know what you think happened that night, but it sure as hell wasn't that."

"Shit, Anna, you are twisting my words. I am not implying that." As our argument escalates, so does the tension behind Tommy's back. The Alverez brothers look like they aren't choosing sides, rather trying to de-escalate the situation to no avail. Ryan manages to push Patrick off but says something that has him winding his fist back. And that is when all hell breaks loose.

Chapter 16

Bobby

Working the night shift with Jones on a Friday night is not my idea of a good time. It's been slow, and to pass the time, I've been teetering on the back legs of this chair, balancing so precariously that a slam of the door could send me to the ground. I am bored out of my mind; I have counted the cracks in the drop ceiling and how many spots of the industrial grey paint on the walls of the bullpen are peeling. *Maybe the gala next week will loosen the budget for some much-needed repairs.* Through the boredom, lunch with my brothers keeps replaying in my head on a loop. *Tommy said he learned a lot from drunk Anna. What the hell does that mean, and why didn't I find out before I hightailed it out of there with my tail between my legs?*

"Why do you look like someone kicked your puppy? You aren't the one to get booted off the most interesting case to happen to this town in years." Jones has had his panties in a twist since Dobbs sent him home to lick his wounds, but he only has himself to blame. *Though if he had gotten me kicked off the case, maybe I could have entertained Operation Penguin—whatever the fuck that is.*

"Brother stuff," I grunt, knowing he won't understand. Jones is an only child. *Explains so much.*

"With your brothers, that can mean anything from a misdemeanor to a felony." He isn't wrong, so I don't call him out; my brothers have a way of finding themselves in the thick of mischief and mayhem. "Whatever it is, can you sulk about it on your own time? It's bad enough being stuck here all night when it is this slow." I let the two front legs of my chair slam down and glare at Jones. Great, *he's gone and done it now.*

"What'cha have to go and say that for? Are you trying to borrow trouble?" Sure, I may have thought the same thing, but every civil servant, medic, or ER nurse will tell you that you never let the word 'slow' slip past your lips unless you want hellfire to rain down on the rest of your shift. And as if he had summoned chaos by some sacred ritual, as soon as I got done admonishing him, the phone rings.

Jones pulls up to Wolf and Whistle a minute before I do, but waits for me before heading in to break up the fight that's been called in. "Fifty bucks says we cart one of your brothers off to the holding cell tonight."

"Hah, it's not a bet when it's a sure thing," I reply, spotting two of my brothers' vehicles in the lot. *But that doesn't mean that all three of them aren't in there.* I've lost count of how many times I have had to haul away one or more of my brothers in the last four years, and lord only knows how many nights they spent on the cots of the holding cells in the eight years I was gone.

"Is it weird?" The question surprises me, but he mistakes my pause for misunderstanding. "Having to take your brothers in? Does it cause animosity?"

"Well, they have been frequent flyers to the sin bin since we were boys, so having them in there is not weird. But if you mean, do they expect me to go easy on them, or do they hold a grudge when I don't? The answer is no. They know it's my job and they know they aren't angels."

"That's putting it mildly."

"They get a little too rowdy sometimes, but they mean well for the most part." The music, as we approach the doors, vibrates my bones and masks whatever mayhem we are about to walk into.

"Well, hometown hero, after you." Jones gestures towards the doors with a smug smirk that does nothing but make me roll my eyes.

"Don't mind if I do," I say as I push open the door. The smell of sweat and spilled drinks smacks me in the face first, but once the shock of it dissipates, the absolute bedlam that we are walking into stills my next step.

"Holy hell, a wrecking crew would wreak less havoc." Jones almost sounds impressed with the wreckage that we are witnessing. I may have been too if, at the eye of the storm, I didn't see two of my brothers actively participating in the brawl with Anna being shielded by the third. *What the actual fuck is happening here?* There are tables toppled and chairs askew, and enough broken glass glinting in the neon lights that you would think these idiots would be covered in nicks.

"Break it up!" I yell as I see Roman throw a bucket of water on the main antagonizers, which happen to be two of my brothers and half of Fire and Rescue.

"What in the hell is going on here?" Jones yells into the din, though the second bucket of water—this time courtesy of Leah Willson—goes a long way in shutting them up.

"Shit, that's cold!" someone exclaims, but I can't discern who; my focus is zoomed in on the blonde with the piercing blue eyes giving my brother hell. The house lights turn on, temporarily blinding everyone, but once the initial shock fades, it illuminates how much glass is on the floor, and all I can think of is getting Anna out of the middle of it unscathed.

"Okay, now that we have your attention, someone start explaining." I will give Jones credit; he really has that authoritative voice down. Not that any of these heathens pay him any mind as they all start pointing accusing fingers at each other.

That's when I notice the two of the Alvarez brothers near the middle—Enzo holding back his partner and Roberto holding back Patrick as they spew vitriol back and forth. Taking in the carnage and their central position to it, I think it's safe to say where this initiated, clocking Anna's proximity. My mind starts to spin a story of what sparked it as well. *If that red-headed fucker laid one finger on her, his face is going to be redder than his hair.*

I make a beeline to them, Jones following close behind. "Tommy, what happened?" I am not even asking as a deputy at the moment.

"That's rich. Ask your brother. Real reliable detective work." Ryan shakes Enzo off and spits blood onto the floor; it looks like he has the start of a fat lip. *Good.*

Ignoring him, Tommy answers, "Murph here doesn't know when no means no." A flush of heat sears through my senses, and all I see is red. I turn to Anna to see if she is alright, but she won't meet my eyes. Murph says something, but I can't hear him as my focus is singular.

"Did he hurt you?"

"I was handling it. They didn't need to step in," she murmurs under her breath.

I grab her chin lightly, turning her head until her glacial gaze meets mine. "Not what I asked. Did he hurt you?"

"Not like you're thinking, no. We were dancing, and he read it as something it wasn't—that's all. Nothing happened."

"You're shitting me with this, right? Anna, there is hard to get, and then there is delusional. What am I supposed to think when you're dressed like that for me? You've been screaming for it all night." The thought that she dressed up to impress this piece of shit enrages me.

"You need to keep better company, Anna." She rolls her eyes at me, and I want to kiss the bratty attitude right off her. Which is a ridiculous thing to want after what she has been through tonight. *She doesn't need more unwanted advances.*

"Like you're one to talk," she spits back at me, and I get the sense that she is pissed at me for more than what I just said, though I can't fathom why. Before I have time to ask, Murph opens his fat trap.

"Oh, good, Officer Cock-block is here to save the day," he mocks

"Ryan, you have the right to remain silent. This may be a wise time to exercise it," I seethe

"You know what I think? I think you can't stand that I was about to go where you never could. I was gonna close the deal, and it was going to be the back of *my* truck rocking, and *my* cock Anna Adkins riding, so you sent your goons here to interfere." He throws his arm out wide, gesturing to my brothers. "Still cock blocking after all these years? You're pathetic." He wipes the blood from his swollen lip as he steps closer to me. The rest of the restaurant goes still. "And you know what? I'm sure it would be even better than if I had gotten to pop that cherry all those years ago, because everyone knows that crazy chicks are wild fucks. Do you think she'd call me Daddy before she chokes on my—"

He doesn't get to finish that sentence before my fist connects with his face and he is on the floor. It takes all three of my brothers to haul me off his sorry, crumpled form. I must have blacked out because I only recall hitting him once, but my bruised knuckles on both hands tell a different story.

"Jesus Christ, Payne, what the fuck do you think you're doing?" Jones asks. "We are supposed to be breaking up a bar fight, not participating in one." I couldn't care less about what I should or shouldn't be doing. The only thing I care about is where Anna is and whether she is okay. *There is no way she didn't hear that shit he was talking. God, he is such a dick.* I am vaguely aware of Jones calling in for backup, but I still can't find Anna. I scour the crowd searching for her.

When I finally find her between Caroline and Leah, shrinking in on herself, a phantom pain passes through my heart. This image of the grown version of her is superimposed with the image of her the night her dad died, and like that night, I go to her. However, before I am halfway across the floor, I am stopped when Leanne steps in my path.

"Oh my God, Bobby, are you okay?" she asks, taking both my hands in hers, bringing my knuckles to eye level to inspect the damage. Her touch makes my stomach roll. The only woman I want to touch me right now is Anna, and Leanne is in the way.

"I'm fine," I murmur, wrenching my hands from her grasp, trying to sidestep her. I catch Anna's gaze and she looks devastated. That's when I notice how close Leanne is to me and how this must look to Anna. She doesn't know this is only concern for a coworker. *I need to explain.*

I step towards her but before I can reach her I feel a yank at my arm pulling it behind my body, and handcuffs clicking into place on my wrist.

"What the hell are you doing?" Leanne's voice goes shrill.

"Sheriff's orders," Jones answers, and then to me he says, "Look man, I get it. If someone said half that shit about Jess, I would beat their face in too, but Dobbs is pissed about you being on call and assaulting civilians. Looks like you're gonna spend the night in the cell with your brothers for a change." It is then that I notice that, in my distraction, Jones called in the cavalry. There are a dozen other deputies here rounding up the perps and loading them into cars and the van. *This is going to be a long fucking night.*

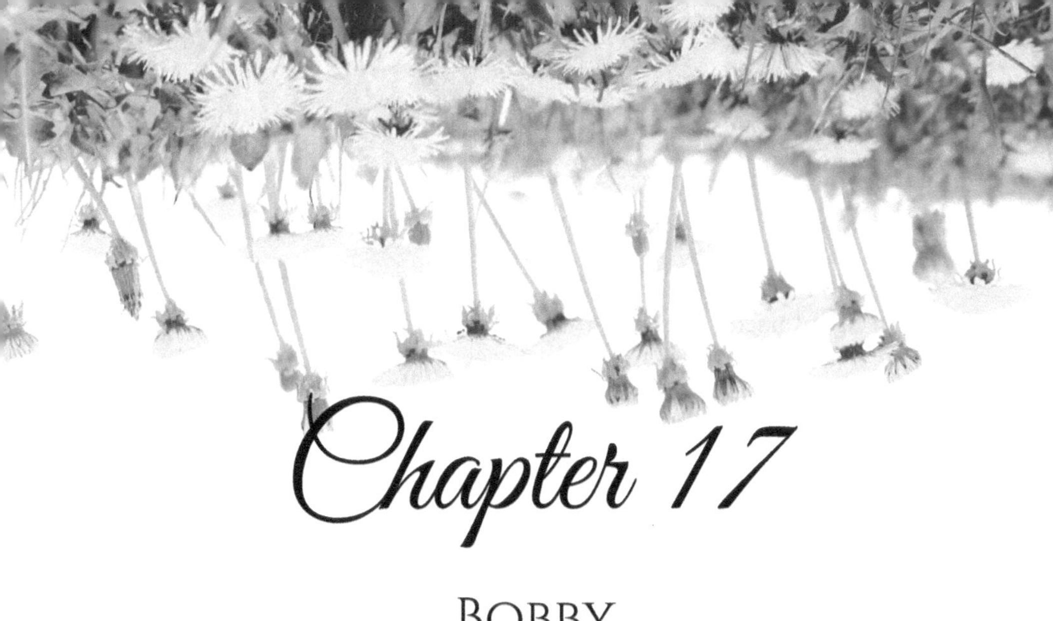

Chapter 17

BOBBY

This is the fullest the town's holding cells have ever been; we don't have enough cells to accommodate all of the occupants. Usually bar fights are between a smaller group or one-on-one. However, half of the town's firemen and medics joined the fight to back up Ryan, out of some misplaced sense of camaraderie causing friends of my brothers to enter the fray without knowing why they were joining in the first place—other than to even the odds. Alcohol has a way of fanning the flames of mob mentality, but there are also a few frequent flyers in here who will fight any chance they get for fun. There is not a lot to do in a town like this and boredom will warp some people's sense of entertainment.

Due to the lack of vacancy and perhaps to avoid any further incident, my brothers and I occupy one of the interrogation rooms instead of the standard holding cell. Smart really; if any of us were in the same room as Ryan right now, I can't say cooler heads would prevail. I can't get the things he said about Anna out of my head. *He doesn't deserve to breathe the same air as her. He never did.* The thought of it ignites a new flame of anger in my belly, fueling a restless energy that isn't satisfied sitting here on this metal chair. I jump up, sending the chair toppling with a clang, but it doesn't stop my momentum as I begin to pace back and forth. Shaky fingers run through my mussed hair, giving them a purpose other than curling into a fist and slamming into the wall out of frustration. My abused knuckles would not fare well if I followed through with the urge, but it would be satisfying all the same.

"Calm down, Bobby. I doubt he'll press charges," Tommy says. I am not sure how he got carted in with the rest of us. From what I could tell, he was on the perimeter protecting Anna and her friends from the maelstrom. It may be muscle memory at this point for my coworkers to put a Payne in cuffs.

A humorless snort escapes me as I turn to him. "Thought never even crossed my mind—til' now, so thanks for that, dick." Typically, in these bar rumble situations, personal charges are not filed. The involved parties are fined for the disruption of peace and ordered to pay for any property damages to the owners. Then, in a few days—or weeks for the more personal feuds—everyone is back to sitting on barstools next to each other, sharing a cold one and a couple of laughs. The town is too small for long-term grudges. *I don't know if I can ever go back to not wanting to knock his freckled face from his shoulders every time I see him,.* However, I wasn't a patron caught up in the drink and a bar fight. I was an acting law officer who lost their cool. *Reckless. I was so reckless.*

I couldn't stand there and let that bullshit spewing from his mouth continue to flow, especially not when she was right there to be caught in the undercurrent of his words. So, I dammed up the stream with my fist—repeatedly. *I should have punched him harder.* The wounded look on her face in the comfort of her friend's arms will haunt me. She looked so small. I had only seen her look that small twice before, and I hate seeing that broken expression on her beautiful face. I hate even more that I couldn't be the one to comfort her this time. And then that makes me think of all the times I don't know about that she has felt small over the years, and how I wasn't there to hold her through any of that either. That thought blows out the restless flame and chills me with a wind of despair that stops me cold.

Before any of my brothers can comment on the obvious change in my momentum, Sheriff Dobbs enters the room. "Did you boys get your phone call yet?" When we all shake our heads, he lets out a tired sigh.

There is no clock in here, so it is impossible to know what time it is, but if my internal clock is still sharp. I would put us at just past two o'clock in the morning. And for the first time since my fist connected with his freckled cheek, I feel a pang of regret for it. Not for him—he deserved it and all the hits that followed, probably the ones my brothers landed as well, but for dragging Sheriff Dobbs out of his bed and into the station at this time of day. Because there is only one reason he was called in, and that is to deal with me.

"Do you all need one? You are each entitled to one, or are you okay to use one call for the four of you?" he asks, making sure to note that he isn't refusing any of us our right to a phone call but is familiar enough with us to know we are all going to be calling the same person anyway. *Mom is going to be so disappointed in me.* Another regret to add to the list. "As you can imagine, we are limited on phones."

"I'll make the call." Johnny pushes back from the table, making brief eye contact with each of us. "If that's alright with y'all?" We each nod our consent; he is the mediator of our little band of misfits after all.

"Peachy," Dobbs responds. "Johnny, you can follow Deputy Jones to the phone bank." Jones steps up, brandishing a pair of cuffs.

"Is this really necessary?" Johnny asks, holding out his wrist in front of him.

"Standard procedure, I'm afraid," Jones answers, but not being able to hold back the dig, he goes on, "Should be used to it by now, John." This earns an eyeroll from my brother; no one calls him that. John is our father, and Johnny hates the reminder that he is a junior. Having thought that he was her last baby, my mother gave in to my father's request for a namesake on the condition that he get snipped. I imagine she was right pissed when she saw the double pink lines a year later, indicating Tommy was on the way. We all know the tale that after me, she made the appointment herself and all but insisted on being in the room when he finally followed through on his promise.

The ratcheting clicks of the cuff tell me Jones made them just a little too tight on purpose. I wonder if this is his standard mode of operation with all perps or only the ones with my last name. He can't touch Max, so he takes it out on the rest of us by being a right prick.

After Jones leads Johnny off, the sheriff's gaze hardens and falls onto me. "If you'll excuse us," he addresses my brothers. "I need to borrow your brother for a moment in my office."

"He has a right to have an attorney to be present for all questioning," Patrick pipes up for the first time since we arrived, sounding like Elle Woods reciting the law. I cringe at the look of utter annoyance Dobbs now wears.

"Or a representative from the Fraternal Order of Police, in his case, if this is about his job," Tommy adds in, and I wish they would both shut up.

"Actually, since your brother is a deputy and not a police officer, he is represented by the West Virginia Deputy Sheriffs' Association. But if it will put your mind at ease, boys, Joe from the WVDSA is already here," Dobbs informs them as if he is placating toddlers who just learned to string together sentences, only to argue with their Ma. If it does put their minds at ease, I can't tell, but all it does for me is create a pit in my stomach.

Moving towards Dobbs and possibly my fate as a deputy in this department, I stop when Tommy adds one last piece of legal advice as if I don't already know. "Remember you still have the right to remain silent." The door shuts behind me, effectively silencing my brothers from me, and I feel more alone than ever before.

"They studying for the bar exam or something?" The attempt at levity falls flat in the quiet of the hallway leading to the sheriff's office. Taking the hint, he leaves me to my riotous thoughts for the time it takes to make it to his office door. It creaks open, in need of some WD-40 or maybe some new hinges altogether, like everything in this town, they have a bit of rust on them. Inside the office sits Joseph Williams, the representative Dobb's spoke of moments ago. He rises from his seat to greet me, and I take his outstretched hand. We have met before; he lives in the next town over and has visited the station a few times prior.

Dobbs sits in his office chair and motions us to take the seats in front of his mahogany desk. On top of its surface sits my gold-plated deputy's badge along with my standard-issued Shadow Systems XR920 9mm pistol—the model the department adopted last year after the state troopers made it their issue of choice. I was stripped of both before Jones secured me in the back of his rig. My sight is glued to them, focused on these symbols of who I've been for the last four years, and I forget to sit.

"Take a seat, son." Dobbs' voice is stern but not unkind, and I wonder if he, in his long career, has ever been on this side of the desk, in the same position as me. I follow the order because even delivered in the gentle tone he used, it is in fact an order from my superior, and I am nothing if not a dutiful soldier. "You are familiar with Joe?" He gestures to the man seated beside me, and at my nod, he continues, "Good. He is mainly here to serve as a witness to the actions the office needs to take in light of your... indiscretion."

"Yes, sir."

"He would also be available to represent you in any criminal or civil case should any be filed, but Mr. Murphy has already stated he has no intention of filing charges for assault or pursuing a civil case for damages. So, what we are left with is the internal investigation of use of excessive force, dereliction of duty, and the general charges of disrupting the peace." It surprises me that Ryan isn't pursuing any further action against me, but it doesn't mean I forgive the things he has said and done. I doubt we will be friendly moving forward.

"It is standard procedure to suspend any deputy involved in excessive use of force for two weeks without pay, pending an internal investigation. During this time, you will be relieved of your weapon and badge, and all duties fitting an officer of the law. You will be prohibited from the premises unless called in for questioning concerning the investigation. Any current case work will be distributed to other officers for the remainder of your suspension, and you are not to investigate the status of any of them on your own. Do you understand?"

"Yes, sir."

"Joseph is available to you as counsel, but you do also have the right to seek individual private representation if you see fit. Do you intend to seek private representation?" the sheriff asks as he clicks his pen, waiting for my response before he ticks off the box on the form in front of him. An incident report, no doubt.

"No, sir," I respond as his eyes flit to my raw knuckles.

"Did you receive medical attention for your injuries?

"No, sir."

"Do you intend to seek treatment for injuries sustained while on duty?" This is the most clinical I have ever seen my boss, and the routine of it all puts me at some kind of ease. If there is anything eight years of service will teach you is to find solace in protocol and procedure. It is mostly why I accepted this position once I rejoined the civilian ranks; I needed the structure. The idea of two weeks without that structure is a little daunting. *I should probably check in with my VA therapist.*

My fingers flex under the scrutiny of his gaze, sending pain signals to my brain, but I've had worse and deserve worse still for letting him down. "No, sir."

Opening a drawer, he pulls out another form, sliding it across the desk. "You still need to fill out this incident report, and if, within the next week, you change your mind about seeking treatment, call the number on the top. That will get you to the county's workman's comp department." Eyes trained on the shake of my hand as I grab for the pen he has placed next to the form, he continues, "If you are unable to fill out the form, you can call the line and dictate the answers, and intake will transcribe them for you." I shake my head as I force my swollen fingers to hold the pen between them. "I'll make sure Jones gets you an icepack when you go back to your cell."

"As for the general disruption of the peace charge, as you are familiar, you will be held on until a bond of 500 dollars is paid for your immediate release, refundable only if found innocent in a court of law. When the clerk's office opens on Monday, you will be expected to show for arraignment, at which time you can enter your plea. If you plead guilty, the magistrate will determine your fines and you can set up payment with them. If you plead innocent, then a date will be set for your trial. Joseph is available to you for these proceedings as well, or again, you are within your rights to appoint private counsel. Do you intend to seek private counsel?"

"No, sir."

"Alright. Joe will be there on Monday." Turning to Mr. Williams, the sheriff asks, "That right, Joe?"

"Yes, I will be there when the clerk's office opens to discuss our options. Unless you want to speak privately now, Deputy Payne?"

"It can wait 'til Monday. I know it's late."

"Or early, depending on how you look at it." The attempted cheer falls flat. Everyone in this room is exhausted, pissed off, or disappointed—or a combination of all three.

"Okay then, I need your statement of events, signature, and I will get you back to your brothers," Dobbs says, pen at the ready as Williams sets a tape recorder down to record this as well, likely so that my words cannot be misrepresented. He looks to me for permission, and I nod, causing him to click the button.

"It started when we got the call..."

Returning to the interrogation room with my brothers, I see Johnny has returned. "Mom coming in the morning?" I ask.

He shrugs, and I assume his call went to voicemail. I know he called our mother; Dad would let us sit here until Monday's arraignment as a form of 'accepting the consequences of our actions'. He is the tough love to our mother's tender care, but they balance each other well.

Jones comes in with some water bottles and an icepack for me. He sets them on the table without a word before leaving again. "Cheery fellow that one," Patrick jokes.

"Yeah, a regular laugh riot," Johnny responds, rubbing at his reddened wrist, no doubt recalling the unnecessarily tight cuffs he has just escaped.

"It's a wonder you don't invite him over to family dinners on Sunday. I'm sure Jess would appreciate the chance at some of Mom's sweet tea again," Tommy joins in, finally breaking through my funk and earning a weak chuckle from me.

"Could you fucking imagine Max's face over the screen when he video-calls in? It would be priceless," I say, grabbing the ice pack as I sit, squeezing it in one hand until I feel the telltale 'pop' of the of the internal pouch releasing the cooling crystals. I shake it up, a sigh passes my lips as I place the soothing pouch onto my knuckles. The second pouch remains in active on the table, I'm saving it for when this one's effects dissipate.

Thinking of family dinners, I am reminded of all the ones that Jess did attend with Max at her side, and how younger me used to dream of the day Anna would be seated next to me with my arm around her shoulder, trading verbal jabs with my brothers. I would imagine her in Jess's place next to my mother, drying the freshly washed dishes and gabbing about local gossip. Not that Anna was much for gossip or doing dishes for that matter.

The fantasy was more about seeing her weave her life in with mine until we created a fabric of family, woven so tight it would be hard to tear apart. Though even if that happened back then, who's to say the months of distance and time the military demanded would not have eaten through the patchwork quilt of my dreams? Max and Jess didn't survive it after all. *But at least they had their chance. We never got that.*

It hits me like a punch to the face. The only thing standing in the way of our chance right now has now been removed from the path, for two weeks—at least. Turning to Johnny, meeting his gaze, his chuckle stops short at the sudden seriousness he must see reflected in mine. "I'm ready."

Perplexed, he asks, "Ready for what?"

And with more seriousness than the name should demand, I state, "To hear about Operation Penguin."

Chapter 18

BOBBY

(Saturday)

The door creaks open, allowing the light from the hallway to illuminate the sleeping forms of my brothers sprawled out on the floor. Thomas is off to my right, curled up on his side, but Patrick and Johnny have somehow found themselves in a cuddle pile through the night. *I wish I had my phone. This is perfect blackmail material.* Years of military training made it easy to sleep propped up against the wall facing the entrance and also explains why the door opening woke me and not my brothers. I have been programmed to sleep light.

"Paynes, your stay has ended. You don't have to go home, but you can't stay here," comes the way too chipper voice of Wojack.

"What time is it?" My voice creaks from my dry throat, and I cough, trying to clear it as my brothers stir awake. It must be after six a.m. if Wojack has relieved Jones.

151

"Quarter to seven. You lot are the first of the jailbirds to get sprung, so c'mon—time to fly the coop."

We follow him out to the hall as he leads us to booking and storage to gather our personal effects. "God, I am hungry. Do you think Mom will mind if we stop at the diner for breakfast before she drops us off at our cars?" Tommy asks.

I am not looking forward to cramming into my mother's sedan with my three grown-ass brothers. "Shotgun," I claim as if we were kids again, and Patrick and Tommy groan in unison. Johnny is oddly silent.

"Oh, it's not your mom who posted bail," Wojack states with a shit-eating grin, and I cannot fathom what could cause such an expression. That is, until I turn the corner and see Anna sitting in the waiting room, glaring daggers at Leanne. *Shit, looks like Operation Penguin starts now.*

"You used your one phone call to call Anna?" Tommy asks Johnny, confused.

"No, he called Max who then called me twenty times until I picked up. I didn't even know he had my phone number," Anna answers in his stead. She is wearing a cropped ACDC tee over high-waisted cutoffs with one side of the shirt hanging off a smooth, pale shoulder. Her golden strands are pulled back in a messy bun with her sunglasses pushed back on top of her head. My eyes travel down, and the sight of rainbow crocs on top of ankle socks makes me smile. This is most she has resembled the version of Anna I remember; since she crashed back into my life like a meteor.

"Oh, well, I shared it in the Payne brother group chat the night we dropped you off at the bar," Patrick provides, attempting to be helpful.

"I didn't get that message," I sulk.

"Oh... um, it must have been chat we have without you in it," He responds

"Rude."

"It's for your own good. Plausible deniability, and all that," Johnny says with a wave of his hand as if that should be a given.

"Great, nice to know you have the means to plot without local law enforcement surveillance," I say.

"Awesome, now that we got that out of the way, can we get moving, please? I have specific instructions to drop you three," she points at my brothers, "Stooges off at Wolf and Whistle to start 'Operation Clean Up' and then drop Deputy Payne off at his apartment. Let's roll out."

She walks past Leanne's desk and shoots her the bird. I need to know what was said between her posting our bail—*shit, that's two grand for all of us*—and when we walked into this waiting room.

"Y'all go ahead, I'll catch up," I yell, moving toward the desk.

Anna rolls her eyes and mutters, "Of course," then louder she says. "You have five minutes—or you can walk." With that statement, she pushes open the door, allowing it to swing shut, almost hitting Tommy in the face before he catches it at the last minute. My brothers shoot me a pitying look before following in her wake.

"Well, she is a ray of sunshine, ain't she?" Leanne snarks as the door shuts with a click.

"Listen, Leanne, Anna is going through a lot right now. What did you say to her to rile her up?"

"Me? What makes you think I said anything to her? She just came in here like a bat out of hell, making demands with her bad attitude," Leanne says on the defense. There is definitely something I am missing here. "Anyway, I am glad you stayed back. I wanted to talk to you about the gala. I was thinking, since you are driving me and all, maybe we call this what it is and make it our official first date." Frozen and slacked jawed, I am so stupefied that it takes Anna's warning beep to get me moving. I need to get out there before she leaves me behind... again.

"First of all, Leanne, I was driving you as a favor, not as a date, and second of all, I'm not going anymore, so you will have to find your own way."

"What do you mean you're not going?" she whispers. "I already told all my friends we were going together. I'll look like a fool if I show up alone."

"As of last night, I am suspended from all duties, including attending the gala. And I'm sorry you had the wrong idea here, Leanne, but it was only a ride on offer." I am distracted by the SUV starting to back out of the space in front of the floor-to-ceiling window. "Shit, gotta go."

I leave her sputtering as I throw myself out the front door into the glaring morning sunlight. Blinded for a moment, I have to reorient my senses. That moment has cost me precious time as I see Anna adjusting the wheel to make her way out of the parking lot. *Shit.*

I start out at a cold sprint. Tommy throws open the back passenger door and sticks his head out of the vehicle, yelling, "Run, Forest, Run!" at the top of his lungs. causing me to bark out a laugh and quicken my pace.

Her getaway is impeded by the stop sign. Blood pumping in my calve muscles I take advantage of my momentum. Bending at the knees in a deep squat I push off the pavement launching myself into the open back door, landing across Tommy and Johnny's laps.

"I thought I called shotgun," I pant. *I need to start running again. This is pathetic.*

Patrick turns around and gives me a meaningful look and says "You snooze, you lose." What he is not saying out loud is I need to get my head out of my ass and get out of my own way. I nod. *Message received loud and clear.* I sit up straight, close the door, and buckle my belt.

Anna looks at me over her sunglasses through the rearview mirror. "Are we ready now?"

"Yes, I'm ready." *Finally.*

Annastasia

"Anna, we're starving. Can we please go to Deb's?" Tommy whines from the back like a five-year-old.

"No."

"Puh-lease? We don't have to sit and eat. We can order to go. I'm so hungry I could die." *Hyperbole, thy name is Thomas.*

"Should have thought of that before you tore a whole bar up over something you should have kept your fat nose out of." Yeah, I am still salty.

"Hey, first of all, my nose is just the right size for my face, slender even. And secondly, I wasn't even in the fight. I was standing right next to you the whole time."

"And yet you spent the night in jail."

"You are being mean this morning, Anna," he pouts, *actually pouts.* I can see him in the rearview crossing his arms, slumping down in the seat between his brothers. His lip juts out quivering. I can remember him making this exact face when we were in grade school, and his brothers made him the monkey in the middle. How Mrs. Payne survived these five is a mystery to me.

Johnny smacks him on the back of the head, also a move I remember from our youth, and says, "Leave Anna be. She just dropped two grand on us. Don't be a brat."

"Yeah, Tommy, don't be a brat," Patrick mocks back, piling on. I am one second from yelling that I am about to turn this car around, but I bite my lips shut. I will not be mothering grown-ass men today. I am half tempted to say fuck it to Max's instructions and drop them all off on the front porch for their *real* mother to deal with, but Max's sincere plea rings in my head.

(Earlier in the morning...)

The ringing of my phone jars me awake.

I crack my eyes open; I swear I just closed them. I look around my room for any indication of the time. It is dark except for the illuminated radius surrounding my phone on the nightstand and the moonbeams trickling in from the window, casting shadows of the swaying trees outside on my floorboards. I reach one hand out of my cocoon of sheets and blankets, preferring to be bundled even in the heat of a fledgling summer, and promptly hit the fuck you button. Once my arm has retreated into the safety of my cozy little nest, I snuggle in to resume my visit to dreamland.

The alert sounds again.

Obviously, someone has other plans for me, but I learned my lesson earlier this week: no good news happens before bankers' hours. I cover my head with the pillow, hoping they will get the hint and give up.

As the tension melts away and I think I am in the clear, the ringing picks up anew.

Both my eyes pop open with the sudden thought that maybe it is Joanie, and maybe it is an emergency. She had changed me to her emergency contact two years ago when she finally went no contact with her family. She is all I have. Well, that isn't true. Caroline has proven that she has always been here too, but it is not the same. Joanie is my sister for all intents and purposes, and now I am picturing her laid up in an emergency department, hooked up to machines with no one to hold her hand as she did for me a few short days ago. Anxiety has me throwing my covers off and reaching for the phone.

I miss the call by seconds, and with shaky fingers, I mess up my swipe code twice before I unlock my phone. Holding my breath, I check my missed calls. Not seeing Joanie's number, I exhale. I actually don't know this number, but the 304-area code tells me it is someone from West Virginia. *Okay? So not a Vegas hospital either. Who the fuck is calling me?*

I do time zone math and decide that it is not an appropriate time to burden Joanie with a phone call because my mind spiraled down a dark hole. I focus on my breathing exercises, clutching my phone tighter. I feel the case indent my hand, grounding me in reality and out of my whirlwind imagination. I jump, my hand spasming and tossing my phone across the room as it rings again right in the middle of my grounding ritual.

"God fucking dammit," I shout, clutching my hand to my chest as if that could calm my racing heart. Right as I had begun to calm down, and the fucking thing went off again, ruining any chill I had. Also, eliminating any chances of falling back into a peaceful slumber. *Maybe the Amish have the right idea about modern technology.*

Now wide awake, I place both feet to the ground and heave myself off the bed to retrieve the cause of all my strife. Checking the phone when I pick it up, I see the same unknown number. I huff in annoyance. Only a handful of people in this state have my number, and half of them are in the sheriff's holding cell right now. *No…It couldn't be one of them, could it? Would one of the fucking Payne brothers have the nerve to call me as their one phone call right now? No, no fucking way. Well, if it is, they can rot, overbearing assholes that they are.*

As if daring me to stick to my convictions, my phone illuminates in my hand, same number. I click answer call, before the ringer can sound. "Hello?"

"Thank fuck. Listen, Anna, I know my brothers are a handful, and you owe us nothing. Well, that isn't exactly true. I did pull your scrawny ass from Coal Miners Creek when the ice broke, and you fell in. You know, after I told you and Bobby that you shouldn't walk on ice over running water, so I guess you do kind of owe me a life debt." I haven't heard his voice in years, but if the story didn't give him away, his condescending attitude did would. *So it* is *a Payne brother, just not the ones that ruined my night. Well, I guess he felt left out.*

"Max, it is too late… or early, oh hell, it is *not* a good time for this—whatever this is. Can we skip to the point where you tell me why you are blowing up my phone at—" I hold my phone away from my ear to check the time. "—four-thirty in the fucking morning."

"Pffft, hearing you swear is like hearing a *Care Bear* drop F bombs." His amusement does nothing but stoke my ire.

"You have ten seconds to start telling me what this is about or I am going to hang up the phone and put it on do not disturb."

"Is that the way you talk to someone who saved your li—"

"Ten," I cut him off, "Nine… Eight."

"Okay, okay. God forbid a guy reminisces."

"Seven."

"*Alright!*" he shouts. "Sorry, you're just so easy to rile up." Hearing my intake of air to resume my countdown, he rushes. "I need a favor."

"No."

"Anna, be reasonable. At least hear me out." His tone has changed from needling to serious, and the swift change stops my finger from hanging up, countdown be damned.

"Fine, what do you need, Max?" I relent, sitting back on the bed, attempting to at least be cozy through this conversation.

"I need you to post bail for my brothers in the morning."

"You must be joking."

"I assure you I am not."

"Why should I?"

"Besides the fact that they were protecting your honor?" The haughty tone is creeping back in, like he can't help himself.

"Max, think of me as the raging rapid and you are the fool walking over me on thin ice this time."

"Okay, yeah. Shit, I'm sorry. I am not used to being the one to ask for favor." He takes a deep, suffering sigh. "It's just I don't want my mom to know the boys are in jail."

"She surely is used to this call by now." Even having been gone for over a decade, I know the Payne boys well enough to suspect they are frequent flyers.

"Yes, but not with Bobby, and I think it would break her heart if she knew that the golden child is as bad as the rest of us." That rings half true, but I don't think he has told me the full story. If I am going to tamp down my anger by sunup and spring the rest of the Paynes in my asses out, I want the whole truth.

"You Payne boys are dramatic as fuck. Rip it off like a bandage and tell me the truth," I say, exasperated by this whole evening.

"Fine, the others don't know, so don't let on, but Dad hasn't been feeling great, had a persistent cough, and Ma finally convinced him to go to the doctors this week. They are waiting on some of the labs to come back. I don't think she can take this added stress right now, even if she is used to it."

I freeze—physically—my mind however, is spinning over time. Mr. Payne was a miner for most of his life. There are so many things that can kill you in that line of work, but one of the slowest and most miserable is BLD—"Black Lung Disease."

"We don't know anything for sure yet, Anna," Max says, tone gentle, as if I am the one who needs comforting. *I didn't even realize I said that out loud.* "Could be anything. Could be only a respiratory infection and some steroids will clear him right up. I'm the only one who knows anything about it. Other than constant phone calls to me, she is dealing with the stress alone. Anna, please, I don't want to add this to her plate. Not right now."

"Yeah. Yeah, of course. What do you need me to do?

(Present)

"Sorry, Anna." Tommy's voice has lost the whine, but it brings me out of my thoughts.

"It's fine, and I didn't drop two grand—Max transferred the money to me this morning," I reply to Johnny's admonishment. I don't need these guys walking around thinking they owe me a debt; it will be more trouble than it's worth.

"Still, you are going out of your way for us. We are grateful," Bobby chimes in for the first time since we pulled away from the sheriff's office.

I can't help some of the annoyance that seeps into my voice when I say, "I am honestly surprised your little girlfriend didn't bail. At least, *you* out, before she clocked in this morning."

Three Payne brothers' heads snap to Bobby; Patrick turning his whole upper half to stare his brother down. *What is that reaction about?*

"What girlfriend, Robert?" Johnny asks with a hostile undertone coating his words. *I don't think I have ever heard Johnny call him that.* This interaction is all kinds of weird, so I keep my mouth shut and watch it play out in the rearview mirror.

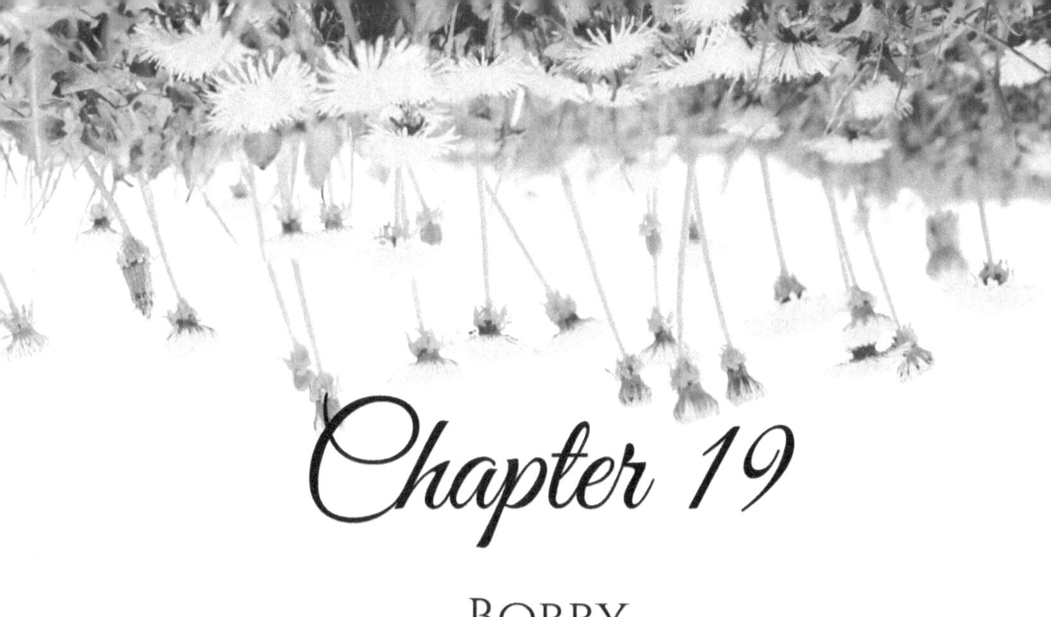

Chapter 19

BOBBY

The weight of all my brothers' stares is bearing down on me like a mudslide down the mountain. They are all ready to jump in and be the judge, jury, and executioner for a crime I did not commit. Holding my hands up in a placating manner, I inform everyone in the car, "I do *not* have a girlfriend."

My brothers seem to accept my proclamation for the truth it is—too much time spent together to not be able to see through each other's bull-shit—but Anna's icy gaze narrows at me over her sunglasses. They have slid down the bridge of her button nose, giving me a clear view of her eyes, judging me through the reflection of the mirror. I know that her ire shouldn't excite me, but it does. *If she is jealous, that means that I have a shot.*

"Sure, okay" Her beautiful ocean eyes roll like tidal waves crashing to the shore before disappearing behind the shades she pushes back into place. "Situationship, friends with benefits, fuck buddy... Whatever label you want to give it, you would think she would have bailed you out."

She doesn't give me the chance to answer as she turns up the volume when *'Manchild'* comes on the radio. She and Patrick start singing at the top of their lungs like it is their own personal episode of *Carpool Karaoke.* Tommy and Johnny join in on the chorus, and I can't help but feel like this is a targeted attack.

It is not soon enough that we are pulling into the lot of Wolf and Whistle. Roman comes out shaking his head as he catches the tail end of their performance. How he deals with all of this town's crazies is beyond me, but at least he takes it in stride. He has a 'you fucked it up, you fix it' policy that he goes to first, not wanting to ostracize his clientele by being the one to file charges. He understands that hefty fines for every scrap that happens here would be bad for his bottom line in the long run.

"Alright, you morons. Tools are in the shed to the side. You're on clean-up and rebuild duty until everyone else gets here. I need this shit cleaned up before noon for the lunch rush." He delivers the orders as well as any drill sergeant, and having never enlisted, that is impressive. If I recall his backstory correctly, he was an Army brat before landing here to live with his grandparents. My brothers spill out of the SUV and I follow suit, wanting to get into the front seat, refusing to let Anna drive me around like some ride share.

Tommy clocks my movements and can't help himself by throwing a jab my way. "I still don't understand how Deputy Dipshit gets out of this. He threw hands, too. Meanwhile, I stayed back and protected Anna and her friends. If anyone gets a free pass on this, it should be me."

"Yeah, well, I think he and Murph need some time away from each other. Chief Johnson called and said that they are sending all the guys up after they've fed them breakfast. We are trying to clean up, not start round two."

"Aww, man. See Anna? They got breakfast. We could have stopped." A hungry Tommy is a whiny Tommy; he always reverts to a child when he is in a calorie deficit.

She leans her head out of her window and yells, "Sucks to suck." It seems like sleep-deprived Anna only regresses to middle school, which coincidentally is the last time I heard that turn of phrase. But seeing her fall into place with my brothers like some long-missing puzzle piece that is essential to getting the whole picture only furthers my feeling that this could work. *She's always been ours. Now I have to figure out how to make her mine.*

Before I reach for the passenger door, Johnny's hand lands on my shoulder. Leaning in close so only I can hear his warning, he says, "I don't know how or why she thinks that harpy you work with has her claws in you but clear it up and clear it up now. There is no room for a miscommunication trope in Operation Penguin." I nod my understanding and open the door before slipping in and buckling my belt with a click.

We sit there for a moment, with only the sound of the ads on the radio filling the vehicle. This is the first time since the hospital that we have been alone in the same space. Anna's thumbs tap the steering wheel to the tune of a jingle about poison control before she turns to me.

"So, Max, in all his micromanaging glory, forgot to tell me where you live. Where to Deputy?" She sounds overly cheery, a false voice, one she must use with customers at the fancy hotel she works for. The voice she uses for strangers. That stings. I may not know what we are or the whole of what we were, but *strangers* is a role we have never played. At least not in our conscious lives. I suppose there was a time that two-year-old me met an infant version of her. Our mothers were best friends. Anna was the closest thing my mother ever had to a daughter, and Mary, while she was here, was a second mother to us as well. We all mourned her when she left. My mother still can't make sense of it. But that is not an aspect of our shared past I want to dwell on. That is only another tick in the column of reasons she has to leave and never look back. *And I am so damn tired of being in her rearview mirror.*

I reach my hand over and push the ignition to cut the idling engine, cutting off the radio and drenching us in silence. I don't want her to be distracted from what I am about to say. Johnny's right—there is no room for miscommunication in this already huge chasm between us. It is already filled with trauma and regrets, but doubt is something I refuse to let come between us.

"What are you doing?" she asks, reaching her hand to hit the ignition to restart the engine, and I grab it in mine before it reaches its destination. I rub a rough thumb over the smooth skin on the back of her hand. I feel a shiver move through her and see the pale, almost translucent hairs on her arm stand up with the tension that little movement causes. It is hard to hide the effect her reaction has on me. It hits me somewhere deep and prehistoric and makes my caveman brain wake up and want to claim this woman as mine, drag her back to my cave to keep for all time. But I have to fight my baser instincts and rely on conversation to move this in a direction that can be considered progress.

"She isn't any of those things," I say soft but sure.

"What—"

I interrupt her before she can ask what I mean. "Leanne. She isn't my 'situationship', friends with benefits, or what was the last one? Oh yeah, fuck buddy. She isn't any of those things, never has been, and she most certainly is *not* my girlfriend. Never even had one of those. Though I was close to getting one back in high school. But as we know, life had other plans."

"God, that's an understatement." She slumps back defeated, taking her hand with her, and I miss the feel of her in my bones.

"I don't know where that idea got into your head, but I'm telling you it's not true."

"So, she made up that you were taking her to some gala on Friday?" She sounds weary and then looks suspicious as I wince.

"Okay, so no, I was *driving* her to the gala, as a favor. She said her car was in the shop and did not want to third-wheel a couple. It sounded plausible at the time. I swear I didn't know until today she even saw me like that." I cross my heart like the scout I never was, earning another one of her eyerolls, but this time it is accompanied by a half smirk, so I count that as a win.

"Nice to see you are still as dense as ever. It is good to know that some things never change," she says as she starts up the car. "So where to?"

I rattle off my address, knowing that she knows where the little row houses are and won't need further direction. I, however, can't let that last comment slide. "What do you mean I'm dense?"

"She has been after you since high school." She lets out a maniacal laugh as she backs out onto the main road. "God, I wonder what other schemes to get your attention over the years she tried that just went right over your block head. She has never been subtle."

"I never paid her any attention, now or then. There has only ever been one girl in this town to catch and keep my attention, and in the spirit of being transparent, she is sitting in this car right now."

"Ha, and it took you forever to even see me." That isn't true, I always saw her, and embarrassingly enough, Johnny wasn't too far off when he called me out for pining for her since I could get a hard-on. What he doesn't realize is that I was gone for her long before that. I just wasn't good enough for her, not then. And I am still ashamed that it took *Ryan fucking*

Murphy's words to give me the push then, and somehow now to go after what I wanted, whether I deserved it or not.

But she isn't ready for me to lay it all out there. We aren't ready to shed the locks on all the secrets we've kept close, so for now I say, "I have always seen you, Anna. Sometimes you were all I could see." Her fair skin does nothing to hide the flush on her face. She doesn't reply, and that is okay; she needs time to process, and I will give her at least until the end of the ride to be in her own head. But I am not going to let her retreat from this. No, we are here, given this chance for a reason, and I refuse to waste it.

Annastasia

My hand aches with phantom tingles from where his thumb drew lazy circles on it. When it happened, I had full-body shivers that radiated from that spot up my arm and then traveled down my spine. *Am I really that touch-starved? Or have I just been starved of his touch?* I have had my share of one-night stands and casual flings over the past decade, nothing serious. No one I wanted to get into the nitty-gritty of the patchwork of trauma that has led me to who I am now, sitting in this car with a white-knuckle grip on this steering wheel. *What is this? What does he want? What do I want?* My head is spinning. I need to call Joanie.

Pulling into the lot of the row houses that Bobby now calls home, I try to reconcile the small footprint dwelling with the sprawling plot of land that he dreamed of as a boy, and come up short.

"Well, here you go. You probably want to get out of that uniform and shower. My good Samaritan deed is done for the day," I say, not looking him in the eye. Even with the shield of my sunglasses, I feel too raw and vulnerable when I am this close to him, sharing the same air, without any buffer between us. His brothers are excellent buffers.

"Anna, let me take you out." It isn't stated as a question, more of a desperate plea that falls from his lips in the form of a demand. I can see that he is frustrated about how it sounded by the tick in his jaw.

"I don't know, Bobby. Isn't that going to be a conflict of interest for you while you are on my case? And when you are off of it, I'll be gone." He winces as if the word *gone* was a physical blow, but he shakes it off.

"Uh, actually, I am off the case now—all cases, really. I am on suspension after last night." I don't want to think about last night, but now I can't stop. It was going so well until it wasn't. I believed, or was starting to, for the first time, that maybe I could belong again to these hills and these people. But that thought crashed and burned in an instant, and now I can't get Murph's words out of my head.

He called me crazy. And that is the bit that I cling to. The advances and crude language were bad enough, sure, but it isn't anything that any woman in this day and age hasn't experienced at least once. *Coming from a notorious paste eater stings a bit,* but it's the crazy bit that sticks with me like a scarlet letter. *Because there is some truth to it, isn't there? Normal people don't spend two years in residential therapy. And if crazy is genetic? Well, no one who has their mental faculties just abandons their child, and no one who isn't insane could do what* he *did and live with themselves. Drunk or not.*

Rough calloused fingers brush a loose strand of hair from my face, tucking it behind my ear with gentle care before they caress my cheek and finally stop at my chin as he tilts my head towards him. My thoughts still at his touch. No, not just still. My thoughts are silenced by the reverent way he touches me, as if I am not only a fragile thing but a precious one.

"Where did you just go?" he asks, eyes darting back and forth, trying to find purchase in my gaze but no doubt only finding his own reflected by my mirrored lenses. With another gentle move, the hand that was holding me in place tilts my glasses up to easily rest upon my head. Then that thumb, the same one that sent tingles down my spine no more than twenty minutes ago, swipes a stray tear that I did not even know had fallen, so enraptured in his touch. "What's wrong?"

"Do you think I am crazy?" His soft hazel eyes sharpen and darken in an instant as his brow furrows and his jaw tics.

"I didn't hit him hard enough." Coming from anyone else, it would be an aim for levity; from him, it is deadly serious.

"If you hit him any harder, he'd be dead." Not an exaggeration; it only took one hit to knock Ryan flat on the floor. The pulverizing that followed, I am not sure was done in complete consciousness. Something unleashed inside of Bobby, and with my past, I should want to run from it, but I don't.

"Yeah, well, he would deserve it."

"You mean that, don't you?"

He nods, then, holding my gaze, he asks, "Does that scare you?"

"Maybe it should, but it doesn't. You want to protect me. You've always wanted to slay my dragons." I think back to days running through the woods with sticks as swords.

"I would lay their heads at your feet if that's what it took."

"But I've never been a princess in a tower. I can slay my own dragons now."

"Well, if you let me, I will fight by your side." He pauses, staring so deep into my eyes that I am sure he will see all the ugly, scarred pieces of my soul. Pieces that I try to keep buried deep. Then he says, "You are not crazy, Anna. You are strong. Lesser people could not rise from the ashes of what you have been through and come out stronger for it. But here you are, a phoenix in the flesh, and *Ryan Murphy,*" he spits his name as if it leaves a foul taste on his tongue, "has never deserved to breathe the same air as you."

"I still have to leave when the case is over, at least for a little while. What do you want out of this, really?"

"So many things, Anna. I want the chance that was snatched away from us. I want you to know that I have always seen you. I want to just hang out with you again, because, God, I missed you. But most of all, I want whatever you can give me for however long that is. I want you, and I want you to know it like you know how to breathe."

"Then yes, I will go out with you." A boyish grin lights up his face, showing that damn dimple that has haunted my dreams, and I sigh as he leans in and kisses my cheek.

Before he pulls back, he whispers in my ear, "You are not going to regret this." He pulls away and exits the car, heading for his door—and I believe him.

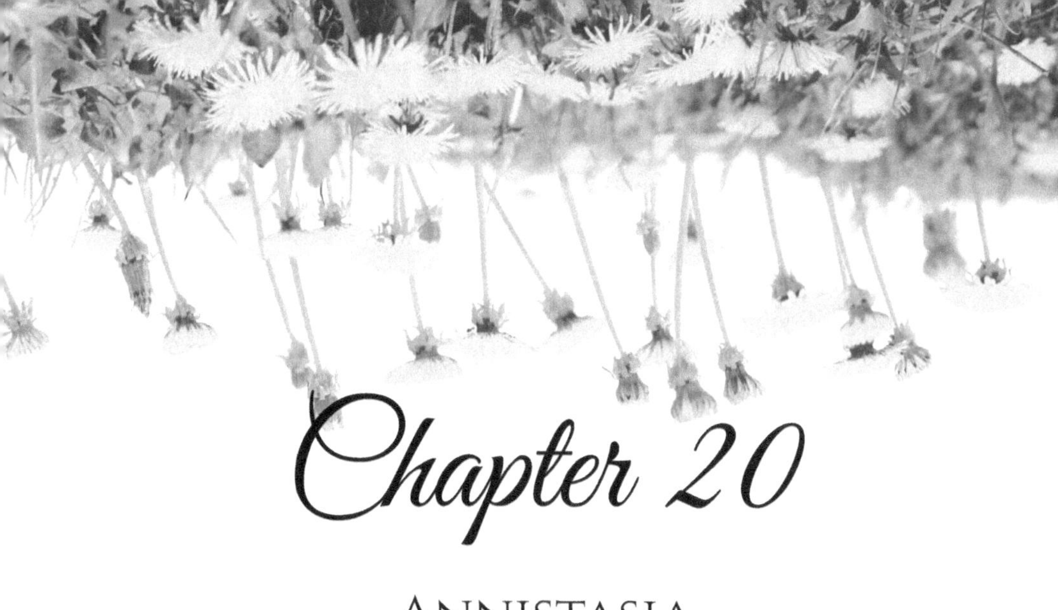

Chapter 20

ANNISTASIA

I made it back to the inn before they put away the continental breakfast. I ate it in the common area, watching the kids decked out in blue and bronze prepare for their summer orientation visits to St. Brigid's. They have a giddy air of anticipation about them, on the precipice of something new. I feel a sort of kinship with them in that sentiment. For once, being in this town is bringing me something other than perpetual nerves and dread. Well, the nerves are there, but instead of the inescapable sinking feeling that is their usual partner, I feel an airy sort of anticipation.

I forced myself to eat slow and take lingering sips of my hazelnut coffee, drawing the ritual out. Anything to keep my twitchy fingers from calling Joanie until a respectable hour. *She is three hours behind,* I remind myself. The sun hasn't even hit the strip yet. Calling at this time of day, for anything short of a catastrophe, would be a good cause for the dissolution of our long-standing friendship.

I could call Caroline, but besides the fact that she is most likely nursing a hangover, it wouldn't feel right to go to her first with this. Joanie has been my one constant since stepping into our shared dorm freshman year. She's the one who held me through the night terrors, grounded me through the storms of my anxieties, and showed me that they were a part of me but didn't define me. It seems unfair, or even a betrayal, if she isn't the first to know of this unexpected positive turn, having been the one to see me through so much negativity. So, I bide my time and busy myself with observing people until Joanie wakes up and has consumed at least one cup of coffee.

I crack after thirty minutes; it's just after six a.m.in Vegas. *Joanie has a huge event today. She should get up early anyway. I'm helping her, really,* I tell myself to purge the last bit of guilt away as the dial tone rings.

"Someone better be dead," Comes the groggy sleep-affected voice of my best friend. "Fuck." She sounds clearer now and there is a rustling noise in the background like she just jumped out of bed. "Sorry Taisa, that was insensitive. Are there more bodies? Did they charge you with something? Is this your one phone call? Do you need bail money?" Her rapid-fire questions don't give me a chance to answer any of them, so instead I tap the button to switch over to video call, hoping that seeing me eases her sudden worry.

"I don't think they let you make phone calls from your personal phone when you're in jail," I say in lieu of a greeting as her sleep-mussed face comes into view. Her golden gaze narrows. Before she can rip into me, I continue. "But I did have to post bail for someone else. For four someone else's, actually" It is fascinating to watch her face flip through emotions in real time, from the panic of when the call first connected, to frustration, and suddenly to interest. *Hot gossip is the only thing to calm the beast,* I muse to myself.

"What in the actual fuck are you talking about? I left..." she pauses, looking at the clock, "you alone for forty hours. Not even two full days, and you are bailing out people from jail?" I am impressed with how fast she did that math. "What is going on?"

As I fill her in on the whirlwind events of my past twenty-four hours, I watch as she runs through the motions of her morning routine. I envy the ritual's results, her dewy, glowing complexion, but not enough to commit the time, energy, and frankly small fortune she has invested into each step in the process. She has me propped up on the counter of the sink as she pours what seems like the seventh serum of the day onto a cotton ball for application. When what I said last registers in her brain, she drops the opened bottle into the sink with a clatter.

"That son of a bitch, did what? He said what?" The decibel of her voice makes me cringe as it is amplified in the echo of her bathroom.

"Isn't that expensive? You are letting it run down the drain," I say, pointing to the bottle that landed face down in the sink.

"Shit." She snatches the bottle up, screwing on the top and then brandishing it at me, emphasizing her point. "Stop deflecting! I can't believe the nerve of that asshole. Are you okay?"

I wave away her concerns, still salty about it but wanting to get to the more important part of the story. *At least what feels most important to me.* "Yeah, it's fine, but listen, there is more."

"No, it is not fine. That could send you into a spiral if you—"

"If I don't take time to process it. Yes, I know," I interrupt, frustrated that she is playing therapist, making me dwell on the negatives when I want to get to the positives. Well, what feels like a positive to me. "And," I soften my tone and continue, "I will call Jennifer after we get off the phone. Can you let me get to the rest of it, please?"

"I am worried about you," she admits. "What if something happens and no one is there for you?" I sigh, now realizing that maybe we have become a little codependent over the past decade. Maybe being the sole person

I trust with my vulnerability, besides my therapist, has been too heavy a burden on my friend. Twisting her role from confidant to caretaker. I am even more resolved in the idea that I need to see this situation through to whatever end, without her here as an emotional crutch. Even if I miss her.

"Jo, I know you are always there for me, no matter how many time zones are between us. But at some point, I need to face the world on my own. You shouldn't have to be burdened with managing my every reaction. I don't want that to be your main focus."

"So, what, I am supposed to kick you out of the nest to fend for yourself, or turn to your new... err, old friend Caroline for support instead? You don't need me anymore?" Her lip juts out in a pout, and if I were not across the continent, I would squish her puffed-out cheeks between my palms.

"I *do* have to learn at some point. And yes, I also need to widen my circle and rely on other people for support. I can't expect you to be my sole source of it. That's not fair to you. But no, I will always need you. You're still the first person I want to run and tell when I am feeling something big on the horizon. Why do you think I waited *hours* until a respectable ti—"

"Six in the morning is not respectable."

Ignoring her, I go on as if she hadn't interrupted me. "A respectable time, instead of calling Caroline, who is right down the street." She seems placated by this.

"I guess. I just feel so far away from you, and I am not coping well with it. I need you too, Tasia. Our relationship is not a one-way street. I have never seen you as a burden. I see you as my sister." The admission brings a sting to my eye, but I refused to cry over a video call.

"I see you that way, too. As the family I choose. Nothing is going to change that, okay?"

"Okay."

"So, if you can refrain from mother henning me, are you ready to hear the rest of the story?" She mimics zipping her lips and turning a key to lock them closed, and holds up three fingers in a mock of the scouts' honor, even though we both know she never made it past Daisies.

I fill her in on the rest of it, starting from the absolute ass kicking Bobby dealt Ryan for his transgressions to the early morning call from Max, then the unpleasant exchange with Leanne in the lobby as I waited for the Payne brothers to exit the holding area. I even went into great detail at my attempts to leave Bobby behind and how they were thwarted by an expressive feat of athleticism on his part. How, even though I was extremely annoyed at the time, it was secretly a turn-on to watch.

I bemoan that if having multiple children is anything as exhausting as having four full-grown brothers interact in a closed-in vehicle for less than twenty minutes, then I think I will stop at one. Then finally, I detail my last interaction with the one and only Deputy Officer Payne. All the while, she keeps her promise to hold her commentary until the end.

She raises her hand as if waiting for the teacher to call on her in class, and at my nod, she asks, "That is all of it?" I nod again. "Holy fucking shit! First of all, I hope Bobby broke that jerk's jaw. Maybe if it is wired shut, he will think again before talking about you like that." I don't think I knew she had this appreciation for violence. "Second, fuck Leanne. I hate her." I nod a third time, fully agreeing with that sentiment. "And finally, holy fucking shit, you are going on a date? When? Where? And most importantly, what are you going to wear?

"I don't know, I don't know, and I really don't know."

"Well, shit, patch Caroline in. We need someone who can be on scene because I know what you packed in that carry-on and no one wants to go business-casual to a first—well, I guess technically second date." I am glad that she doesn't hate Caroline, only the idea that she is being replaced. We can work on that. I will bring it up to Jennifer. I am done segmenting parts of me. I think it is past time that I let everything fall in together, despite what chaos it may cause. If anything, having the Payne boys back in my life has taught me that sometimes a little chaos is exactly what you need.

Chapter 21

BOBBY

(Sunday)

Driving past Anna's property on the way to my parents for Sunday dinner is a test of my willpower. It is instinct to stop and check with the deputy on duty to see if there have been any developments, but I am no longer privy to that information. It will be hard enough to keep what I do know from Anna on our date on Tuesday. If it wasn't for this mandatory court appearance tomorrow, I would have made it for then. *What a fucking mess.*

After she pulled away, I realized I still didn't have her number. *Rookie fucking mistake.* If I still had access to the station and its files, I could have gotten it from that. As ethically questionable as that may be, it would have at least saved me from asking any of my brothers for it. I went with the one least likely to give me shit for it and contacted Johnny. He has been oddly invested in this whole 'Operation Penguin' idea. *I can't believe I am actually calling it that.* I knew he would give me her number with no questions asked, if only as part of furthering the operation.

I have an objective to accomplish towards the plan while I am at my parents tonight. When we were locked in that investigation room for hours, my brothers were able to debrief me on everything they learned from the loose lips of a drunk Anna and her friends. Apparently, when they first approached the girls, they overheard Caroline and Anna reminisce over the past. They were lamenting never having tried the wine we all spent days of our childhood gathering wildflowers to make. It was part of a bucket list we made at the start of my senior year. It was right after I had told Anna of my plans to enlist. I remember it like it was yesterday.

(Senior year)

I can't shake this restless feeling gnawing in the pit of my stomach as I replay the words that bastard said to me after church last week.

"She's too good for you. You'd do best to stop sniffing around. Everyone knows you're worthless, destined for the mines like your pa. You and your miscreant brothers should all just stay away."

I try not to heed the words of a notorious drunk, but I can't find fault in the first part of his statement. She *is* too good for me, and I *don't* have much to offer her. I am not good with numbers like Max, so there will be no scholarship for me, and as the youngest of five, there are not too many pennies left over to trickle down into my college fund. So yeah, maybe I can't argue the point that I am destined for the mine either. I will never agree that my father is worthless or that he hasn't provided a life for my mother and us, but is life as a coal miner's wife, tending to his children, good enough for someone as bright and shining as Anna Adkins? *I'm not sure.*

That is why I am sitting at this lunch table reading this packet. I picked it up from our local recruitment office last night. Skimming over how I can be 'Army strong', I miss when the object of all my internal struggles slides into the seat next to me at the lunch table.

"What's got you so broody today?" Anna asks as she snatches the brochure from the table. "Army? Are you signing up?" Her surprised tone catches me off guard. I glance over to see her wearing a brooding expression now. "Whatcha wanna go and do that for?"

"Yeah, if you want to risk death every day, just become a miner. Least your corpse will be closer to bury," Caroline adds her two cents, having taken up the seat across from us. "Ow," she exclaims. "What did you kick me for, Anna? I'm just saying is all."

"You are being insensitive. Mr. Payne works the mines. It is a fully respectable job and a lot safer than it used to be. Bobby doesn't need to worry 'bout his pa not coming home, 'cause of something dumb that fell out of your mouth." Seeing Anna fighting mad for any reason always gets me going. It is the flash of frost so cold it could burn you in her eyes that sends chills tingling over my body. Having her get that way on my account has me shifting the book bag on my lap so she doesn't see the effect it has on me.

Turning to me, the ice melts in her eyes, changing into liquid pools of blue. "But really, what's all this about? I have never heard you talk about joining up before."

"Well, it is senior year, and I have no plan, no direction, and most of all no money for school. Figured it was a good enough option—see the world, learn something, make something of myself." *Make myself into a man worthy of you.*

"Well, that last part is done. You already are something. You're Bobby Payne, a good son and brother. A sweet, caring friend, and anyone should be glad to be someone like you." For some reason, her ringing endorsement of my character sounds like the death knell ringing as the last nail is hammered into the coffin of the friend zone. I shake it off. I am not ready to be anything more than her friend right now; that is what all this is about. "But is this something that you want? Truly? Not just because you think you are out of options?"

Do I want to become someone who deserves her, who she looks at as more than a sweet and caring friend? "Absolutely." I answer a question she didn't ask, but it serves as a response to the one she did.

"Well, that settles it then. Caroline, rip me a piece of paper, would you? And I need a pen." I am confused as to what we have settled and what she plans to write down.

"For what?" It seems that Caroline is as lost as I am.

"For a list," Anna deadpans as though it should be obvious—it is not.

"A list of what exactly?" I give voice to my confusion.

"A list of all the things we need to do around here before you leave, of course."

"Like a bucket list?" Caroline asks, excited at the idea as she rips a page out of her notebook and fishes through her bag for a pen. "You guys start listing, I'll write it down. No offense, but my chickens scratch is better than either of yours." She isn't wrong; my penmanship is atrocious, and Anna always scribbles things down so fast you'd think she'd lose her thought if she took her time.

"Exactly like a bucket list," Anna beams, pleased that we finally caught up to her thought process. "I'll start. We need to share a bottle of Mrs. Bianchi's dandelion wine."

(Present Day)

We spent the rest of that lunch period listing everything we wanted to do before I joined basic training after graduation. We took it very seriously and pricked our fingers at the end, sealing our pact in blood. It is a pact that has been left unfulfilled for the past twelve years, and the list has been collecting dust on a shelf in my childhood room.

When I called Anna yesterday to make plans for tomorrow, I told her that what we would be doing was a surprise. It wasn't a lie, because at the time, I didn't know what the plan was either. *I still don't know actually. Not 'til I get my hands on that list.* Good thing my mother has kept our rooms as shrines to our childhoods, even all this time later. Objective one: retrieving the bucket list; should be easy. Deciding what off that list will make a suitable first date may be the real challenge.

I park the car and notice that I have arrived before my brothers. I wonder how they got on with the cleanup efforts yesterday. Since the quick text to Johnny to get Anna's number, I haven't talked to any of them.

I reach in the back seat to grab the bouquet of flowers I grabbed for my mother on the way over. My father instilled in us from a young age that if you find what makes a woman smile, and it is within your means to do so, do it every chance you get. My mother loves wildflowers, and since we have emptied the nest, my brothers and I take turns refreshing her bouquet every week. It is a routine now, and you think it would lose its impact, but each week it lights up her face like she is surprised to see it. I want to learn what lights Anna's face up like that.

Stepping on the second step of the porch, I feel a slight shift as it creaks underfoot and make a mental note to fix it sometime next week. *Lord knows I'll have the time.* I am a little concerned about what all this free time will do to my mental health. I have needed routine and framework since I left the Army, or I get a sense of anxiety or unease. 'Loss of structural scaffolding' is how my therapist referred to it. I type out a reminder to make an appointment to see my therapist as I turn the doorknob of the front door.

I am greeted with the aroma of baking bread and a combination of spices that make my mouth water and stomach rumble in anticipation of the home-cooked meal my mother has prepared. The best part of leaving the service and returning to civilian life is undoubtedly the weekly meals she makes with loving care. I survive the rest of the week on a combination of take-out and the civilian equivalent of MREs. Culinary mastery is not one of the skills I learned in my time in the service. *I can scratch any thoughts of impressing Anna with a homemade meal off the date list, unless I bring her here.* That idea has merit; it has been a long-standing daydream of mine to have her seated next to me during family dinner. *But as a date? Maybe not.* I think high school Anna would have been thrilled. I am not so sure of what will thrill adult Anna, *but God, do I want to find out.*

Hearing the door open summons my mother from the kitchen. She pulls up the base of her apron, using it to wipe off her hands as she approaches me. We meet in the foyer where I am toeing off my shoes with the bouquet behind my back, and I pull her into a one-armed hug. She pulls out of the embrace as I kiss her cheek and present her with the flowers. Right on cue, her eyes alight, and a smile cracks her face.

"Oh, honey! They are beautiful! Come with me to change out the vase." She holds the bouquet in one hand, breathing them in as she threads her arm through mine. "I love how the orange of the butterfly weed complements the bright yellow of the ox-eye. What a happy little bouquet." I don't know which of the flowers in the mix are either of the ones she named, but I can't argue that the arrangement does capture the feeling of happiness. *I wonder if Anna would want flowers?*

As kids, the only use for them she ever expressed was the five dollars a basket Mrs. Bianchi would pay for dandelions picked two days every spring. Anna had a field full and always came out on top of the earnings list of all the kids who gathered them. I suspect she also spent the most time picking them as well, since most of us could only be bothered to fill one basket a year.

"Grab the vase from the table, will you, Bobby? I'll cut the stems while you refresh the water. Set the old ones in the sink. I'll hang them to dry after dinner." I know it is childish, but seeing my bouquet replace one of my brothers on the dinner table always gives me a sense of smug satisfaction, even though I know there is no priority in her mind. My mother chooses no favorites.

As the water gurgles and bubbles, filling the vase, my father walks into the kitchen and chuckles when he sees Mom trimming her stems while humming a tune.

"Those are nice, dear. Very cheery." He bends down and kisses her on the cheek. It is a picture I have seen painted in front of my eyes more times than I can count, and I can't think of anything I envy more than this quiet sort of love that my parents share. Their main priority is to make each other smile. *I want this.* I can now admit for the first time in a long time that I have always wanted this. Now I know why I never tried for it, because if it was not with Anna, I didn't want it at all. *Son of a bitch, I think my brother was right. I gave her my rock—I mean my heart, away a long time ago.*

I walk the now full vase to the dining room table, followed by my mother with the freshly cut arrangement. She's fussing with the arrangement when I hear the creak of the door announcing the arrival of one of my brothers. With a glance, I realize it is all of them; they must have decided to ride together, which is not rare, but I would have thought they would have had enough of each other after the events of the last two days.

My mother finishes perfecting her display and gives them the same warm greeting that she gave me. Patrick lifts her off her feet and spins her, setting her off in a fit of giggles that warms my heart. For as much trouble that my brothers and I have caused my mom over the years, we have made sure that we bring her double the amount of joy to tip the scales.

My father coughs behind me, and I turn to him, concerned. A cough is never just a cough when you worked in the mines for as long as my dad had.

He waves me off. "I'm fine. Your mother made me go to the doctors at the beginning of the week. Just a respiratory infection, don't sound the alarm." I exhale as my shoulders loosen from a tension I didn't realize they had taken on.

We settle around the table, occupying the same seats we did as children. My father even sets the tablet in front of the chair that has always been Max's before connecting into a video call with him. Even a state away, you can't skip Sunday dinner. Patrick remotes in as well when his job takes him away for weeks, as did I during my military career, whenever I was stateside.

Once we are all seated, and Mom and Dad take their respective spots at either end of the table, we bow our heads for grace. None of us are particularly devout, but it appeases my mother, so the ritual has stuck.

After a chorus of "Amen", we grab our forks to dig into the shepherd's pie my mother no doubt has poured her love and care into.

We all freeze—Tommy with his fork halfway to his mouth, Patrick with his hand reaching across the table for the salt, Johnny mid sip of water—when my mother asks, "So, boys, anyone want to tell me why I had to hear from Max that you *all* spent the night in jail?"

If it were a few hours later, you would be able to hear the crickets near the creek; that is how quiet it is. All four of us turn our heads to Max, who is wearing a shit-eating grin as he shovels mac and cheese into his face. *The smug bastard.* She continues, but this time laser-focused on me. "And Robert." I cringe knowing the use of my government name cannot bode well for me. "Why did I have to hear from Max, who, mind you, is not even in this state, that the daughter of my best friend is back in town? And involved in some kind of criminal investigation? And most importantly, staying at the inn?"

"Don't leave out the part where he is suspended from the force for punching some guy," my father interjects unhelpfully around a mouthful of potatoes.

"Yes, while the suspension is concerning, I can't be mad at you for defending a lady's honor," she demurs. "But, letting her stay in an inn when we have a perfectly good guest room down the hall is unforgivable."

"Mom, I was investigating the case. It would be a conflict of interest if she stayed in my childhood home while I did it."

"Well, from what Max tells me, you are officially off the case, so why didn't you bring her home?" She doesn't tack on *with you,* just leaves it as *home,* as if this is Anna's home too, and it warms my heart to know that if this works out, my whole family already loves her.

"Well, it would be pretty awkward to pick her up for our date tomorrow from my mother's house." My mother's stern face dissolves into a bigger smile than the one I got for the flowers.

"Finally! So, what's the plan? How are you going to woo her?" My mother is a hopeless romantic.

"Wooing is very important. Remember when I wooed you, Lucy?" my father says, and we all groan. Seeing my parents in love is endearing. Hearing them talk about the wooing stage of their relationship is nauseating.

"Wooing *is* important," Johnny pipes up before we hear anything we can't unhear from our parents. "Which is why we came up with Operation Penguin."

And that's how family dinner turned into a strategy meeting, the dining room acting as a war room, with the whole family chipping in.

Standing in my childhood room I stare at my shelf, full of memories of a me I hardly recognize. A folded piece of paper, yellowed with age, sits under a framed picture of Anna and me. You can tell I took it myself, with how my arm is stretched out. I smile at the shocked look on the face of a younger me as she kisses my cheek. She did it at the last moment, I recall, right before the flash went off, and then ran off after leaving me dumbfounded and dizzy.

I lift the frame and pocket the list to take with me. I notice a sealed envelope that was tucked behind the frame. Stamped across its face is 'Return to Sender' and on sight, a trickle of doubt enters my mind. I shake my head, refusing to let the feeling take root and turn towards the door, leaving the letter along with the doubt in the past where it belongs.

Chapter 22

BOBBY

(Monday)

It is 6:30 a.m. and there is a pounding at my door. I have two and a half hours before the magistrate office opens, and I have to meet Joe, my appointed advocate, to enter my plea. I was looking forward to sleeping in an extra hour to recoup from the hurricane of a weekend I just experienced. *I can't be too mad about it. I did get a date out of the ordeal, and Murph has needed a good punch to the face—or five—since high school.*

"Wake up, dipshit, we are having a strategy meeting at the diner before court." Of course, it's my brothers. I roll over and put the pillow over my head. If I don't respond, maybe they will think I went for a morning run. *I should start doing those again after how winded I got from a sprint on Saturday. Disgraceful.*

The doorknob jingles, and I hear a faint *click, click, click* as the tumblers of the lock are engaged one by one. *Right, I forgot who I was dealing with. Miscreants.* They are picking the lock. I throw off my covers and make my

191

way to the living room right as the door swings open, and my brothers pile in.

"Breaking and entering is a felony, you know? Punishable from one to fifteen years," I deadpan, leaning against the door frame of my bedroom.

"We don't intend to commit a crime, so it would be trespassing at best, and that's a misdemeanor," Tommy retorts unbothered.

"One could argue that picking the lock is already committing a crime." I push off of the door jamb, heading to my tiny galley kitchen. I need coffee if I am going to deal with them this early. Reaching for the cupboard I keep the grounds in, I flex my knuckles, pleased that the swelling has gone down and the bruising is minimal. I don't think I did any lasting damage. After the scabs heal, it should be good as new.

"We'll call it a wellness check, then. You weren't answering your phone," Patrick chimes in.

"It is hard to answer the phone when you are sleeping," I snap back.

"Someone is crabby before their coffee. I forgot what a bear you were in the mornings," Johnny gripes, opening a cupboard after cupboard until I close the one he reaches for next, glaring at him.

"What are you doing?"

"Looking for extra mugs."

"Only have the one."

He looks at me, head tilted as if he is trying to figure out a scrambled word puzzle. "You only have one mug?"

"I only have one mouth."

"What if a lady friend wants coffee the morning after?"

"The morning after what?"

Tommy laughs, adding his two cents, "If you have to ask, I have no faith in you pulling a girl like Anna."

Johnny sighs like he is stuck dealing with a sullen toddler. "After a girl spends the night."

"No one ever has. I don't shit where I eat."

"God, you are a charmer. Let him make his coffee so he can maintain a conversation like a human," Patrick says.

"What I mean is I have no need for mugs because any... *entertaining*, I partake in is outside city limits and is a one-off."

"Ahh," they chorus in unison, and it is honestly a little creepy.

"What about Anna?" Tommy asks.

I narrow my eyes at him. "What about her?"

"God, you're annoying. See, this is why we came over—well, that and to get breakfast before court. I am starving, but we need to have a strategy meeting on how you are going to 'entertain' Anna. Good thing we are here because you don't even have a mug to offer her coffee in the morning after."

"First off, we had a strategy meeting yesterday, remember? Whole family affair, there were flow charts and everything. Second of all, you can refrain from thinking about Anna and *entertainment* in any capacity before I reopen the cuts on my knuckles on your face."

"True, we did have a strategy meeting yesterday, but that was the PG stuff. We were not going to coach you on game with Mom and Dad in the room. Gross."

"This whole conversation is gross. I am a thirty-year-old man who has done my share *entertaining,* and if I don't know what I am doing by now, then I am beyond help."

"But do you know what you are doing?" Johnny asks, "You are thirty and still single."

"And you are all *over* thirty and still single. So why would I ask any of you for tips to improve my dick game?" *I have never seriously contemplated fratricide until this very moment. With this lot, that is actually impressive.*

"If I promise to go get dressed right now, and buy you all breakfast, can we please drop this whole conversation and never speak of it again?" I implore, finally pouring my fresh coffee into my *only* mug,

"Deal," Tommy agrees, always down for a free meal.

"Fine, but only if you promise to buy another mug before you bring Anna here." I nod because it *is* a fair point.

"I guess it doesn't matter. I am outnumbered anyway," Johnny pouts, and I don't have the energy to figure out why he is so invested in this.

"Alright, I'll meet you at Deb's in ten. I had enough carpool karaoke on Saturday to last me a lifetime." They all nod their agreement and file out of my door. I make a mental note to install a deadbolt or two to prevent this in the future. *Or at least slow them down a bit.*

Breakfast was had with little fanfare, my brothers keeping to their promise to stay away from the intimate aspects of my future with Anna, and I try to erase the morning from my memory. We all head over to the magistrate early, knowing that it is going to be a packed docket from all the parties involved in the brawl. I hope that they will follow a first come, first serve order of things. Walking up, I see that Joe had the same idea as he is sitting on the bench waiting for the doors to open. He nods to me in greeting as I take up the seat next to him on the bench.

"Okay, Bobby, I am here for you in whatever capacity you need me. Do you know how you want to plead?"

"Well, I don't see much point in pleading innocent. We have a bar full of witnesses that saw what went down."

"True, but intoxicated witnesses can be proven unreliable if you were to want to go that route."

"Nah, I'll tell the truth and take my licks, come what may."

"Alright, but there is also a plea of temporary insanity. I did see in your file that you suffer from PTSD from your time in the military."

"That isn't what this was." I shut down immediately on the defensive. "He ran his mouth, I got mad, made a dumb choice. End of."

I am a little pissed that he would want me to leverage my service and trauma in that way. Yes, it is something I struggle with—daily. But it is not something that informs my every decision, and not something I am comfortable using as an excuse for every bad behavior. This is how people with mental health issues get a bad stigma, and I refused to play into that narrative. However, the mention of it does remind me to shoot a text to my therapist to see if he can get me in for an emergency video session. I don't want this upcoming lull in routine to set back my hard work. I need an action plan to keep myself grounded.

"Okay, I understand. I only am here to make sure you know all your options." Just then, the magistrate's door opens. "I am going to go in ahead and enter your plea for you, then see if we can get an early time slot. Hang tight." I take the opportunity to shoot Richard, my therapist, a text.

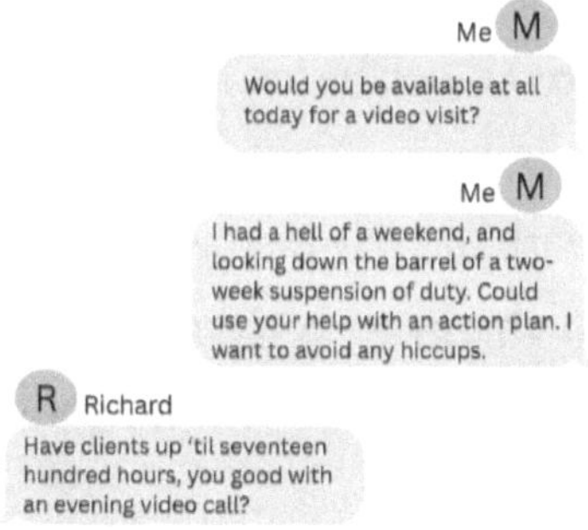

That is actually perfect, in case I am waiting here all day.

Joe and my brothers rejoin me at the bench. We got here early enough that we are the first four on the docket. This works out in our favor as I see some of the fire and EMS guys fill in the parking lot. I hope I can get in and out before a run-in with Ryan. It is a small town, and it is bound to happen, but a little breathing room between now and then would be nice.

"Some of the guys apologized to us on Saturday, for escalating the matter. They saw me pinning their friend and jumped in, no questions asked. They didn't know he was being a drunken idiot," Patrick states, leaning against the brick wall, one foot propped up, spinning the keys to his trunk around his finger; a nervous tick he has had since we were young.

"That excuses them, but I don't think Ryan can get a 'I'm sorry I was drunk hall pass'. Not with the way he was talking about her when she got here. Maybe he wouldn't have acted on them if he were sober, but he hasn't been shy or quiet about his intentions," Tommy says, blunt as ever, and I am in full agreement with him.

"Payne Brothers, you're up. We are gonna take this in birth order. Patrick, you are up first," Penny, the court clerk, calls out, and we file into the building to wait for our individual turns in the lobby. *Let's get this shit over with.*

Walking out of the hearing, I look down at my phone with Anna's latest attempts at getting me to spoil my plans for us tomorrow.

That is true. She has had one hell of a week, but I want this to be a good surprise; we could both use a tick in the win column. Especially after the two grand in fines hit my bank account. That was with taking into consideration that I was a first-time offender. I was fortunate that they decided to defer adjudication. Provided I pay my fines and complete the court-ordered community service, as well as adhere to any terms that come from the internal investigation, they will dismiss all charges from my record. *A deputy with a record, at least temporarily—a real hometown hero I turned out to be.* Though I am lucky, it could have ended so much worse.

I did manage to get out of there without running into Murph and with enough time to get supplies for our date tomorrow, so there is a silver lining to the early morning wake-up call my brothers graced me with.

My phone alerts me to an incoming video call, interrupting my text thread with Anna right when it was getting interesting. I type out a quick goodbye message before I connect the call.

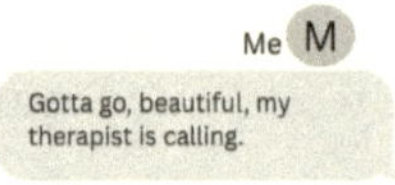

Richard's face fills my phone screen as her reply scrolls across the top.

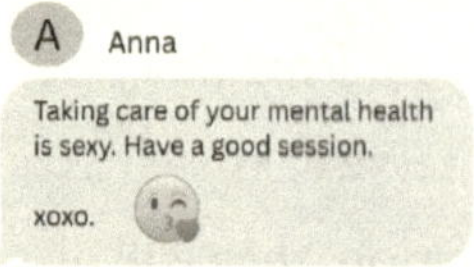

I can't contain the smile the message brings to my face.

"For someone who just got suspended from work, you sure look happy about it," Richard jokes in way of greeting.

"Hey man, you would not believe the week I've had."

"I'm all ears, buddy. Tell me all about it," he says, sincere as always. What I like most about Richard is that he reminds me of my Army buddies. Talking to him is like shooting the shit with one of them. Probably because he served as well. He gets it; more than the civilian therapist I've tried. There are some things that you can't explain to someone who hasn't walked a mile in your boots. Richard has.

I sit back and settle in, ready to fill him in on all the things that have been bouncing around my mind nonstop. And I am confident that when this conversation is over, we will have an action plan in place to counter any missteps hiding around the corner.

Chapter 23

BOBBY

(Tuesday)

*W*as I this nervous before homecoming? I can't recall, but my palms are sweating now, slipping their grip on the steering wheel as I pull up to the inn. The parking lot is full of people packing up their cars, fresh from checking out. It is amazing Anna found a room here at all last week. Pretty soon, our sleepy little town will be thrumming with college students. The local businesses benefit from the boost, but I swear it makes my job a thousand percent more difficult. The one thing worse than dealing with a bunch of unruly college kids is dealing with their entitled parents.

When these guests file out, Anna will have the run of the place alone. The idea of her having to pay for this inn for the foreseeable future doesn't sit well. I mull over my mother's request to offer her their spare room. *I guess it doesn't hurt to ask.*

My phone pings with back to back notifications as I back into a spot. They are texts from Caitie; *I wonder if she doesn't know about my suspension.* I was sure it would be all the gossip this morning, but Caitie doesn't interact much with the rest of the station unless it involves a case. She is pretty content to remain among her lab equipment and samples like some crazy mad scientist, so there is a chance she doesn't know.

Conflicted, I stare at the screen, debating whether I should open the thread or call her and tell her I am off the case. Burning curiosity wins out as I swipe the notification open.

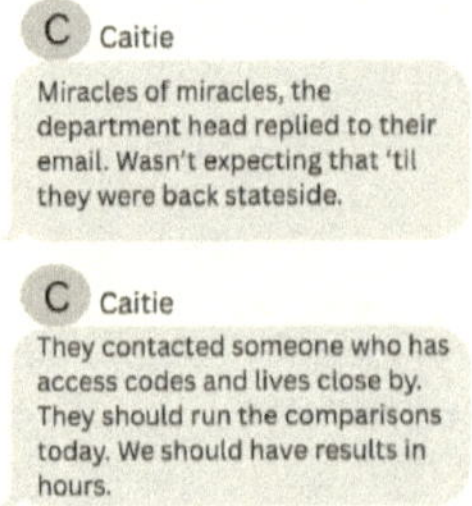

If the results come back and show the remains are from the body farm, and the dogs don't find anything, Anna could be completely off the hook. I want to jump for joy and run in and tell her, but I know nothing is sure yet, and that would be a gross breach of ethics. I want to be the one to take one stress off her shoulders if I can. *This case could be closed in a week—well, at least the murder investigation. There is still the matter of the theft, but any reason to suspect Anna would be put to rest.*

On the back of that revelation comes another one, *by the end of the week, she may have no reason to stay here.* That thought sobers me from my elation. I decide it's best not to know when my time is up and make the best of the time that I have with her. *It will have to be enough.*

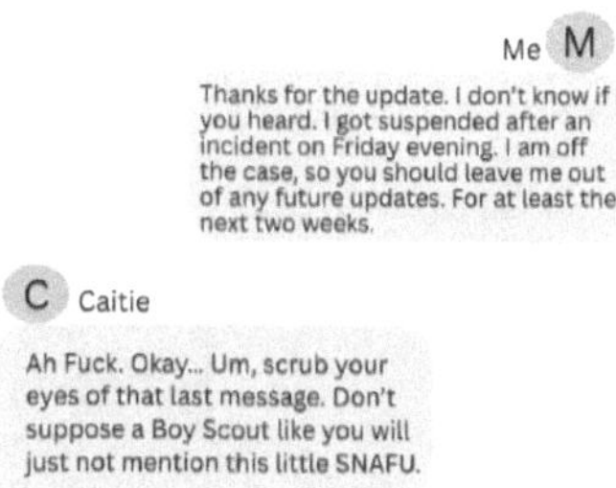

Normally, I would, and I should report this to Dobbs, but in this one instance, I am fine with scrubbing the message. *If only I could scrub it from my mind.*

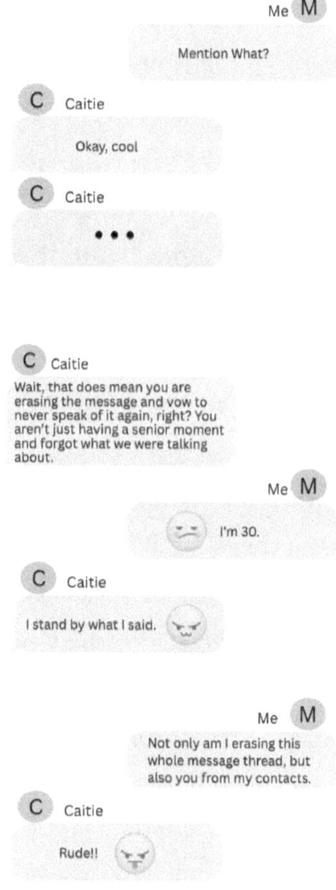

I delete the last few messages and then set my phone to 'Do Not Disturb'. If she is still texting, she will get the hint soon enough. At least I am no longer nervous for this date. Instead, I am more determined than ever to make it count.

Resolve renewed, I grab the bouquet sitting next to me and make my way into the inn. I stop at the front desk and greet Leslie, the owner. "Hey Leslie, do you think you have a spare vase lying around I could borrow for these? They are for one of your guests."

"Oh, aren't you sweet! I think I have something perfect." She motions me to wait while she disappears for a bit behind a door marked 'Employees Only', returning moments later with a bright blue glass vase. "This cobalt trumpet should fit it well. The blue will contrast with the orange of the stargazers. It'll make them pop." Not sure what any of that means, but trusting her nonetheless, I grab the vase from her outstretched hand and stick the bouquet inside to carry up to the room.

"Thank you, ma'am. I sure do appreciate it." I offer her a genuine smile.

"Oh, that dimple. I swear if I was ten years younger, I would give your lady friend a run for her money," she says on a sigh. Laughing her off, bidding her goodbye as I make my way to the room number Anna texted me this morning.

Shifting the vase to one arm, my knuckles rap on the door, earning a faint "Coming" from the other side. With my free hand, I fiddle with the neckline of my shirt as I wait in the hall, suddenly sure it is suffocating me. The door swings open, and I am greeted with a vision so stunning I fumble, almost dropping the vase. Years of training and quick reflexes save me that embarrassment, plus whatever this 'cobalt trumpet' costs.

Anna looks radiant in a pale purple sundress. It hugs the curves of her chest, flaring out at her hips and ending mid-thigh with a ruffled hem flirting with the line of decency. The two straps holding the top up are tied in bows at her delicate shoulders, and I get a maddening urge to pull the string just to see what happens. I put my free hand in my pocket to keep myself from acting on that impulse. She looks so good that I am reconsidering all my plans for this date as I take her in again, from the meticulously curled hair on top of her head to her manicured toes in white wedge sandals. She looks perfect. Like a dream come true, except it is all wrong for a day spent stomping around the wilderness of West Virginia.

"Oh, wow, those are pretty. Are they for me?"

"You look beautiful."

We speak over each other, and it breaks me out of my stupor when she chuckles. reaching out for the vase.

"I don't have anything to cut the stems with. Do you think they will be okay until we get back—" She pauses one thin manicured brow arching higher, "from wherever we are going?"

Having watched my mother prepare bouquets for a vase my whole life, I came prepared. Stepping over the threshold, I reach for the foldable shears I grabbed from a safety kit in my truck. "It's fine, I'll trim them while you fill the vase."

"Hmm, that is very 'Semper Paratus' of you," she jokes. "Oh wait, that is the Coast Guard motto. What was the Army's again?" she muses as she leads me into the ensuite.

Looking around I see everything is organized in a meticulous way, as if she were concerned that I'd judge her if her room were a mess, and she overcompensated for it.

"Oh yeah, it is 'This We'll Defend' right?" God, she is so sexy when she spits random facts. She has always been smart, but I wonder where this knowledge of random military mottos comes from.

"Know a lot of military men?" Did I just sound jealous of men I've never met? *I mean, I am jealous of anyone who has the privilege to breathe the same air as her in the last decade, but it is probably best not to let her know that.*

"Not particularly, no. I just remember them from when I looked them up in high school. When you were still deciding what branch you wanted to join."

"You looked that up?"

"Well, no, not specifically the mottos. But the different branches? Yeah. If you were going to be away and out of touch, I wanted to have some idea of what you may be off doing." Then with a voice low and somber, so quiet I have to strain to hear, she adds, "I wanted to feel close to you, no matter where you were." She shakes her head and picks up the conversation as if her tone never shifted at all—voice clear she says, "The mottos were plastered all over everything, so I kind of absorbed them into my knowledge bank."

I focus on cutting the stems of the flowers to stop myself from kissing her senseless before we even go on this date. She is so fucking cute. Deciding to change the topic before I throw all my plans and caution to the wind and lay her out on that king-size bed and spend the rest of the day in it.

"I told you that I think you look beautiful, right?" The pink that flushes her cheeks is adorable.

"I think I recall you saying something to that effect at the door."

"Okay, so don't take this the wrong way when I tell you, and it pains me to tell you—believe me—but you need to change."

She turns away from what she is doing, eyes meeting mine head tilted in confusion. "What?" she asks, not paying attention to her task, and the vase starts to overflow. Reaching over, I turn off the faucet, taking the vase from her hand and spilling out a third of the water before I set it on the counter placing the fresh trimmed flowers inside.

Not wanting to give away the whole plan for the day, I go with, "We are going hiking." We are doing more than that, but I want to see how long it takes her to realize I am working off that list. I know she remembers every unticked item; that is how her mind has always worked.

"Hiking?" she repeats the word as a question.

"Hiking," I respond.

"And you didn't think, seeing any of the texts I sent you pleading for clarity, that maybe just saying 'hiking' or 'dress for an outdoor activity', could have prevented this situation? I spent an hour curling my hair."

Her bottom lip juts out in a pout and I have an urge to bite it. Instead, I wince because I see she has a point, but I never expected *this* when she opened the door. I only ever saw her in a dress once, and that was at homecoming. She even wore pants to church when we were kids. First, because her mom couldn't keep her from running and hanging off the monkey bars in the church's playground, and later, because her father wouldn't buy her anything but thrift-store boys clothes. Not that she cared about style back then.

"I don't even think I have any shoes suitable for hiking in my bag. I already had to borrow these and the dress from Caroline." That explains the snug fit around her breast; she always has been bustier than Caroline. Not that I am complaining. *God, not complaining at all.*

"You're right, this is my fault. I should have been more transparent. We can pivot—do something else. We can go down to Aberville. I hear they have a brand-new bakery that everyone is raving about, Karlie's Konfectionery. We can go eat some sweets, walk around town, take in the sights, and you can see how much it has changed since you've been here last," I rush out, words tumbling from my lips as the thoughts form, trying to repair this before it is too late. I didn't even notice that I had begun pacing until she stops me with a hand on my shoulder.

"Bobby, stop. Calm down. It is okay. I let Caroline and Joanie get in my head about this. I told them this was too much." She waves down at herself, and I shake my head, because I need her to know that I love that she put in the effort. Love that she spent time talking to her friends about this. Preparing for this—for me.

Grabbing her hand from my shoulder, I kiss her palm, breathing in the vanilla scent of whatever lotion she rubbed into her skin, resisting the urge to dart my tongue out and taste her. Inhaling a calming breath, I lower our now joined hands and meet her gaze head-on.

"It's not, it is not too much. I appreciate the effort you took to look nice for me. God, *nice* is such a weak word for how you look right now. Beautiful, radiant, stunning, fucking sexy as hell—just pick an adjective. But you also looked sexy as hell Saturday in cut-off shorts, wearing Crocs with socks." She scrunches up her nose at that like a little squirrel, and it is so fucking adorable I can't stop the smile that spreads across my face. "What I am trying to say is there is no 'too much' or 'too little'. Whatever you wear is just right."

"Except for hiking," she snarks, and I can't help the snort I let out.

"Yes, smart-ass, except for hiking. But I already told you we can pivot. My plans don't have to be so rigid."

"Can I confess something?"

"Anything."

"These heels are already killing me, and I am afraid that if I bend over, I am going to fall out of this dress."

"Want to test out that theory, you know, for science?" I try not to glance at her tits and fail. *I am just a man after all.* She rolls her eyes and punches me on the shoulder with her free hand. My grin grows wider. I love that she didn't drop the hand I am holding and sever our physical connection.

"What I mean is, if you think the pair of tennis shoes I have in my bag can withstand this 'hike' you have planned, I only need ten minutes to change." She leads me out of the bathroom by our still connected hands but sadly drops mine when she steps to the bag sitting on top of the dresser. She takes a minute before pulling out a white pair of low tops and hands them to me. They wouldn't stand up to rough terrain, but where we are going is all marked paths, so I think we are in the clear.

"These will work, and if you get tired, I'll give you a piggyback ride." Thinking of her thighs wrapped around me, I clear my throat of its sudden dryness. *That doesn't sound like a hardship at all.*

"Okay then," she says, grabbing her bag. "I'll be right back." But before she heads off to the bathroom, she leans over, kisses me on the cheek and whispers in my ear, "I appreciate the effort you put into this, too. The planning, the wanting to surprise me. Our signals got crossed, but I am happy to meet you in the middle."

With that, she turns away, leaving me with memories of a much younger Anna calling and asking to meet me in the middle; meaning the old oak tree that stood between our properties. Feeling the corners of my mouth curving into a grin, I try to manage the dopey expression I know I must be wearing by the time she steps back into the room, knowing it may be a lost cause.

Annastasia

I eye the pack Bobby grabs from the bed of his truck. It's a huge army rucksack, which in itself isn't strange—he is ex-army—but it is filled to the brim with accessories clipped and strapped to all sides. Is that rope? What do we need rope for?

"We are only hiking for one day, right?" I ask, concerned. I like hiking as much as the next person, but in reasonable amounts with lots of breaks.

"Yeah, why?" he asks, heaving the sack onto his back and securing the waist strap, which up to this very minute I was sure was superfluous and no one actually used. *I don't hate the way his forearms flexed with that motion, though.*

The waist strap has brought my attention to the way his compression shirt clings to his abs, and the tips of my fingers tingle at the thought of tracing each individual one. Distracted, I forget to answer the question until I feel a calloused finger brush against my chin.

"If you walk around with your jaw dropped, you'll catch flies," he says as he tilts my chin up so I meet his amused but sharp, hazel gaze. "I asked you a question, Annastasia." The way my full name drips from his lips sends a shiver down my spine.

"Hhhmm? Could you ask it again?"

"I asked you why you questioned if we were hiking for more than one day."

Stepping back, shaking the ab-induced fog from my brain, I respond, "Oh yeah, right. I was just wondering because it looks like you've packed enough to survive for a week when I think some water bottles and protein bars would suffice."

"Trust me, okay? I have everything we need for today." Nodding, because I do trust him, I always have. I wave to him to lead the way on this excursion and follow him into the wilderness.

Breathing in the fresh mountain air calms me in a way I haven't felt in years. It is hot today, I realize as the sweat beads down my neck to collect in the collar of my shirt, but it is different from the dry arid heat of Vegas. At least the trees offer shade from the sun beating down on us. I missed this. I realize I missed the sound of the critters rustling in the underbrush, and the breeze making the leaves flutter on their branches and wicking the sweat from my skin. I can't believe I am thinking it, but I even missed the way the humid air wraps around me, clinging like a second skin. It feels like home.

At first, we exchange light conversation. I ask him about his parents. Trying to respect Max's wishes I avoid any inquiry about their health, though the worry sits in my stomach like a stone. He askes about Joanie and how we met, leading us to my college experience.

"How did you end up in Las Vegas anyway?" he asks, taking my hand in his as he helps me down from a boulder.

Feet firmly on the solid path again, I reply, "Midway through junior year," I say as if I attended any regular high school, "we kinda had a career day. A bunch of fancy professionals set up booths we could peruse and ask them questions. The tourism and hospitality booth caught my eye. I thought, knowing the same handful of people my whole life, that it would be cool to have a job where you could meet a lot of people. Different people." I glance at him out of my peripheral as I continue, "And something you said had stuck in my head, about getting out there and seeing the world. Well, there are hotels everywhere, so I figured it was a job I could do no matter where I ended up."

Thick brows furrowed like he is trying to solve a particularly perplexing math program he asks, "Okay, that explains why you chose your profession, but how did you end up in Vegas? I'm sure you could study that anywhere."

"Vegas has the most impressive program and one of the most voracious tourist industries. It offered the most varied experiences and opportunities, all in a one-mile strip. And if you want the more vulnerable answer—"

"Always."

"Well, there was nothing left for me here, not really. No family, all my friends off living their lives. I wanted to experience something somewhere different from what I always knew. I needed a change."

"And so you went to Vegas, the exact opposite of boring Boremanton," he jokes, "and became Tasia, leaving Anna in the past."

I roll my eyes at his over-dramatic delivery; he spends too much time with Johnny. I nudge his shoulder with mine, trying to ignore the electric charge that lingers anywhere my skin touches his. "Actually, I tried to be Annastasia. You know, to come off more sophisticated and worldly, but on day one, Joanie declared it was too long and shortened it to Tasia. I was actually so shocked Anna wasn't her immediate choice that I decided to run with it, and it stuck."

"Do you want me to call you that?" he asks in an echo of the question that Ryan asked me last week.

If I'm being honest, I would rather him call me Annastasia, in that low gravel and sandpaper tone he used earlier, but that is far too embarrassing to say. Instead I reply, "No, Anna is fine." He lets out a breath as if he is relieved and nods.

"We're almost there. We can take a break for water and something to eat," he says as if we were approaching the destination of our activity. I thought hiking *was* the activity, and at some point, we would decide to turn around and hike back.

"Get where exactly? I thought we were hiking, and well, we are already doing that," I voice my confusion.

Winking at me he says, "Trust me." Ah, so part of the surprise then.

"Okay, fine, Mr. Man of Mystery, why don't you tell me a little about your time in the military? Did you see the world—like you wanted?" He pauses his step and looks at me, his eyes going a little unfocused before he shakes it off.

"It's complicated. I did see a lot of the world, some of it wonderful, yes. But some of it..." His fists tighten around the straps of his pack, scabbed knuckles turning white.

"Hey," I step closer, prying one closed fist from the strap to hold in mine, soothing over his knuckles with my thumb. My other hand caresses his face, the stubble on his jaw a pleasant prickle beneath my palm. "You don't have to talk about it. Not if it is too hard, but I want you to know that you can. Even if it is hard."

He nods and exhales. "Some of it I just—" He pauses, his throat working as if he is swallowing his words before they can make it past his lips. "I just wish I could unsee some of it is all. Not exactly great date conversation," he finally gets out, fingers mussing through his wind-swept hair.

"Okay." I pause, considering how to approach this. "Tell me the good parts then. The friends, the wonderful sites—just the good things for now."

He releases his white-knuckle grip on the other strap, placing his hand on top of mine, resting on his jaw. He grasps it, moving it to his mouth where he places a gentle kiss on my palm. My insides melt into a puddle on the well-worn path we stand upon. I could get used to these tender shows of affection.

"Just the good parts," he agrees as we continue down the path hand in hand.

He tells me of the friends he made and the antics they got up to. Some sound much like the shenanigans he and his brothers have been known for, which makes me smile. I am glad he had people to trust and laugh with, even through the tough times. He tells me of the hearty food and beer in Germany and the beautiful views in the Philippines. He tells me of the two years he spent in Fort Irwin, in the heart of the Mojave Desert and how he wished he knew I was so close. Apparently, he wouldn't have even needed a Liberty Pass to travel that distance.

Before I notice, a half hour has passed and he comes to a stop so abrupt I almost trip over myself at the loss of momentum. He drops my hand to slide off his pack. I pretend I don't miss the contact and hook the thumb of my abandoned limb into my front pocket.

"We're here," he says, rummaging in his pack, pulling out two bottles of electrolyte enhanced water and two foil-wrapped bundles. Next, he spreads out a tarp, gesturing for me to sit. Handing me one of the bundles, he says, "It's nothing fancy, just some turkey and hummus wraps, but they are full of protein to keep us going."

"At this point, I'd eat a horse. I didn't realize how hungry I was until we stopped." Peeling back the foil, I get a whiff of the savory spread and my mouth waters. I dig in, enjoying the way the creamy, nutty flavor of the hummus pairs with the turkey. The water has a faint, undefinable mineral flavor but is refreshing all the same. Once our wraps are finished, he pulls out baggies of trail mix and some apples to top off our meal.

Finishing up, I watch as he places our trash in a zip seal bag to store in his pack on the way back. He is meticulous in his motions, as if it is ingrained in his marrow to leave no trace behind. A remnant of his training, no doubt. For the first time, I wonder how much of the man before me was forged on memories he can't bear to share. I am distracted from the thought as he starts pulling out a bunch of gear I don't recognize.

"What is all that for?"

"You haven't figured it out yet?" he asks, referring to the surprise. He points to a cave mouth with a wooden sign posted in front. It reads

'Miller's Falls'. Memories click in place, connecting the name to knowledge long buried of the underground waterfall not far from town.

"We are going to see the falls?" I question, excited. I have always wanted to see the underground waterfall. Turning to look at him, he is holding out some kind of harness to me.

"Sure are, now go on and step into this."

"What for?"

"Well, the falls aren't just down some path—we are going to need to rappel." My eyes widen as I look from his face to the apparatus he is holding out. *He* must be joking. When I see no hint of mirth, I lift one leg to step into it. Wobbling slightly, I steady myself on his shoulders as I thread my other leg through. He shimmies it up until it is comfortable, cradled between my thighs. He takes his time adjusting straps, making sure everything is secure. The act is intimate with his gentle caressing and the firm tug of the harness here and there. It is hard to concentrate as he describes the process, and by the time he asks if I understand, I ask him to run me through it again.

Laughing, he places a helmet on my head, tightening the strap beneath my chin, and says, "This is a highly used rappel spot, so there are permanent rigs set up. It is pretty straightforward, but I will go over it first so you can watch, and then I'll be able to talk you through it when it's your turn."

He goes through the basic steps again, this time coming around me and taking my hands to show me the motions as he explains them. I focus this time, only slightly distracted by wondering about other scenarios he might 'talk me through'. We run through the whole scenario multiple times until I am comfortable enough to show him that I can do it on my own. I am blown away by the patience and care he shows, even in this. Never once showing frustration or annoyance at how many times it takes me to get it.

Pleased with my last run through, he beams at me. That devastating dimple weakens my knees on sight.

"Good girl." *Okay, new kink unlocked. I am learning lots of new things today. Didn't realize praise was my thing.* Or maybe it is only praise from this particular man that is my thing. It takes him half the time to gear up as it did me, but I admire the competence of his sure hands as he tightens his own harness into place. No preparations left to be made, we make our way into the cave.

Squeezing through narrow corridors here and ducking down in low ceilings there, we follow the marked path illuminated by the headlamps attached to our headlights. As an afterthought, I muse that I am glad that claustrophobia is not one of my many triggers, or this could have taken a different turn. As it is, I can't recall a better time I had on a date. There is a lot to do in Las Vegas, but after over a decade, it feels like I have done it all. And while there is hiking to do, it is in the desert and not the best conditions for my fair complexion. I would never have let one of the guys I've gone out with take me rappelling, of all things. I never got to know any of them to trust them with my literal life, but as I told him, I have always trusted Bobby Payne.

The further we descend into the cavern, the cooler the air becomes; it is almost refreshing. I hear the rushing of water that has been echoing in the distance this whole time, roaring louder and louder until Bobby has to shout to be heard over the noise.

"Just up around the corner is where we'll rappel from," he shouts, looking back at me having taken the lead, showing me where is best to step. I give him a thumbs up as we continue. There is an opening that requires us to enter sideways, and I hold my breath as if stilling my breathing will help me to fit through the passage better. On the other side, the cave opens up, and above us a canopy of stalactites hang from the ceiling, illuminated by sunbeams filtering in through a hole in the top of the cave where the water is cascading down. The air is moist and smells of minerals and earth. There is a man-made rail separating us from a steep drop. I lean over it and see where the billowing water pools on the cavern's floor.

"It is beautiful," I say in awe, taking in the way the light is reflected by the running water.

"Sure is" is Bobby's reply. When I turn to look at him, he is not even looking at the falls; his full attention is on me. The flush I feel forming on my face sends waves of heat through my body and settles in my core. I was unaware how having a man's—having *this* man's full focus could be such a turn on.

Bobby makes quick work of rappelling down, years of military training making it second nature to him. I find after the first maddening step backwards, where I have the briefest worry that my harness won't hold my weight, that it is exhilarating. Gaining confidence towards the bottom of the decline, I start to allow myself to drop at a quicker pace. The whole way, Bobby is there coaching and cheering me along, making sure to point out the man-made foot and hand holds we will use to climb back up when we are done exploring. When my feet touch solid ground, he grabs me in a bear hug and spins me around, tangling us up in my ropes. My thighs find a natural purchase around his hips, and he leans us against the cave wall for balance.

"You were amazing," he says, peering into my eyes as if he can see down to the root of me, the breath of his words tingling on my lips, causing my thighs to clench on reflex. He stills for a moment, seeming to have only now realized the position we have found ourselves in, and steps back to let me slide down his body. Then he steps away, giving me some breathing room. Room I didn't ask for or particularly want at that moment.

"Sorry, I got a little carried away," he says sheepishly, rubbing the back of his neck. He looks so much like the boy I once knew that I forgive the unwanted distance and smile.

"S'okay. Want to explore?" He smiles back, working on untangling us from the ropes. I try to conceal the havoc each unintentional brush of his hand is wreaking in my body. Each graze sends shockwaves through my nervous system and shivers down my spine. I play it off as chill from the spray of the falls, unsure if he buys the ruse.

For the next few hours, we bask in the majesty of this hidden gem that lives outside our sleepy little town, discovering all the secrets it keeps. When we are done, we make our way back up. I find I much prefer repelling to climbing, my muscles straining from disuse. Halfway on our hike back to the truck, my legs are shaky with exhaustion, I run into the solid planes of Bobby's back as he comes to an abrupt halt. I can't get a protest out before he has the rucksack swung around his front, and he is squatting down in front of me.

"Hop on," he says, gesturing to his back, and I am too tired to argue, so I do as he says. He lifts me as if I weigh nothing and hikes us the rest of the way back to the truck. Each shift of his muscles against my thighs is sweet torture, providing just enough friction to have me holding back moans, but not enough to find relief. It is the oddest form of edging I have ever been through and I am equal parts humiliated and turned on.

Reaching the truck, he does not let me slide down his body until he has the door open and ready for me to fall into the passenger seat. I use the moment it takes him to round the vehicle to compose myself, though that composure is hard won as he drives me home with one hand on the steering wheel, the other holding my own, sending thrills up my arm with every pass of his thumb.

He walks me all the way to the door to my room, never letting go of my hand. Leaning in, he presses a kiss on my cheek and says, "I had a really good time with you today."

"I had a good time too."

"Can I see you again tomorrow?"

"Yes," I answer before he even finishes his question. "What do you have in mind?"

"It's a—"

"Surprise. I am sensing a theme. Can you tell me what to wear at least?"

"Something casual is fine but bring a sweater in case it gets chilly at night. "

"Oh, an evening surprise. I am intrigued."

"Good, that means I'm doing my job."

"Your job is to make me intrigued?"

"Nah, my job is to make you happy. That is just part of it." With that, he leans in and kisses my cheek again. "See you tomorrow, Anna."

"See you tomorrow."

I open my door and close it behind me, listening to his footfalls as he walks down the hall. I lean against the door and press a palm to my cheek, wishing I could seal the heat of his kiss into my skin to keep me warm for the rest of the night.

My phone beeps; it is a message from Joanie.

The phone alert indicates an incoming video call, and I move away from the door to get comfortable as I recount the best date I have ever been on to my best friend.

Chapter 24

ANNASTASIA

Five o'clock sharp and there's a knock on my door, Bobby's right on time. I open the door to see him standing there with a bouquet of white roses.

"More flowers?" I ask, feeling the corners of my lips twitch into a smile.

"I saw them and thought they'd look nice next to the ones from yesterday. I already cut the stems in the parking lot," he says, tilting the flowers to show the freshly sheared stems. *Thoughtful.*

Taking them from him, I say, "I'll be right back." I make my way to my nightstand where yesterday's flowers sit, adding the new ones to the vase. Once placed, I lean in and inhale, savoring the sweet aroma and basking in the happiness they inspire. *He did say he wanted to make me happy.* Pulling out my phone, I snap a quick picture to send to Caroline and Joanie, receiving a chorus of heart emojis in reply. Heading back to meet him at the door, I grab my sweater, and I am ready for wherever this adventure takes me.

Pulling up to Deb's diner minutes later is not what I was expecting, especially after yesterday's excursion. *I hadn't thought about Miller Falls since high school. I am glad I didn't miss out on that.* I try to keep any reaction to this drastic change of pace off my face. It isn't that I don't like Deb's, it just doesn't quite meet up to the hype he was building. My efforts must fail because, as he opens my car door, *like a gentleman,* he laughs.

"Annastasia," he chides. The use of my full name again has the same shivers sprinting down my spine, and I wonder if he has caught on to my reaction yet. "Are you pouting?" The pad of his thumb flicks off my bottom lip, prompting my tongue to slip out and chase its path, tasting the salt his skin left behind. *Actually, this is fine. We can get dinner and go back to my room, and I can find out what the rest of him tastes like. That's a surprise I can get behind.* He tisks and reaches for my hand to help me down from his truck. "I thought you learned to trust me."

"I do," I immediately reply. There has never been a time I can recall that I did not trust this man.

"Then *trust me* when I say that this is only the first stop. We need to fuel up before we go and the wraps from yesterday are about the extent of my culinary prowess."

"I didn't say anything," I protest.

"You don't have to. That little pout says it all," he replies, opening the door and setting off the chime to announce our entrance. I breathe in the familiar smells of the oil from the deep fryer permeating the air, and my mouth waters as my stomach growls. Bobby doesn't say anything, but the knowing look he shoots me speaks for itself.

We are seated and served fast, considering how packed the place is for a Wednesday night. It doesn't take long for us to finish up our food over light dinner talk. When the check comes, Bobby gets up to pay at the counter, telling me to stay and finish my milkshake.

"I want to settle up while there's no line so that when you're ready, we can leave, but no rush. Enjoy it." I don't know what is sweeter, the triple chocolate milkshake I am slurping through a straw, or the way he is treating me. Taking another sip, I decide that maybe it is a tie.

I am distracted, staring out the window, fiddling with the straw paper. I tear it up into little pieces and create a pile—a habit I've had since I was young—when a body slips into the other side of the booth. Thinking it is Bobby, I say, "Wow, that was fast. You weren't even gone a minute." Looking up, I am shocked to be staring into green eyes instead of hazel. "Ryan," I deadpan. "What do you want?"

"I wanted to apologize about last week," he says, holding up his hands in a placating manner. His black eye has faded to a sickly greenish yellow that clashes garishly with his red hair.

"For what part, *specifically*?" I ask, leaning back as I cross my arms over my chest, narrow my eyes at him.

"Erm, all of it?" The upward inflection at the end, paired with the look of confusion on his face does nothing to soften me towards him. My mother may have left me early, but she did teach me that if you are going to apologize, you ought to know what exactly you are apologizing for. If you can't put a pin on it, then you aren't sorry.

"Not forgiven," I say as a flat-out dismissal.

"Anna, be reasonable. I was drunk and we were dancing. It got a little heated and I misread your signals. I'm sorry."

Ma also taught me that apologies don't come with excuses, so I say, "That's not an apology. It is a heap of excuses, and besides the point, it isn't even what I'm most mad about anyway." He looks at me like I have grown two heads and started talking Latin. Like he hasn't the foggiest idea what, besides hearing no and pushing for more, could have me upset. *This guy is a real piece of work.* "What about all that crude shit you were spittin' about me and how I was crazy?"

He casts his eyes down, his freckled face flushing under the bruise as he rubs the back of his neck and says, "You heard all that, huh?"

"Be for real. The whole fuckin' county heard it, Ryan."

"I didn't mean to say all that. It is just Bobby gets me so mad, riding in playing white knight all the time. He and his brothers have had a wall around you since high school—before even. Blocking out anyone who wanted a chance and not even acting on it until someone else was interested. Why do you think you were a virgin through high school?"

"Um, because I chose not to fucking open my legs? Not that there is anything wrong with girls who did." *Is he serious right now?*

"No! It's because those Payne brothers kept you on the shelf playing goal tender but never intending to take a shot themselves."

"You're delusional," I seethe. *Who does this guy think he is?*

"Everything alright here, Anna?" Tension I didn't realize I was building melts from my shoulders like my forgotten milkshake on the table at hearing his voice.

"Un-fucking-believable. So you are gonna sit here and tell me I'm wrong? When it's happening right in front of your face?" His voice rises, attracting a crowd, and I do not want to be at the center of another incident. I especially don't want Bobby to get in any more trouble than he already is in.

Luckily, Miranda chooses the exact right moment to interject. "Ryan, come on, man. I said to apologize, not start World War three. If you can't do it right—just don't." She shoots me a long-suffering look, like she is gently parenting a rowdy toddler and is fed up with it. *At least her mother taught her about proper apologies.*

"You know what? Fuck this and fuck you two." Gesturing between Bobby and me, he continues, "Y'all deserve each other." With that, he slides out of the booth and storms out the door.

Deb yells out, "Hey, you didn't pay your check!"

Miranda, rubbing her temples like she has the start of the world's worst headache, sighs and then tilts her head backwards, looking up to the ceiling as if she is praying for whatever deity is listening to give her patience. "I got it, Deb," she calls back, and then to us she says, "Sorry if he ruined your evening. He was supposed to apologize and then leave you alone. Looks like he is getting enrolled in an interpersonal skills one-on-one. Did you already pay? I'll grab your check if you haven't."

"Just got back," Bobby replies, sounding more like himself now that Ryan has removed himself from the equation.

"Ah, okay, well you two have a good rest of your night. I'll see to it that he doesn't bother you again." She leaves us to settle up with Deb.

Squatting down so he is at eye level with me, he brushes a stray strand of hair behind my ear. "You okay?" he asks, his voice firm. I nod. "You want me to take you back to the inn?" I know he doesn't mean for sexy fun times, so I shake my head. "You still want to go on an adventure with me?" I nod again and see the reappearance of that distracting dimple. "Good girl." *He has got to know what he is doing to me.* He pulls me up by both hands and then wraps his arm around my shoulders as he leads me off to our adventure.

When the car turns off the road an hour later at the rusty and worn sign that reads 'Lake Shawnee Park', that is when it clicks in my head. Visions of a high school lunchroom table and a bunch of military recruitment packets spread out in front of Bobby. I remember panic swirling around my stomach as I spoke about a list of things we needed to see and do before he left. I framed it like it was all for him, but it was really my desperate attempt of holding onto him as long as I could. Making as many memories as we could while we still had the time.

It was the first time in my young life that the tick of a clock felt like a death sentence marching ever onward to demise. Miller Falls and Shawnee Lake Park were on that list. *Has he kept it all this time?*

Nonchalantly, I say, "Caroline is gonna be pissed she missed out on this."

"She won't," he replies, smirking. "After yesterday's wardrobe SNAFU, I messaged her to make sure we are on the same page in case you consult her for wardrobe advice in the future."

"So, you *do* still have the list?"

"Of course I do," he says, his eyes earnest as they glance at me before he parks the car. "It was so important to you then. I could never bring myself to throw away anything that meant so much to you."

"It was doing things with you that was important to me. Still is," I say, voice nothing but a murmur, but he hears it anyway.

Lifting my hand from my lap, he kisses my knuckles. "Then it's a good thing that we are here together."

To resist jumping over the console and jumping his bones with an audience of ghosts, I lean over, pecking him on the cheek, and say, "Let's go see if the boy in the red shirt greets us. Oh, and I hope you came prepared with some offerings. It's only right if we are invading their peace."

He points his thumb to his trusty rucksack in the back, only slightly less full than yesterday, and says, "Haven't you figured it out by now, babe? I am always prepared." The easy way the endearment rolls off his tongue sets butterflies afloat in my stomach.

We wander around using the tools and trinkets that Bobby packed to try to coax out spirits. He even has an old transistor radio, he says, that will work like a spirit box. We take turns asking it questions, getting static words and white noise in reply. The sun has set, and that signature West Virginia mist casts everything in an eerie glow, highlighted by the full moon high in the sky. I won't say it out loud, but I am starting to get the creeps. I mask my nervous shaking as shivering due to the bite of chill in the air. This has a bonus effect of Bobby drawing me in close, rubbing a muscular, capable hand up and down my arm.

We are serenaded by crickets as we sit on the defunct swings, said to be a hotspot of paranormal activity. It is almost serene as if even the restless spirits are at peace tonight under the blanket of mist and endless stars. Our conversation has meandered from ghosts back to us in the here and now. Bobby asks me about my plans for the land as he had back in that investigation room. *God, that was only a week ago, it seems like forever.*

I answer in more detail this time. "Vegas is a temporary situation, and the time clock is ticking down. A person can only be out there so long before the city changes you, makes you jaded. I want to settle down someplace quieter, maybe someplace I could raise a family. I already own the land, so it is the logical choice, but what really pushed my hand is the uptick in developers hounding me all the time in the last two years to sell. Don't get me wrong, I think progress is something that should be strived for, a real effort to offer more jobs than the mine or the military to kids."

I give him a meaningful look, and he nods in agreement. "But not at the cost of our ecosystems, both natural and economic. Growing too fast will price folks out of their homes, and then only wealthy transplants will be able to afford any property. People with long-standing roots will have to find somewhere else to go, or worse, have to rent under increasingly unfair rental agreements."

I pause briefly to gauge if he is still with me or if I have bored him to death. *He is probably regretting this line of questioning. I could go on all day about the nationwide affordable housing issues.* I shouldn't have worried; his gaze is entirely focused on me. Blushing under his attention I continue, "Pretty soon, you will have a 'Vail-ifcation' effect where even nurses and teachers won't be able to afford to live in the area they serve. In Colorado, some of them are having to travel outside of ninety minutes just to commute to work. So, while yes, growth is necessary, it also has to be measured, or else your balloon will pop."

I stop my rant to see a dopey grin on his face. He saves me from asking what it is all about by saying, "God, you're so sexy when you get up on a soapbox. Hand me a ballot. Forget hospitality, you could be our next mayor—hell, senator even."

"Psssh." I wave him off. "And have to deal with slimy sycophants all day? No, thank you."

"So, how many developers have been calling you? Had there been an uptick recently?"

"Oh loads, but yes, within days of filing my reno permits, six different companies reached out, each with a more ridiculous offer than the last, but I'd rather let the whole plot go to seed than let them build a strip mall. It wouldn't be right." I find that I am shivering for real now and not merely to cover the heebie-jeebies I am experiencing.

"You're cold," he says as a statement, not a question, no doubt noticing me hiding my hands in my sleeves. "Let's get you home. Unless you want to give the Ouija board a go before we leave?"

"Not on your life."

Walking me up to my door this time, he bypasses my cheek and goes for an innocent peck on my lips, but I am having none of that. When he goes to pull away, I grab him by the shirt and pull him into me, his forearm hitting the door above my head to support his weight and keep himself from crushing me. *But God, do I want to be crushed by this man.* I lick the seam of his lips the same time that his thigh is pressed between my spread legs, barely hinting at the friction I want—no need.

He groans as my tongue enters his mouth, and it is deep and guttural and *all* man. It sends a message straight below the belt that it is time to open the floodgates. I whimper, *actually whimper,* in response to that sound.

"Come inside," I pant, breaking apart our lip lock for a moment to get the words out and suck in some air. I swear I feel his knees buckle in that moment.

"Fuck," he curses, low and breathy. "Fuck, Annastasia, you can't say shit like that when you're riding my thigh."

"Inside the room. I meant the room…" I stop for a second and decide to be bold, "Actually, both. Come inside the room, and then come inside me. I have an IUD."

"Jesus fucking Christ, Anna. I am trying to be a gentleman."

"I'll let you open the door. Problem solved." That causes him to snort as he kisses down my neck, sending a raspberry in that spot. The sensation does nothing to cool the rising tide of my libido.

"Puuhhleeese." I drag out the word as he drags his thumb across my pebbled nipple. I am burning from the inside out. "I need, uh, I need," I stammer, struggling to get coherent thoughts to pass through my lips.

They have much more important tasks to attend to than talking, like kissing up the column of his neck to nibble on his ear.

"What do you need, Anastasia?" he asks, and I am certain now he has caught on to what my name dripping from his lips does to me, especially in such close proximity. I am sure he feels the shivers racking through my body at the combination of growling my name and the way he is rolling my nipples between his forefinger and thumb. "Be a good girl and tell me what you need."

Fuck me. I don't say it out loud, but it is a near thing. He's hit two of my newly unlocked kinks in two murmured sentences. Can words bring you to an orgasm? If we continue, we just might find out.

"I need you to come inside... the room. We need the bed. I need *you.*"

"You're so good for me, telling me what you want, but unfortunately, I am not going to be able to do that."

I freeze on a pant. "You're not?" My voice comes out as a needy whine that I don't recognize.

"No," he says firmly, and I have never been so turned on by the word no in my life. "If I go in there, I am going to fuck you raw and fast. You have me too worked up."

"I like raw and fast." That causes him to chuckle.

"I'm sure you do, but for this time, Annastasia," the son of a bitch whispers it to me, the breath of my name ghosting over the shell of my ear, followed by a swipe of his slick, hot tongue. "For the first time, I want to take my time. I want to shatter you piece by piece. And savor every. Fucking. Minute. I have waited too long to rush this now."

I collapse back into the door a needy puddle of goo. "But I need..." I beg. I have never begged for it before, but he can have me on my knees in this hotel hallway if he wants it.

"I know, baby. I know what you need," he soothes. "You have a choice. You can either ride my thigh or my fingers, but either way, I need you to promise to be quiet."

"Fingers," I say automatically and he wastes no time unbuttoning my jeans and delving his hand into my pants. There are no slow soft touches to warm me up. He was right. We are both too far past that.

I am already drenched, and as soon as he comes in contact with my damp panties to push them aside, he tells me how hot it makes him, groaning into my hair as he breathes me in. The rough scrape of his callused finger finds my clit, and I bite down on his collarbone to fight off an instinctive scream.

"Such a fucking good girl," he growls out. "Using me to muffle your cries. You follow instructions so fucking well. I want you to mark me up, baby. I want the world to see your claim on me."

I have only ever had one heated teenage make-out session; all my adult encounters getting straight to the point. It just so happens that I was with the man now spreading two fingers inside of me while his thumb is sketching maddening circles around my clit. That time ended far too abruptly, so I never had the chance to leave my mark on anyone. That he wants me to—is asking me to—flips some sort of primal switch in my brain, and I clamp down harder until a little bit of iron is mixed in with the salt of his sweat.

A string of curses cascades from his lips like the rushing waters of Miller Falls, and he redoubles his efforts, curling his fingers in and up, reaching the spot that I have only reached myself with my favorite toy. He begins to saw his fingers in and out, hitting that spot each time, giving me exactly the right amount of friction I need on my clit. It doesn't take long until I am clamping down anew onto his neck as my core clamps down on his fingers, and my vision whites out to a misty abyss.

"God, the way you're gripping me. I can't fucking wait till you're milking my cock with this tight cunt. You are such a good fucking girl." His words make me clench again, and he groans into my shoulder this time but does not bite. As I come down from my little brush with death, my gaze locks on his dripping fingers as they disappear inside of his mouth, and he moans, "So fucking good, next time I need to taste it straight from the source."

His newly sucked dry fingers move to button my pants back up as he kisses me on the forehead. "But what about you?" I ask.

He smirks and takes my hand, rubbing it unashamedly against the front of his pants where I can feel a sizeable wet spot grow. "Already taken care of, babe."

And why the fuck do I find his confidence in coming in his pants so fucking hot? I am clearly gone for him—perhaps I always was.

"Now you are going to take your sexy ass into your room, shower, and go to bed. We have a big day ahead of us."

Standing on my tiptoes, I give him a chaste kiss on the lips, allowing my mouth to form the words "Yes, sir," and then proceed to follow his orders, certain I hear a muffled curse from behind the closed door.

Chapter 25

ANNASTASIA

(Thursday)

Hugging the Mothman plush to my chest as we leave Point Pleasant for our next destination, I cannot keep the smile from my face. I twist its fuzzy little antennae between my fingers while Bobby traces absent patterns on my inner thigh with his right hand as we cruise down the highway. I chuckle to myself, remembering the text that woke me this morning.

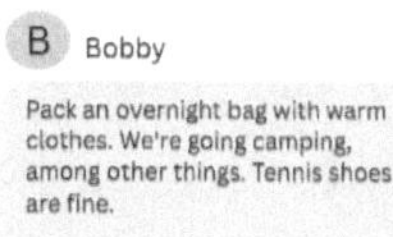

He has been diligent in setting my wardrobe expectations since the little hiccup in communication a couple of days ago. *It's sweet.* I thought on the heels of where we left off last night. 'Among other things' was code for sex, but apparently it is not, well, at least not yet. This is a 'multi-list item date'. That is how he referred to it as he stowed my bag into the compartment beneath the floor of the truck bed. He has been sticking to keeping up the mystery, even though I am on to the game after last night. Just because there is a list he is working from doesn't mean I have any clue what item he will choose next.

We spent the morning into late afternoon in the little town of Point Pleasant, about an hour or two north of Boremanton. I think I almost burst his eardrums with the squeal I let out seeing the exit sign on the highway. As a kid, I had an obsession with local folklore, so when I realized he was taking me to the home of Mothman, well, I may have done an embarrassing little seat dance in the car to accompany my squealing. I had almost forgotten that we had put it on the list at all.

We traipsed through the town, perusing little shops and visiting the Mothman Museum. I made a point of getting several pictures with the infamous statue, sending them off to Joanie and Caroline. Joanie's instant reply of "Damn, why is Mothman so caked up?" followed by Caroline's continuing thread of screenshots of Mothman-inspired romance books still has me giggling.

Bobby glances over at me as I stare down at the latest title on my phone. "What is it now?"

"It's called *Sweet Berries*. It is a follow-up to *Morning Glory Milking Farm*." I cannot stop giggling at the growing monster romance TBR Caroline is supplying Joanie with. Her reply of "Mind blown" with the accompanying emoji sets me off again.

"Do I even want to know what that one is about?" he asked, amused.

"Minotaur," is my brief reply. I am not going to get into the finer details of the plot with him; if he is that curious, he can read it himself. I'll even give him my copy.

"Should have known this is how it would go when you two were so disappointed at the end of Beauty and the Beast when we were kids."

"The opinion that the prince was a downgrade is clearly the only correct answer. I mean, he should have at least had a beard or some stubble," I say, grazing my hand over his stubbled jaw. I have noticed he is letting it grow in since his forced time off started. Can't say that I am torn up about it. Feeling the texture prick against the palm of my hand, I can't help but imagine what the sensation would feel like on other, more sensitive parts of me.

The sun is low as we pull off the highway into Coal Creek Park and I rack my brain trying to recall what list items we may be crossing off here. Bobby sets up some camping chairs first, instructing me to take a seat as he prepares the rest of our campsite. I offer to help, but he insists that I am getting the princess treatment today. He sets up a tent in half the time that it has ever taken me with the help of a group of people.

The sheer competency that he shows in every motion has me rubbing my thighs together. *I guess we can add a competency kink to my growing list.* Or maybe it is time I face it and be honest with myself. I don't think any of these things in particular from any man other than him would do it for me like this. *Maybe I just have a Bobby Payne kink.*

As I watch him make a cozy little camp for us in this open patch of green dotted with clusters of yellow and white wildflowers, I breathe in the crisp mountain air and zone out. Focused on the tune of the breeze through the trees and the bubbling flow of the nearby creek. I am at peace in a way that I haven't been in years. By all accounts, I have no right to be now, with this investigation looming over my head, but growing up in the tumultuous state of my childhood, these mountains have always been my sanctuary. I am relieved to find that they still have that effect on me.

Having finished with his setup, Bobby settles in the chair next to my own and rummages in the cooler until he pulls out a wine bottle with a homemade label. He hands it to me with a smug look on his face as I read the bottle. *There is no fucking way!* Out loud, I say, "Is this what I think it is?"

"If you are thinking it is a batch of Mrs. Bianchi's own home-brewed dandelion wine, then you'd be correct."

"How did you get this? Caroline said she had passed."

"Nicked it from my mom. I think it is from the last batch Mrs. Bianchi made. Her kids were unloading it at the wake."

"Bobby, we can't drink this. This is funeral wine. What if it has sentimental value to your mom and that's why she hasn't drunk it yet?"

"She has like, four other bottles of the stuff. It wasn't her only one," he insists.

I eye him dubiously. "Well, if Mrs. Bianchi, God rest her soul, haunts me for drinking this wine, you'll have hell to pay, Bobby Payne."

"I honestly think she might haunt us if we don't." And knowing the old lady, there might be some truth to that statement.

As he uncorks the wine and pours us both a serving in plastic cups, I think about all the time I spent on spring days filling baskets upon baskets of the little yellow flowers for Mrs. Bianchi to make this wine. *With all of my time spent plucking those damn dandelions for years, it is only fair that I at least get to taste the fruits of my labor.* He hands me a cup and tips his towards mine.

"What should we toast to?" he asks

"To Mrs. Bianchi, may she rest in peace," is my automatic response. He touches his cup to mine, and we both take our first tentative sips.

Home-made booze is not a novel idea in these parts, but the quality and taste of it runs the gamut. I am pleasantly surprised at its smoothness as it coats my tongue in notes of floral and citrus. No doubt the prolonged time on the shelf has allowed it to age out some of the bitterness that home brews are known for. I hum, enjoying the lingering taste of honey that is left behind.

"This is surprisingly good." He takes another healthy gulp, and I am transfixed at the way his Adam's apple bulges with the motion. It also brings my attention to the rather swollen marks he wears as a reminder of last night. Maybe I should feel shame at the wonton mess he had me reduced to, but I only feel pride that he wears my marks so confidently with no urge to hide them or me from the world.

"Okay, man of mystery and intrigue, we've crossed off 'visit Mothman' and 'try Mrs. Bianchi's famous dandelion wine'. What other teenage dreams are we fulfilling tonight?" I meant it to be an innocent inquiry referring to our list, but by the way his pupils dilate, and his nostrils flare, I can tell the thoughts behind those focused hazel eyes are nowhere near innocent.

Bobby

If we are talking about fulfilling my teenage dreams, *well, I have plans for that, too.* Only now do I have the experience and confidence to bring those dreams to life.

I cough, clearing my desert dry throat to answer the question the way she intended it. "Well, I recall sleeping under the stars was one of them—the tent is just in case it rains—and if I remember correctly, 'skinny dip in Coal Miners Creek' was on there too, and well," I gesture to the babbling creek mere yards away, "there is Coal Miners Creek."

The flush on her face, framed by the golden hour glow of sunset on the mountain, is something worth remembering, so I snap a quick picture of her on my phone before she notices and attempts to swat it away. I have been taking random pictures of her over the last three days, making up for the years of memories I've missed. I think she is growing used to it because she doesn't question it anymore.

Instead, she says, "I am going to need to see this list, because while I recall 'swimming in Coal Miners Creak' as an item, I think someone is taking liberties and amending the text. There is no way sixteen-year-old me wrote skinny dipping on there."

"To be fair, Caroline wrote the list we just dictated."

"Caroline didn't write that either. I'll text her right now and tell her how you are throwing her under the bus," she threatens

"Okay, okay, you got me. Maybe I did take some liberties and amended this *one* item to fit both my teenage dreams and my current fantasies, but we can just swim if you would rather."

She raises one eyebrow at me and says, "Convenient that you left 'swimsuit' off my wardrobe list. Not that I packed one anyway."

"Oh? What a shame."

"You just want to get me naked," she accuses.

"If you are asking for a plea, then I'll be honest—guilty as charged."

"Sounds like maybe I should cuff you. You didn't happen to pack any handcuffs, did you?"

"No, but if that is something that you are into, Annastasia—" I love the way she looks at me when I say her full name; I want to see what other reactions she has to it in a more intimate context. "We can certainly explore that more later. But back to the point. Where did we land on skinny dipping? What's the verdict? "

She doesn't answer me with words, but she does throw back her cup, downing what's left of her wine. Standing, she starts to lift her shirt as she walks away from me, revealing lines of ink I never knew she was hiding. I am rooted to my chair, mesmerized by each inch revealed.

It is when she has it hiked up beneath her rib cage that she turns her head over her shoulder and says, "Well, are you coming or not?" removing the rest of the shirt and taking her bra with it as it falls to the ground in a heap. Her bare skin reveals an entire back piece of twisted branches and delicate blossoms of a cherry tree, right as the blooms begin to fall. It is beautiful. I have never been envious of the tattoos on someone's body before, but this ink gets to caress the curvature of her spine in a way that I have only dreamed of.

When her shorts join the fate of her top, I am jolted out of my reverence. As the denim hits the ground, I am up and out of my chair kicking off my boots in a single motion. A few large strides eat up the distance that she has put between us. I shed my shirt and unbuckle my belt on the way. Anna is standing with her back to me in nothing but pale blue panties that match her eyes when she smiles, and I scoop her up, throwing her over my shoulder, my pants falling to the ground. Stepping out of them, I take off running. Pushing off the bank, I leap into the creek with my prize.

Anna is laughing, pure unadulterated joy spilling from her lips. The sound is an aphrodisiac that I want to find the endless well of and baptize myself in. Her laughter, her happiness, has made me brand new. It is at this precise moment that I understand everything my dad has ever said about making a woman happy. I heard it wrong; he never said 'a woman' at all. All this time, he has said, "Find what makes *your* woman happy and do it as often as you can." I get it now because Anna is my woman as surely as I am her man, even if she doesn't know it yet. That's fine. I will use the time I have between now and forever, making sure she gets there, too.

Once fully submerged, we disengage, both of us propelling ourselves up to breach the surface. Anna beams at me before she splashes me in the face in retaliation.

"Not fair! What if I wanted to ease my way in?" she asks chattering as the breeze meets the droplets of water on her shoulders causing her to duck under to escape the chill. The sun sinks over the mountains, the sky changing from oranges and pinks to deep violet and indigo, the brightest, bravest stars peeking through the lingering rays of the day.

"Aren't you the one always saying to rip it off like a bandage? I'm just helping you live up to your own expectations." I don't tell her I couldn't wait, that if I didn't have my hands on her in some way that instant, I would implode and cease to exist. I know it is foolish; she hasn't promised to stay. We haven't had the big talk that we need to, but I am irrevocably in love with this girl. She rolls her eyes, never liking her wise words thrown back at her. She splashes me again and kicks off in a swim, daring me to chase. So, I do.

We play in the water, sharing light kisses and touches, and playing a game of catch and release. It is maddening, and it is wonderful. When the night fully overtakes the sky, and we can only see by the light of the stars and the moon, we make our way back to camp, grabbing our disregarded clothes along the way.

Wrapping her in a towel, I notice more ink that I missed in our games, but I am not able to make it out in the dark. She sits back in a chair draped in terry cloth, wearing nothing but soaked panties that do nothing to hide her from me. I kiss her on the forehead and then start a fire to provide us with light and warmth. I feel her eyes on my back as I throw some blankets down to give us somewhere to lie and observe the sky and explore each other, if that's what she wants. But if all she wants is to lie in my arms and rest her head on my shoulder as we name constellations, I am fine with that, too. *Whatever makes her happy.* It is now my motto to live by.

I invite her over with a wave of my hand. She reaches down and grabs the discarded bottle of wine, and forgoes the cups, snuggling into my side. I pull a blanket over to drape over both of us to aid the fire in warming us up. She drops the wet towel outside of our protective cocoon. A comfortable silence has fallen over us, no sound but the crackle of the fire accompanying the chirp of the crickets filling the air.

We sit there for a while, letting the mountain sing us a song when a far-off howl has me going still. Not out of my own fear, but what the sound will stir in her. Will it remind her of that night? You don't watch a wolf kill your father and not have it affect you for the rest of your life, that is for sure.

Sensing my shift, she turns toward me, half her face cast in the glow of the firelight, and my heart stops but for an entirely different reason than the echoing call of the wolf. God, she is magnificent. I tuck a strand of still-damp hair behind her ear and say, "It's far off. The howl," I clarify, seeing questions in her eyes. "The sound echoes off the mountain. I won't let anything happen to you."

"You think I am scared of the wolf?" she asks.

"Well, you would be within reason if you were," I say in response.

"That wolf doesn't star in my nightmares, Bobby—she ended them."

"I don't understand."

She sheds the blanket, baring herself to me for the first time without the shroud of the creek to keep her modest. Her breasts are spectacular, and my palms itch to caress them, to feel their weight in my hands, but I sense that this is important, so I refrain from acting on the urge. In between her breasts sits the tattoo I couldn't make out before. The face of a wolf framed by a bed of wildflowers and linework filigree, all in shades of grey except for the pair of glowing golden eyes staring back at me. She turns so her back piece is now in my view, close up, and at this distance, I can see that the texture of her skin under the ink is not smooth. Under most blossoms, the skin is raised at their center. I reach out to feel it under my fingertips.

"Cigarette burns," she states, her voice small.

I retract my hand as though it is burned by the mere thought of it, but she does not let me recoil from her fully. She turns and grabs my hand and sets it on the trunk of the tree.

"Trace the bark lines," she instructs.

Unable and unwilling to deny her this—anything really. I follow her instructions and realize that there, beneath the beauty I was admiring earlier, are scars. From what, I don't know.

"Belt lashes," she answers the question I hadn't realized I voiced aloud, and suddenly every bruise I ever chalked up to her clumsy nature and adventurous spirit comes into question.

"How long?" My voice cracks. "How long did it go on?" *How long did I not know?*

"Since she left." *Since her mother left? Fuck.*

"That motherfucker. If he wasn't long dead, I'd kill him."

"Well, you don't have to. The wolf took care of it for us. I think she was repaying a favor. She had the same scars of the wolf my dad had penned up in his shed some years prior. I released her, freed her, and then she freed me in kind. So no, Bobby, I don't fear wolves."

"Did he ever—" I have no right to ask, to make her dredge all this up, but she answers anyway.

"No, he never touched me. Not like that anyway. Even if he would say things that made me feel like it was an inevitability, that he'd try if he was lost too deep in the bottle. He was always saying how much I looked like her." She means her mother. A hazy memory of the night he died smacks me in the face. He had called Anna 'Mary' that night, right before the wolf struck.

I am shaking. In anger? In grief? Both? I am not sure. The only thing I am sure of is, "I am sorry. Sorry, I didn't know. Sorry I didn't stop him."

She whirls around, taking my face between her palms. "No. Don't you do that. It isn't on you. You were a child. He didn't leave a lasting mark where anyone would see. I didn't tell you, or anyone for that matter because I didn't want you to know how weak I was."

"You are the strongest person I know—then and now. I wish I could take this from you is all."

"I don't need you to take it from me."

"What do you need?"

"I need you. I need you to touch me. Show me that you want me still, despite this."

It is my turn to take her cheeks between my palms as I smash my lips to hers in a brutal kiss that can leave no question as to whether or not I want her. I break away and tell her anyway because she deserves to know—to hear me say it, "All I have ever wanted was you, *is* you."

I trail my hand from her face down her neck and trace a line between her breasts with my fingertips, paying the reverence that is due to the effigy of her savior. Her nipples peak, from chill or anticipation, I am not sure. Either way, I lean in and take one between my teeth to warm it with my tongue. She moans, moving her hands to find purchase in my hair, and she tugs, the slight pain sending jolts directly to my already hardening cock.

"Yes, Annastasia, baby. I love it when you get rough with me," I say around her nipple, feeling her whole body shutter. I take advantage of her momentary distraction to tip her onto her back and continue my path downward over the plane of her stomach to my intended destination.

On another night, I would toy with her, use her panties to provide her with just enough friction to drive her mad, but tonight they are in my way. Sliding my thumbs beneath each side, I grasp the lacy material in my fists and pull, tearing them right off her. Her gasp of surprise spurring me on.

"Hey—" I don't wait for her to chide me; I dive right in, stealing the reprimand from her voice. Any words she meant to say dissolve into a moan as I swipe my tongue through her folds. My tastebuds explode with the earthy essence of her. I change my focus to sucking her clit into my mouth as my fingers find her warm, slick heat.

I break off to take a breath. "You're so fucking sexy, I love how fucking wet you are for me."

"Don't stop, please, I... ah... I am so close," she pants, and it drives me wild.

"Are you gonna be a good girl for me, Annastasia? Are you gonna come like a good girl?" With that, she comes undone, as if triggered by my words alone.

"Fuuuuuck." She drags out the curse as she drenches my hand, back arching her off our nest of blankets, breast tipped up like an offering to the moon above. Spread out for me in this field of wildflowers; I don't think I have ever seen anything more beautiful.

She takes advantage of my distraction, clenching her thick thighs around my torso and flipping me onto my back. I am impressed by her strength, but all thought leaves my mind as she shimmies down, her wet center meeting my hard cock.

She sits up, leaning back, soaking my length with every movement of her hips, the engorged head of my dick bracketed between her folds. Scanning my eyes up, I am gifted with the vision of her toying with her tits, twisting her peaked nipples between her thumbs and pointer as she grinds down on me, using me for her own pleasure. And while I am immensely enjoying the view, *this won't do.* I halt her hands with my own, taking over the task, and she leans back further, placing her hands on the top of my thighs.

The moon is a halo behind her, casting her usually pale golden strands in a silvery light. She looks ethereal. This goddess among us has allowed me to worship at her altar, and I am grateful for the opportunity to be her acolyte.

"I need you," she moans, hips writhing, seeking out friction.

"You have me, baby. I'm yours."

"I need more."

"Take anything you need. Take all of me."

"I need you inside." She is killing me. I am absolutely shattered by her. On a growl, I flip us, returning her to her back, and I hover over her, one hand on my cock, circling the tip around her clit as she whimpers with need.

A need I intend to meet vigorously and repeatedly, as soon as I clear one thing up. I grab her jaw to get her attention. When her blown out pupils focus on me, I say, "I know what you said yesterday, but I need to hear what you want now, I have condoms we can use—"

"I want you to fill me up," she interrupts, and fuck if that isn't the sexiest thing she could say to me. "I trust you." And there she goes proving me wrong, *Because that is the sexiest thing she could say.*

Not needing to be told twice, I line up and thrust, and it feels like coming home. She is wet enough from her previous orgasm that she accepts the intrusion effortlessly and her walls instantly grip me on the withdraw as if they don't want me to leave—as if I should spend the rest of my days buried to the hilt inside her comforting warmth. I couldn't think of a better way to spend the rest of my life than in the cradle of her thighs.

I swallow her moan with my kiss as I pick up the pace, the bite of her nails digging into my back spurring me on. Yesterday, against her door, I needed her silence, but tonight, I want to make her scream.

Moving my mouth to her neck and licking a trail to her ear, I say, "Come on, good girl, let me hear you. Scream. For. Me," I punctuate each word with a thrust.

"Oh my fucking God, yes, just like that. Fuck me," she yells, but I want more.

My one hand goes to her throat so I can feel the vibrations of her moans as she makes them. I squeeze a little when I feel her grip me tighter. My girl likes a little rough play, and I am all here for it. My other hand travels down her abdomen, ending its journey on her clit, and I circle the little bud in time with my thrusts

"That's it, Annastasia. You're doing so good, you take me so well," I whisper to her, following it up with a swipe of my tongue to the shell of her ear. I feel her tight cunt squeeze me as I increase pressure on her clit, and I know that I'm close, but there is not a chance in hell I go before she is coming with me. "God, baby, I love when you squeeze me. I want you to come baby. I want you to drench my fucking cock." Her whimper tells me she is close, so I increase the speed and force of impact.

Her nails dig in deep; the pain mixes with the pleasure, and my vision spins. "Right there, Bobby, right thereeee. Don't fucking stop."

Stop? Why in fuck would I stop? She feels so fucking good. I increase the pressure on her throat, and I fucking feel the shudder as it travels down her body until her core is clenching around my cock like a vice. Like the good girl she is, she screams for me, and I come to the sound of it echoing off the surrounding mountains.

After catching my breath, I clean us both up with some wipes from my bag. I pull one of my shirts over her head. We snuggle close, the fire crackling down to embers, the crickets serenading us with their lullaby, and I fall asleep with her by my side underneath a West Virginia sky.

Chapter 26

ANNASTASIA

(Friday)

I wish I could have stayed in the cocoon of warmth that Bobby's arms offered in our cozy nest on a bed of wildflowers. I can't find the words to describe last night. Between the fun we had in the creek, shedding the responsibilities of adulthood for one night as we frolicked and played, to the vulnerable moment when I explained my scars, to the mind-blowing, life-altering sex. I saw stars and not only the ones that painted the sky above us. It was perfect. I am riding the high of a woman who was well and truly fucked, but with the light of day comes new responsibilities that need attention.

I woke up to a call from Diane asking me to meet her as soon as I could at the sheriff's office. She couldn't give me more information than that, and it makes my stomach roll and my anxiety spike. This could be very good news or very bad, and the anticipation is killing me. I am also slightly pressed about not being able to shower or dress appropriately for this meeting, but

I would rather get this over with than put it on hold in favor of stopping at the inn to clean up.

"I feel bad if this cuts into whatever plan you have for the day," I tell Bobby as we travel down the hallway toward home. *Home. When had I started thinking of it like that?*

He lifts our conjoined hands so that he can kiss my knuckles. "The only plan that matters is spending my time with you. I'll be waiting outside no matter what happens in there today. Okay?"

I want to tell him it's okay, he can go home and clean up, that I am a big girl and can handle this on my own, but instead, I say, "Thank you." The idea of him waiting outside calms my nerves. It isn't long before we are back in the town center and he is walking me to the door.

"You got this, Anna. Trust the process and I will be right here," he says, pulling me in for a reassuring hug. The door swings open, almost knocking us over, and of course, it is Leanne, here to be the raincloud to my picnic.

Seeing our embrace, she sends a scowl our way and storms off down the street. The sun is high in the sky, indicating that it is almost noon. I assume she is on her lunch break. *Good, hopefully this goes fast and I will be done before she gets back.*

Palm to my face, Bobby turns my gaze back to his. "Don't worry about her. She doesn't matter." He is right; I can't let her wind me up. Not when this is so important.

I give him a quick peck and pull away from him. It almost physically hurts me to do so. *How will it feel to go back to Vegas if I don't even want an exterior wall to separate us?*

"You'll be right here when I am done?" I ask, and he responds with a nod. Taking a grounding breath, I open the door to see what news is waiting for me on the other side.

I sit next to Diane in the same interrogation room as I did when I got here over a week ago. *God, it has only been that long; it feels like a lifetime between then and now.* Sheriff Dobbs enters with a woman I've never seen wearing a lab coat. I do a perfunctory scan, seeing that she is also wearing neon green Chuck Taylors instantly puts me at ease. I don't think that is the footwear of choice for someone about to deliver damning news. The grip I have on my locket eases, and I instead slide it back and forth on its chain. My anxiety is still present, but not as sharp in my gut as it was moments ago.

The sheriff nods at us in greeting. "Miss Adkins, Ms. Montgomery, thank you for joining us on such short notice. Anna, this is Caitlin Bryant. She works in our forensic lab. Diane, I believe you are familiar." Of course they are. There are no strangers when you live in a small town like this, unless of course you leave for over a decade like me.

Diane shakes her hand and confirms this with a curt but respectful. "Yes. A pleasure as always, Miss. Bryant."

"Caitie, please," she insists, taking my hand next in a firm, no-nonsense grip.

"Nice to meet you, Caitie. You can call me Anna." We may as well all be on a first-name basis. I feel that whatever Caitie is about to say is going to trigger an emotional response from me one way or another. Might as well not stand on circumstance. Except for the sheriff. The day I refer to him as 'Dwight' is the day I file for social security, so not in his lifetime.

"If we can all have a seat, we will get straight to the point," Sheriff Dobbs states, waiting for us to sit before taking up his own chair.

For the next twenty minutes, Caitie explains in great detail the nuances of soil, displacement, and decomposition rates. I try to keep up, but when she details statistics on larva reproduction, she loses me a little. What I do get from the impromptu science lecture is that the bodies they have found on my property were not killed there but planted, and actually, they were not killed at all but rather stolen from a body farm; a nauseating term I wish I could scrub from my memory banks, much like the slide show images she showed us to make sure we grasped the concept.

They inform me that this could have been cleared up a week ago, if only there were someone at the university to run the comparisons at the time. In short, I am cleared of all suspicion and free to go about my life as usual. The murder case is being downgraded to theft. My airtight alibi for the time frame and having no access to the university or motive to sabotage my own renovation project clears me from the suspect pool.

"So, I am free to go back to Vegas?" I question, and more to be clear, I tack on, "And the construction can resume?"

"Essentially, yes, though we would like you to hold off for another week so we can finish collecting any evidence we can," the sheriff states. "We still have some remains that need to be analyzed that are coming in from the search today. As long as they follow the same pattern, there is no reason that you should have to stay. Being a Friday, we will need a few days for the labs to come in once we get them to forensics, but we did not want to leave you in the dark any longer with this hanging over your head."

"I appreciate that," I say honestly. One week in Boremanton would have felt like forever a mere week ago, but now it almost seems too short.

"And if you wouldn't mind answering a few questions that may help us find who is responsible for all of this."

I look to Diane and she nods. As long as she is fine with it, I am happy to help in any way I can, and I tell them as much. They ask me if anyone has contacted me about my land and if I could give them a detailed list of dates and the intensity of their interest. The questions seem super familiar, and I wonder if Bobby had been privy to this theory before his suspension.

"Well, that is all we have for now. We will let you know next week about when you can start your project again. Sorry that you got dragged into this mess." The sheriff shakes my hand and asks Diane if she could stay behind for a bit.

"Yes, Sheriff, of course. I will just walk Miss Adkins out. Shall I meet you in your office?" Diane asks. Sherriff Dobbs agrees, and he and Caitie go their separate ways.

I hug Diane and thank her for all her help.

"Nonsense. If you need anything in the future, don't hesitate to call. I hope this means that you are moving forward with your project. It would be lovely to see you around town on a more permanent basis." She walks me to the lobby, and we say our goodbyes. This must be my lucky day because the reception desk is empty, and I make it out of the station without a confrontation with Leanne.

Bobby is leaning on the grill of his truck, eyes on his phone, so he doesn't notice when I open the door. I take a moment to appreciate him in all his tousled glory with a baseball cap backward on his head, wearing yesterday's shirt. I am currently wearing the one he packed for today. He put it on me to sleep, and in the haste to get home, I didn't change into my spare clothes, just slipped a pair of shorts on underneath. I am giddy with excitement about all the possibilities before me, but first, I think we need to get washed up.

As if he senses my approach, he looks up when I take a step toward him. "How did it go?"

"For all intents and purposes, I'm cleared. They are downgrading the case from murder to theft. But you already knew that didn't you, Deputy Payne?"

"It was only being tossed around as a theory before my suspension." He holds his hands up as if trying to placate a wild animal. So I stalk him like one with each slow step I take in his direction. "And even if I am suspended, I still can't talk about the details of a ongoing investigation," he pleads his case.

When we are toe-to-toe, I stand up on mine, wrapping my arms around his neck, still having to tilt my head to meet his eyes. "How are you going to make it up to me, Deputy?"

"Take you on our date?" he questions, and I shake my head; his face falls, misunderstanding my intentions.

"I am filthy, I need a shower," I pull him down to my level so my lips hover over his, "and so do you. Take me back to your place, Deputy, and help me conserve water."

"That, Miss Adkins, can be arranged."

We spent the rest of Friday afternoon into the evening in a cycle of cleaning ourselves up and getting dirty again. In the end, we probably didn't do anything to help with the water conservation efforts, but I don't regret it.

Chapter 27

ANNASTASIA

(Saturday)

The aroma of coffee brewing fills the air of Bobby's small apartment on Saturday morning. I didn't get the full tour, but in between bouts of sex, he did tell me that he uses the upstairs bedroom as an at-home gym, leaving his main living space to consist of the room I am currently stretching my limbs awake in, a small living room, and a galley kitchen. It's nothing like the farmhouse with the wraparound porch he used to dream about as a kid, but we aren't children anymore, and it isn't fair to hold him to his childhood ideals. Lord knows I have not stuck to mine.

The sizzling of bacon and the aroma of fried eggs join the coffee in enticing me from the comfort of Bobby's bed. I look around and grab a button-down flannel hanging behind his door. I button it enough to be decent. The shirt hanging off my shoulders and brushing down past my thighs could be styled as a mini dress with the addition of a belt. My bare feet pad across the hardwood as I follow my stomach to the source of the heavenly aroma.

"I thought you said you don't cook."

"Bacon and eggs are hardly a gourmet meal", he deadpans, portioning off the eggs and plating the bacon. He sets it on the peninsula that separates the kitchen from the living room. "Coffee?"

"The day I turn down caffeine is the day I die," I reply.

He pours it into a mug and sets it next to my plate, then curiously, he grabs a glass measuring cup and pours himself some coffee. "What's with that?" I gesture to his makeshift coffee vessel.

"I gave you my mug." He shrugs like it makes perfect sense, and then it dawns on me.

"Your *only* mug?"

"Don't start."

"Start what?"

"My brothers already gave me shit about it. I haven't had time to get a second mug. I hadn't needed one 'til now." He means 'til me. It is then that I realize, looking around, that there are no personal touches here. We were a little preoccupied last night. I wasn't exactly looking, but now I see no pictures on the wall, no personal items. Nothing to show that the place is lived in. Nothing to show that he has laid claim to this space.

"Did you just move in?"

Warily, he responds, "No, why?"

"How long have you lived here?"

"Since I moved back home. So 'bout four years."

"There isn't anything here that screams *you* here."

"You learn to live light when you move from place to place." He shrugs, and it seems I have hit a sore spot.

"Can we talk?" he asks. I freeze with a fork full of eggs halfway to my lips. I drop it back down to the plate, sensing this is going to be serious.

"I'm listening."

"Now that you are almost free to leave, are you going back to Vegas?"

"I live in Vegas. I have to go back." His face is a mask, and I can't read what he is feeling. "I have responsibilities and a lease, so yes, I am going back to Vegas. But I already told you that this was my exit plan. Since it looks like I can resume construction, my end goal is to be here. Recent developments," I give him a meaningful look, "have encouraged me to move up that timeline, but there will be some back and forth for a while." Hearing that, the mask cracks and he relaxes on an exhale.

"So, this thing between you and me isn't just a fling for you?"

Oh, I know what this is. I have been there through enough of Joanie's relationships to recognize the signs of a 'defining –the –relationship' moment. "No, you are not just a fling. I don't think I could ever think of you that way."

"Good, because it would kill me inside if all we have is now. I wouldn't stop it, I couldn't. It would kill me when you left. I can do distance, Annastasia. I can make that work. I want you to know that I'm all in on this."

I nod. "I am all in on this, too."

"There is one more thing I have to know, then we can resume the marathon sex we have been having."

"I like the sound of that," I say coyly, sipping from this man's only mug, already planning to buy him a new one any chance I get until his cupboards are full.

"I need to know why you never wrote me back."

I freeze, muscles locking, my stomach dropping at the serious look on his face. I know I can't dodge this, but I didn't know I would be waking up to this particular line of questioning.

"When Caroline told me where you were, I wrote you a letter—well, I wrote you a lot of letters. You never replied. Not once. Did you even get them?"

"I got them." I won't lie to this man ever, but I hate the way it looks like I just kicked his puppy. So, I rush to explain. "You wouldn't have gone. You would not have finished your paperwork, and you would have stayed for me. You would have given up on your dream of seeing the world to be there for me. I was not okay, Bobby. You would have seen how broken I was. I wasn't ready to talk about it—hell, I couldn't even talk at all. My mother abandoned me. My father tortured me. I had so much I needed to work through on my own. You would have wanted to be there for me, and as weak as I was, I would have clung to you and let you miss out on everything you wanted for yourself. I couldn't let you give up your dreams."

My word vomit has shocked him still; he isn't moving a muscle. Then he laughs. It is a humorless hollow noise, and I hate it—hate that I caused it.

Then he says, "That son of a bitch. Dying was too good for him."

"What?" I ask, confused.

"Your fucking father. Sory for speaking ill of the dead, but this one time I think God will forgive me." He is pacing back and forth, a caged tiger primed to strike, only his prey is a ghost. I track his movements as he continues, "I only joined up for you. To be worthy of you—it was all for you."

"I don't understand."

My voice stops his steps. He drags a calloused hand down his face, and after a long exhale he continues, "The Sunday before you saw me with all the recruitment papers…" He pauses to make sure I am following. I nod to reassure him that I am. "Your pa cornered me outside church to warn me off you, told me I was worthless, destined for the mine or for jail. Basically that you were too good for me. That was the only part of his fucking tirade that I could agree with."

I open my mouth to protest, but he silences me with a finger to my lips and says, "You were and are too good for me, but I am done pretending I don't want you anyway." Moving his finger from my lips to instead cup my jaw, tilting my head to meet his gaze he says, "I joined up so I could make a better life for us. Then with his dying act, he took you from me anyway. Put you out of my reach."

"You joined for me?" It is his turn to nod. "God, we've wasted so much time."

He nods again then whisks me off my feet, heading toward the bedroom, breakfast be damned and says, "Let's not waste another moment then."

Chapter 28

ANNASTASIA

(Sunday)

Bobby has been giving me heated stares all through dinner. We stopped at my room so I could change before arriving at his parents' house for dinner. I decided not to waste Caroline's borrowed dress; it was more suitable for a family dinner than hiking through the woods. I knew I made the right choice when I walked out of the ensuite and caught his pupils dilating and his hand clenching as if he had to physically stop himself from reaching for me.

Any nerves about attending this family dinner were swept away when Lucy, as Mrs. Payne insisted I call her, engulfed me in a tender hug and whispered to me, "Welcome home."

I hum around a forkful of creamy ricotta stuffed shells. The garlic and rosemary spices are dancing on my tongue from the homemade sauce. It is almost enough to distract me from the strong hand currently trying to work its way up my skirt—almost. I stop its ascent with a not-so-subtle swat of my free hand and a stomp to his left foot. Bobby takes my rejection in stride, but his focused gaze lets me know that we will revisit this later.

Across from me sits a tablet with Max's smug face filling the screen; he keeps looking between Bobby and I like a proud yenta who has made a successful match. Pulling my phone from my pocket, *I love a dress with pockets,* I shoot him a text.

I was relieved when Bobby asked his father how his cold was faring to learn that John was on the mend from a simple respiratory infection, but it tipped me off to the manipulation tactics of the oldest Payne brother.

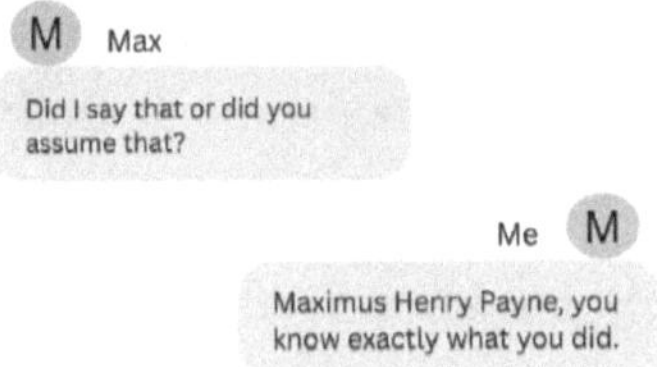

I see the man wince on-screen, eyes scanning the text in real-time. He looks up from his phone at the same time mine vibrates in my palm.

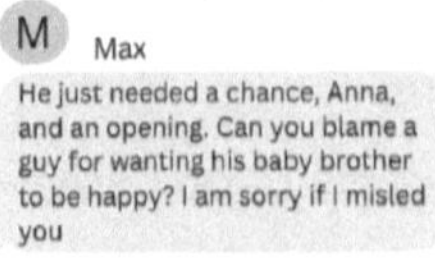

I nod in acceptance. I can't be mad at his machinations—not with how much I am enjoying the outcome.

The rest of dinner carries on with small talk and jokes; each brother contributing stories from their work throughout the week. A sense of belonging I have not felt besides when I am with Joanie washes over me. Family. This feels like family, and I am lucky enough to be a part of it.

"Anna, dear," Lucy interrupts my thoughts. "Has Bobby extended my offer for you to stay here for the rest of your visit?" All heads turn to Bobby when I return the question with a confused look.

"It hasn't come up yet," Bobby defends.

"Yeah Mom," Tommy interjects, "I am sure Bobby's been real busy. Must have slipped his mind." That earns him a snort from Patrick and a smack to the back of his head from Johnny.

"Actually, Anna, I was going to ask you tonight if you'd spend the rest of your time at my place." We have spent the better part of the last two days tangled in his sheets; it doesn't make sense for me to continue paying for a room to go unused.

"Yeah, I would like that." Of course, the brothers revert to children at any given opportunity, and my response is met with some friendly chiding.

"Well, as long as you carve out some girl time for me. We have a lot to catch up on," Lucy says. I am giddy at the chance for a maternal influence in my life. The corners of my mouth tip in a smile I can't hide as a comfortable warmth settles over me.

Before we leave, I excuse myself to use the restroom. I can barely recognize the girl in the mirror. The reflection is showing a woman glowing with happiness, and I wonder if I have ever felt as content as I do in this moment. *Have I been going through the motions of a half-life up until now?* I shake my head as the soap lathers in my hands, intent not to dwell on morose thoughts.

On my way back to the others, I pass a door. Taped on its surface is a torn sheet of notebook paper with a hastily scribbled message written in black marker. *'Bobby's Room. Stay out'* and this is a warning I cannot heed. The pull of curiosity to know what secrets Bobby's childhood room keeps is too strong. I twist the knob, cool in my palm, and push open the door.

What greets me is a room frozen in the past with sports posters on the wall and figurines on a shelf otherwise full of memorabilia of accomplishments long since passed. My eye catches on a frame, and suddenly I am staring at a younger me, forever captured in a stolen moment. The moment right before the flash faded and I ran off. The moment when I stole my first kiss from Bobby Payne; granted it was only on the cheek. It is surreal to think that after all these years, I am still here chasing the feeling of fluttering butterflies that this boy—no, this man still inspires in me.

Setting the memory back in its home for safekeeping, I notice a disturbance in the settled dust. There is a letter out of place, unopened and addressed to Annastasia Adkins with a big red 'Return to Sender' notice stamped across its face. When I left Westly Hall, I told them not to forward my mail. This must have come after I left for school.

My palm itches. I may not have sent a reply to any of Bobby's letters, but there was not one left unopened. Reading and rereading his words grounded me when I was at risk of floating away, lost to grief and pain. Before I can think better of it, to leave the past in the past, I snatch the letter. Folding it in half, I place it in my pocket, rushing to join the others before Bobby comes looking for me.

When we return to the inn, I intend to get my money's worth and put this honeymoon suite to the test since I can't check out until morning anyway.

"The tub is a jacuzzi big enough for two if you want to join me for a bath," I say, backing into the room. He matches me step for step, a hungry look in his eyes.

"I'll keep that in mind for when we need to clean up," he says, his voice comes out gritty like two boulders rubbing together in its intensity. "You wore this dress to drive me crazy, didn't you, Annastasia?" He trails his fingertips up my arm, leaving goosebumps in their wake, stopping at the strap holding up the top of my dress.

"There is a strong possibility," I reply, unrepentant. The back of my calves hit the bed, and he pushes my shoulder slightly, tipping me backwards, forcing me to land with a bounce on the mattress below.

"Is that what a good girl would have done, Annastasia?" I shrug, playing up the bratty role he has cast me in, and he shakes his head with a tisk.

His hand goes to his belt buckle, and in one motion that seems like magic, he has it unbuckled and slipped out of his belt loop with a whoosh. Given my history, that move from any other man might make me flinch, but no part of me fears this man. I trust him with my body, but more importantly, with my heart.

"Do you know what good girls get?" I nod my head, having heard it multiple times over the last few days. I feel my panties get wet at the sight of him reaching behind his head and pulling his T-shirt off in a move that screams masculinity. "I need your words, baby."

"They get to come."

"That's right. And often. So what do you think brats get?"

"I don't know," I whisper, transfixed as he pulls his pants and boxers down in one go, and his hard length springs up, bouncing off the trail of hair that dusts his lower abs.

"Brats get tied up and brought to the brink. Over. And. Over. Until I say they can come." That sounds like delicious torture, and I am salivating at the thought. "Now, do you think you've been a good girl, or do you think you have been a brat?" I shrug again, knowing he will take it as my response. He gives a low chuckle like that is exactly what he wanted. The sound sends electricity straight to my core. "Okay, Annastasia, you've clearly made your choice. Scoot up that bed and grab the headboard."

Walking around the bed to the headboard, he takes the belt still in his clenched fist then wraps it around my wrists and the spindles of the wrought iron frame. He tightens it enough to restrain, but not enough to cut into my circulation or be uncomfortable. I tell him as much when he asks, licking my lips at the engorged member leaking precum just beyond my reach.

"Your safe word is 'red'. 'Yellow' if you need a break. Got it?" I nod but verbally repeat it back to him, knowing it is important to test the words out loud. "Good. If you can't talk then you snap your fingers and I will stop everything and check in with you. Show me that you can snap." I do so immediately, the clear crack of friction sounding in the room. He smiles, pleased by my sudden obedience.

I am still fully clothed, held captive by his belt. He hasn't even touched me yet, but I am primed and feel like I could orgasm from a light breeze. Sensing this, he tilts his head, assessing me as his fist takes one long, slow stroke of his thick cock.

"You look a little worked up, Annastasia, so first I am going to fuck that pretty little mouth of yours, give you something to focus on besides coming at a hair trigger touch."

"Yes, please." That's all I get out before he is climbing on the bed, thighs bracketing me. His cock juts out of reach of my questing tongue. I want to lick that drop of precum, taste the saltiness before it falls and is wasted.

"God, it turns me on when you use your manners." It is a throwaway compliment because it turns him off when I don't use my manners, too. I am not sure if I could do something to turn this man off. "Open wide," he demands, and I do, moaning around the tip at the taste of him.

He is slowly thrusting in and out of the shallow cavern of my mouth, being careful not to overwhelm me all at once. But I want to be overwhelmed. He promised to fuck my face, and I want him buried in my throat. So, I do the only thing I can think of that may goad him on and I scrape my teeth along his shaft, causing him to freeze.

Just when I think I may have miscalculated his usual inclination towards pain, he says, "Oh Anna, I was trying to go easy on you, but if you want it rough, who am I to deny you?"

He grabs the headboard for leverage, fucking my face in earnest, each thrust penetrating deep into my throat. I relax my muscles there as best as I can. However, I cannot resist the reflex to swallow, inciting a string of muttered expletives growled out like sandpaper scraping stone. It is a heady feeling being the one to bring out this wild, primal side of someone usually so controlled. I am loving every minute of it.

It is not long before he is flooding me with his salty come, the essence of him overflowing from my spread lips as he continues to thrust through the last dregs of his orgasm. I would think he was spent. That he would need time to recover before he made good on his promise to edge me, but it seems that I thought wrong, because now that his own need for release is no longer riding him, he is free to take his time with me.

And take his time he does, over and over he builds me up just to back off until the point that I am sobbing. Within the first fifteen minutes, he had torn my dress off me with a promise to reimburse Caroline for her trouble. He then proceeded to use my panties as floss to apply delicious friction to my clit. When I thought he had forgotten his threat and was going to let me ride the wave over the edge, he stopped, backing away completely, watching as I writhed alone on the bed to the sight of him stroking his own cock nice and slow.

He then moved his attention to my nipples, having pulled my breast out of the cups of my lace bra while leaving it on. I am sure I made quite the lewd tableau. Tits out, panties sodden, restrained to the headboard, writhing in need. He would lap one nipple with the warm flat of his tongue and then blow on it until it was a hardened peak and repeat the action on its twin. Taking both between calloused fingers, he'd tug, making me moan and kick out from the stimulation.

All the while he talked—God how he talked—telling me every filthy thing he was doing to me as he did it, praising me for how well I was taking it. And when he finally decided I had had enough, he flipped me over, driving his shaft in from behind. his erratic thrusts at odds with the reverent way he stroked the lines of my tattoo. It wasn't long before I was soaking us both and he followed me soon after into the sweet bliss of release.

He pulled out of me slowly, and I could feel the combination of us leaking down my thighs. He stroked my hair with one hand, whispering sweet nothings to me as his other hand undid my bindings. Diligently, he rubbed the circulation back into my wrist and hands and left me for a moment only to prepare us a bath.

Returning, he scooped me up, carrying me over the threshold of the ensuite and lowered us both into the warm, scented water, having used the oils provided by the inn. He washed every inch of me, soothing muscles that I was unaware ached until right then. I don't think I have ever felt so relaxed and cared for, and most of all, loved as I did in this man's arms. *I am in love with this man,* is the last conscious thought I have before I drift off to dreams.

Bobby

I jolt awake, cold sweat dripping down my spine. I can't make out where I am, but I hear the banging against glass and a soft voice murmuring soothing words. I grasp onto that voice, allowing it to sweep away the bloody images staining my sight. I jerk again when a loud boom echoes through the air, shaking me to my core.

"It's just thunder, Bobby—only a storm. Can you hear the rain tapping on the glass?" the voice, Anna's voice, says. "Can you feel the cotton sheet under your palm? Tell me what you see." As the haze lifts, I begin to understand what she is doing. She is guiding me to ground myself in the here and now. It is a coping mechanism I learned in therapy; she must use it, too.

Once my vision clears, I see her standing at the edge of the bed, out of reach, "I see you in my T-shirt, standing too far from me." She exhales and takes a tentative step closer.

"Are you back with me?" she asks. At my nod, she closes the distance, wrapping me in her comforting embrace. "I didn't want to crowd you. Joanie says I tend to swing when I wake from a night terror." It guts me that she has to experience anything like this. "Want to tell me what this was about?" she asks in a soft voice, not demanding. I know she will accept whatever answer I give.

Do I want to tell her about the horrors that plague me in my dreams? Not particularly, but I am also so tired of managing them alone. Anna was brave with me that night by the creek laying her vulnerabilities bare for me to witness. It is only fair that I brave this with her, too.

Settling down on the mattress with her snuggled into my side, tracing lazy patterns on my chest, I tell her all of it. The names of ghosts that didn't make it home. The guilt I hold that I did. I tell her how loud noises in the dead of night, like thunder, morph into explosions in my mind. Through it all, she is there; those lazy circles traced on my chest soothing the ache from my heavy heart.

Chapter 29

ANNASTASIA

(Wednesday)

These last few days have been a dream. Since Bobby opened up to me about his time in the military, we have gotten even closer. Like a barrier between us has lifted. PTSD of any kind is a heavy cross to bear. I think we both find comfort knowing that this is a mental weight we can help each other carry.

I spend a couple of hours each day with Lucy, as she requested. For the first time, I feel what it may be like to have a mother's influence. The first couple of days, we just chatted over lunch, but today we are getting our hands dirty. The evenings always end in the comfort of Bobby's arms.

Lucy, concerned that her youngest child is lacking in proper dinnerware to entertain guests, suggested we go to a paint and sip day that the local pottery studio is holding. We get to choose from already bisque-fired pieces to paint, then the studio will glaze fire them for pickup at a later date. Caroline had the day off work today, so she is tagging along.

It is a 'trust the process' kind of endeavor. Some of the glazes look quite different in their raw form than they do in their final finish, but we have samples as guides. I hope mine turns out like I am imagining. I chose a mountain motif with a black sky with white speckles to represent stars; a reminder of the night Bobby and I spent sleeping under the stars in each other's arms. My face heats thinking of what else those stars witnessed that night. Caroline immediately clocks it.

"Someone is having impure thoughts," she sing-songs, painting dandelions on a ceramic wine chalice; a clear reminder that she remains the only one of us original bucket list creators not to have had the chance to partake in the libation. Apparently, when she told Bobby that she was fine with us going through it without her, she was unaware that there were any bottles left in existence. She has been slightly salty with me since.

She is sitting directly in front of me, so I take the opportunity to discreetly kick her in the shin, tilting my head towards Lucy and mouthing, "Stop."

"Ouch, bitch that hurt." She is clearly going to ignore my plea. "I am sure Lucy has heard it all before."

"Oh, yes and likely done it. I do have five children after all. Do you know how many practice rounds it took to end up with that number?"

I would rather a sinkhole open up beneath me and swallow me whole than answer that, but no need because she provides the answer herself. "The honest answer is never enough." She chuckles at our aghast expressions. "Honestly, you two, it is fine. I am all for a little girl chatter."

"Yeah well, it is different when it is referring to a person you grew from scratch, I am sure," I murmur, mortified.

"Fine, fine, let's change the subject," Lucy replies amicably, and I am relieved for all of two seconds until she asks, "Caroline, dear, I just love what you are going for. What made you choose dandelions?"

I try to communicate with my mind alone, to not rat us out. I still feel bad at partaking in something that cannot be replaced.

I either fail spectacularly or Caroline is in a cheeky mood because she carries on without missing a beat. "Well, I had a high school oath with certain parties to share a bottle of Mrs. Bianchi's dandelion wine; may she rest in peace. But I was under the impression that there wasn't any left after her passing. I have since come to realize that there was still a bottle. And they—the other parties in the oath—drank it without me. So, the closest I am ever going to get is to drink my regular old wine out of this dandelion cup." She ends the sad story with a pout, and I roll my eyes. *Laying it on extra thick aren't you, Care?*

"Oh, well here. I have some with me. You can try it right now. I had actually forgot they were in my wine cupboard from the funeral until Bobby asked me for one last week."

I sputter the sip of Cab I was drinking, causing it to go down the wrong pipe. Lucy lovingly rubs circles on my back as I chough and wheeze out, "So he didn't steal it?"

"Steal it? Bobby? No. If it were any of the others, they might have tried. I'll let you in on a little secret." Leaning in, she whispers, "My boys are not that stealthy. Why do you think they have spent so many nights in a holding cell? They always get caught." That causes a case of the giggles to erupt as she pours us new glasses of the dandelion wine. "You know, before you kids collected her dandelions, both of your mothers and I did, too," she says, and I am reminded that she was once best friends with my mother. Lucy was always one of the few around town to never utter a disparaging word toward her.

"You did?" I ask, wanting to glean any information I can about my mom.

"Yes, though back then she only paid us a dollar per basket. You kids made out. It is too bad that Ritchie, her son, didn't want to take up the mantle. Kids today could use something to keep them busy, even if it is only two days out of the year. Though he did give me the recipe. Said he had no use for it. Maybe come next spring, I'll try my hand at it."

"I think that would be a lovely idea," I say.

"I'll drink to that." Caroline raises her plastic cup, and we follow suit. "To Mrs. Bianchi. God grant her peace, and to carrying on a Boremanton tradition."

We clink cups and shout, "Here! Here!"

Caroline throws it back like it is a shot. "Oh, that is good. Fill me up, Mrs. Payne." Lucy laughs and obliges my boisterous friend.

We spend the next twenty minutes chatting, painting, and sipping on dandelion wine. When we are wrapping up, I send a text message to Joanie with a picture of our work.

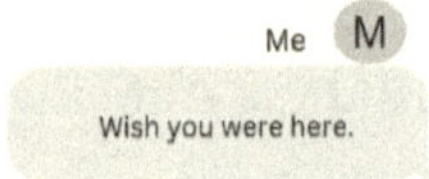

I get up to gather our items and place them in the designated spot our instructor set aside for us. My phone rings, and thinking that it is Joanie calling to reply to my picture, I don't even look at the caller ID.

"I know the colors look strange, but according to the samples, it should turn out just right."

"Um... Mrs. Adkins?" a deep voice, who is decidedly not Joanie, replies. "This is Sheriff Dobbs. Normally I would call your council to get in touch with you, but Ms. Montgomery's assistant said that she is in the Capitol for a deposition and won't be back until Friday. There has been an update in the case. Can you please come into the office?"

"Oh," I say, surprised. I look outside to see that the sun is shining. My car is parked right outside, but I decide that a walk could do me some good. "Yeah, I am actually not far. I can be there in ten minutes, give or take."

"Okay, see you soon." The call disconnects, and I stare at it for a second, an odd feeling settling around me.

"Who was that, dear?" Lucy asks.

"Um, the sheriff needs me to stop down for a bit. "

"Want us to go with you?" Caroline asks.

"No, you guys can go on. I don't know how long this will take. You don't have to wait on me."

"If you're sure," Lucy says with a maternal rub to my arm.

I tamp down on my emotions. "Yeah, I'm sure. It's a nice day. I am going to walk." We settle our bills and go our separate ways. For some reason, I can't shake the feeling that my life is about to be turned on its head. *Again.*

Luck is not on my side as I enter the station. Leanne is sitting at her post, and she is glaring daggers at me. I thought professionalism and the fact that she is at her job would stay her tongue for once, but of course I thought wrong.

"Do you really think this little thing you have going with Bobby is going to last?" she sneers.

I was having such a good day. I am not going to let her bring it down. I act as if she did not address me at all and say, "Sheriff Dobbs is expecting me."

"Payne boys don't do long distance. Look at how Max and Jess worked out."

"Can you please tell him I am here?"

"I don't—" Thankfully, whatever she was going to say is cut off when the door behind her opens to reveal Sheriff Dobbs.

"Oh, you're here, good. You can follow me." Thankful for the reprieve, I do so without a backward glance at Leanne. We head toward what I am beginning to think of as *my* interview room with as much time as I have spent there lately.

"Have a seat, dear." The soft quality in his tone is one I haven't heard in these last weeks. In fact, I haven't heard it since I was a scared sixteen-year-old girl who had just witnessed something gruesome. This tone makes me anxious. I know that I am not going to like what comes next.

"Remember how I told you that we had a few remains left to analyze." I nod my ascent and signal for him to continue. "Well, one of those is a full body we found out by that shed you warned us about." Any warmth that was pumping through my veins runs cold, and my vision swims. Blood rushes to my head as my anxiety ramps up, making it hard to hear his next words, but I focus my vision on his lips to watch them form. "It didn't follow the same pattern as the rest. There was no recent disturbance in the soil. The DNA did not match any listed in the body farm's records. I... I'm unsure how to say this tactfully."

"Rip it off like a bandage," I hear my own voice say, but don't recall permitting my mouth to move.

Before he says anything, I notice a locket in an evidence bag. It's covered in dirt and tarnished with age and neglect, but I would know it anywhere. Its twin is currently grasped in the palm of my hand. The chain I have used as a tool to ground myself for years suddenly feels heavy around my neck. It's turned into a noose choking off my words but one gets through anyway.

"Mom?" The question comes as a broken gasp. The sheriff nods, solemn in the face of the news

"Right, there is no easy way to say this so I will just come out with it. The body is that of Mary Monroe Adkins, and we suspect she was killed by your father Scott Gilbert Adkins. The cause of death was a rifle shot to the gut."

"You're sure? The locket it..." I swallow my mouth instantly dry, "the locket was on the body?" The twin to my own, it is a locket I've recalled in my dreams, hanging from her neck as she tucked me in on countless nights. I know if I were to open it, there would be a picture of a three-year-old pigtailed version of myself staring back at me.

"Yes, the locket was with the remains. When I saw it, I thought it looked familiar." He gestures to my firm grip on my own locket. "When the labs didn't match the others, they did some soil testing to determine a time of death, which placed it close to when everyone thought your mother left. But more conclusively," he sets an open file down in front of me with X-rays of teeth, "these are your mother's dental records. They are a match. It's why I waited a few days to contact you. I didn't want to put you through a DNA test if we didn't have to. The state of West Virginia only requires dentists to keep records for ten years after the last visit of an adult patient. There was no guarantee they would have them, but sometimes in these small towns, offices aren't too quick to get rid of old files. Not having a surplus of patients doesn't make clearing files a priority. Doc Jameson still had her records on file."

A thousand sneered whispers run through my memory. Everything from, *"That girl ain't right, not even her mother loved her,"* to, *"Bet she'll turn tramp just like her ma,"* whirl around inside my mind.

Meek as a lamb, I say, "She didn't leave me?"

"No, Anna, she didn't leave you."

Shaking, I continue, "And you're certain it was my pa?"

"Yes, the bullet we found lodged in her spine." *Oh God I'm going to be sick.* "It matched one of the rifles in the shed. I am sorry, Anna." He places his hand on top of mine, a move meant to be comforting, but it makes me feel claustrophobic right now. *I can't breathe. I gotta get out of here.*

"I have to go. Am I allowed to go?" Anxiety is washing over me in the form of a cold sweat, and pins and needles start creeping up my arm, starting at my fingertips

"Yes, but—" I don't wait to hear the condition that would make me have to stay in this room a second longer. I run for the door. Slamming it open, I take off for the lobby.

I think I hear Deputy Jones call after me, but it is muffled and faraway. I don't stop. *Can't stop.*

I make it to the lobby, but Leanne is waiting there for me, blocking the exit. Blocking my way out of this nightmare. "What is wrong with you? God, you look pathetic. Ryan is right, you know. Once the novelty of fucking the crazy slut wears off, Bobby is gonna drop you like yesterday's news."

All I see is red as I let out an unholy screech and make a mad leap at her. *If she wants to see crazy, I will fucking show her crazy.*

Mid-air, a strong arm wraps around my stomach, halting me by mere inches from scratching out Leanne's stupid eyes. "Whoa there, wild cat. Payne will kill me if I let you go down for aggravated assault."

"Get that crazy bitch away from me," Leanne shouts.

"Why don't you just get out of her fucking way and leave her alone. Maybe then she wouldn't want to rip your face off." It is strange that Jones is defending me. He has been nothing but apathetic at best to me since I arrived, but I am not going to fight it, or him.

"Get her out of the way. I want to leave," I plead.

"Bobby is on his way. I'll let you go with him. Leanne, take a walk." She huffs but storms behind her desk, opening the door directly behind her station and slamming it shut behind her.

"Okay, I'm gonna put you down. You can sit and cool down til' Bobby gets here."

He makes the mistake of thinking I am one to obey orders—*well outside of the bedroom; and even then, only if Bobby is the one giving them*—and turns his back to me for a split second to check his phone. I take the opportunity to run for the door, and I don't stop until I am in my car driving away.

Bobby

Anna and my mom are out having girl time. For some reason, they are being very hush-hush about what that entails. For the last two days, they have stayed at the house for lunch. I've spent the time split between utilizing my home gym and checking in with my therapist. This suspension is going smoothly. I know it is because I am distracting myself with the newness of this thing with Anna, but sooner rather than later, she will be leaving, and I don't know what my status with the force is going to be after their decision on Friday. I am still trying to hold onto some routine.

The first stretch when she leaves is going to be the hardest. I don't know if you can feel withdrawal from the absence of a person, but I think it is going to be something like that. We have had long talks on what this looks like for the foreseeable future. It is going to be a lot of scheduling over video calls across different time zones. *Good thing, I thrive with a schedule.* I am optimistic that with work and effort, we can get through the distance portion of our relationship and make it to the other side; when she is here full-time in my arms.

A crumpled-up napkin hits me right between my eyes and Tommy's smug face lets me know which of my brothers is the responsible party. Instead of a workout, my brothers and I offered to help my father out with some repairs around the house. We had just taken a break for lunch, but it seems I was in my head and not paying attention to the conversation thread.

"You back from daydreaming about Anna?" Tommy asks

"I wasn't daydreaming about her. Just going over logistics in my head."

"Logistics of what?"

"How this will work when she is gone."

"That's depressing thinking. It seems like you are borrowing trouble. She is here now. Let that be tomorrow's problem," Patrick says like someone who has never followed through on a plan a day in his life. It is amazing he keeps his work schedule straight.

"No, he is right. They are gonna be over three thousand miles apart and three separate time zones. They have to have a plan if it is going to work. Especially since she probably burned through a lot of PTO for this little trip," Johnny, for once, the serious voice of reason, chimes in.

"Shit, I hadn't thought about that. How is she going to keep an eye on the project if she can't get time off to check in?"

"Well, that part is easy—she has us here to be her eyes and ears and muscle if she needs it," Tommy states as if it is a forgone conclusion that they would automatically take on that workload without even being asked.

My other brothers nod their agreement, and for the first time in a while, I think brothers aren't so bad after all.

We get back to work lining the hole we dug with pavers and extending them out to a little patio. Dad saw Mom looking at this fire pit set up on Pinterest, said it would make her smile to have a place for us to gather round the fire making smores and shooting the shit. I can see it; I can see sitting on one of the little benches with Anna roasting marshmallows over an open flame, watching her ingrain herself even more into the fabric of this family. One day, maybe a kid or two who look like her running around as the adults tell tales of the good ole' days. *I can see us building a life here—together.*

"So, you are in it, right? This is it?" Patrick asks, a strange tone to the question. Almost vulnerable.

"Yeah, this is it. I love her—think I always have."

"But when did you know, like for sure, that this was it?"

"When I heard her laugh," I say without needing any time to respond. "All I could do was think of ways to make her do it again. To see her so happy and find the blueprint to repeat it forever. That is when I knew."

My father passes by with a wheelbarrow full of sand to tamp between the pavers. He stops and looks at me, proud in a way I have never seen before. "That about sums it up, my boy. When what makes you happy is making them happy, that is when you know."

On the tail of that sage advice, my phone rings and the name across the ID reads 'Jones'. *What in the hell could he be calling me for?*

I connect to the call and don't even get to offer a greeting before Jones speaks. "Payne you need to get to the station, *now*. Your girl needs you." I drop the paver I am holding, and it almost lands on Patrick's foot.

"What the fuck Bo—" He cuts off abruptly when he gets a look at me. I feel like all the life force has drained out of me. I must look it too as all my brothers go silent—eyes on me.

"What is going on?" I ask, desperate for any crumb of information.

"I can't get into it on the phone. Just trust me, get here." The line goes dead, and I don't waste time with goodbyes.

I get to the station in record time and fling open the door. Everything is in absolute bedlam: Leanne is crying, Jones is reprimanding Dobbs, and Anna is nowhere in sight.

"Payne, you are suspended. You can't be here," Dobbs says, the first of the trio to notice me.

"I called him. I can't believe you didn't," Jones interjects.

"He is on suspension."

"So what? You didn't have to tell him about the case, just that he needed to be here for his girl."

"I thought he would be outside waiting for her. He was the last time."

"Are you going senile, old man? You can't drop a bomb like that on someone without them having anyone there for support. You shouldn't have assumed, especially with someone with PTSD. She literally passed out from a panic attack less than three weeks ago, and that was just from her own memories." I watch them volley back and forth, and I know I am missing crucial information. "Leanne, stop your crying. Didn't you hear the sheriff? You are done here."

"Bobby, please, I didn't know. I wouldn't have started with her if I knew the news she just heard. I'll apologize, whatever it takes. I can't lose this job," Leanne sobs. *What in the hell is happening right now?*

"Leanne," Dobbs says, exasperated, "I already told you that it doesn't matter if someone has had bad news or not. You cannot talk to people who walk through that door like you did. This is a professional position, and it is not the first time that you have not acted professionally. Please go."

"Fine, whatever. I am going to call HR and fight this." She storms past me and out the door, and I am even more confused than ever.

"Will someone tell me what the fuck is going on, and where the hell my woman is?"

"Anna left ten minutes ago, and as for what upset her, that is classified, and you're on suspension," Dobbs insists. I have never had the urge to hit a superior, but I do now. I have a white-knuckle grip on my keys, hoping the bite of metal to my skin will help reign in some of the simmering rage that is building at being left in the dark.

"That part of the case is closed, and when he finds her, he is going to find out anyway. Hang the rules, old man." That Jones is the voice of reason here just shows what bizarro dimension I've stepped into. "Long story short, we found a body, but it wasn't one from the body farm. Dobbs had his suspicions, followed the lead, and got dental records. It was Anna's mom, man. Her old man killed her and buried her by that rundown shed." The news hits me in the gut like a physical blow.

He continues, "Leanne being the harpy she is, chose the worst time to sharpen her claws. Your girl almost ripped her face off, but I intervened, took my eyes off her for one second to text you, and she slipped out the door."

I want to rage and shout and point fingers, but I don't do any of that. I let the calm before a mission settle into my bones, I text my brothers tell them to spread out and look for any signs of Anna, and I step out the door. I have one objective: to find my woman, and I won't rest until she is in my arms.

The sun is setting when I find her, hazy pinks and vivid oranges paint-ing her in a golden glow. The gate at the bottom of the water tower is wide open, the padlock lying uselessly on the ground. I notice a hairpin sticking out of its locking mechanism. I am relieved that I found her, that she is within my sight, but all the things that could have gone wrong—climbing this thing in the state she is in—run through my mind. I take a steadying breath, reminding myself she doesn't need a reprimand right now. *She just needs me.*

I start the long climb and think of what the first thing I need to say to her is. What comes out of my mouth is, "I see you can still pick a lock."

"I had a good teacher," she says, staring off into the distance. I taught her when we were kids, hand-me-down knowledge that had trickled down to me from my brothers. I exhale some of the tension I had been holding. At least she is responsive.

"How did you find me?" she asks, even-toned, still staring at the horizon straight ahead. I take the seat next to her, letting my shoulder graze against hers but not making any other move to touch her. This is about what she needs from me, not the other way around.

"It was the last thing on the list," I say with a shrug, trying to ignore the weight of prophecy crossing off the last item brings. As kids, we wrote that list as our goodbye letter to Borementon. Now that it is complete, does that mean this is goodbye?

"She never left me." It isn't a question, just a declaration, but it comes out timid and meek as she fiddles with her locket.

"No, she didn't."

"But she still isn't coming back." Her voice breaks on the last word, turning the one-syllable word into two, and my heart breaks for her as two twin tears wind their way down her cheeks.

"No, she's not." A sob breaks free from her and that is when she turns her head to face me.

"I'm sorry," she says. Her voice is strained, and I know what she is apologizing for even before she tells me.

"I can't do it. I can't build a life here on the ashes of hers."

All I can say is, "I know."

Because I do. I know that she would be overrun with the ghosts of her past. The light of hope that maybe her mom may come back is now extinguished, leaving her nothing to cling to but the darkness of the abuse at the hands of her father. People talk, and they will talk about this. She'll hear it whispered from the church ladies on Sundays or boldly thrown in her face by the likes of Leanne and her crew. She will die a little more inside, each and every time. No, she can't build a life here. It will make her miserable. And if it is my life's mission to make her happy, I can't tie her down to a place, to a life that brings her so much pain. So, I will have to let her go. Tomorrow.

But for today, I ask, "Can I hold you?"

"Please." is her reply. So I do.

I hold her 'til the sun sets and the stars light the sky, and after we've climbed down and replaced the lock, as I carry her to my truck, leaving her rental a problem for another day. I hold her hand the whole way home, where I hold her tight through the night. And in the early rays of morning when we've gone as far as someone without a ticket can, I hold her—clinging to her one last time, as if I can sear the feel of her into my skin. Then I let her go.

Chapter 30

BOBBY

(Thursday)

I'm drunk. I put the love of my life on a plane to the other side of the country, never to return less than two hours ago, and I am drunk. She isn't even at her destination yet, and I am lying on my floor, counting the rotations of the fan blades, drinking moonshine straight from the jug. I am so drunk that I don't even flinch when I hear the telltale rattle of my lock being picked, or when Johnny looms over me, looking down on me both figuratively and physically. He kicks the bottle out of my hand. At that, I flinch.

"What is happening here?" he asks, waving a hand and referring to the state of my living room—*trashed*—or maybe to the state he has found me in, *also trashed*. "Where is Anna? You had us looking all over town for her. Without telling us why, mind you."

All I do, all I *can* do is mumble incoherently in response,

"Jesus man, you're a fucking mess."

More incoherent mumbles spill over and out of my lips. This time in agreement.

I jackhammer straight up, sputtering, dripping wet, and I am shaking. My brother is standing before me holding a now empty bucket, its frigid contents now soaking into my clothes and dripping from me to a puddle on my floor.

"Fuck!"

"Good. Now you are at least making sense. Now I am going to brew your coffee and put it in your one mug. You are going to sober up and tell me what the fuck is going on here," he says, leaving me in a puddle on my living room floor.

"I have two mugs now," I pout, trying to make a point, but just ending up upsetting myself further. She isn't here to use her mug; it will sit there lonely and useless in the cupboard. Like me sitting on this floor.

Three cups of coffee, two glasses of water—*ingested not worn*—and one slap to the face later, I can articulate to my brother exactly what happened. I tell him everything from the scene I stumbled upon at the station, to finding her at the water tower, to holding her through the night as she fell apart, sobbing in my arms. And finally, to watching her walk away from me at the airport gate... forever.

He doesn't interrupt. He doesn't interject. He lets me get everything out until I have nothing left. *I have nothing left.*

"Did you tell her that you love her?" is the first thing that he asks me.

"No," I reply honestly

"Well, why the hell not?"

"It wouldn't be fair to burden her with my feelings when there is no hope that anything will come of it."

"Bullshit," he spits

"What?"

"I said that is bullshit. Just hours ago, you were making plans. She was still going to be in Vegas then too, but you were putting in the work. What happened to that?"

"That was when she could still see building a life here with me. But I can't make her do that. This place would kill her slowly. It is too much to ask."

"Okay, then don't build your life here. Go to her."

"I can't just up and move across the country. I have responsibilities. A, a job—a life here."

"Do you?" I think he is doing this only to be a dick at this point, so I don't dignify that with a response. I just glare. "No, really, do you have a life here?"

"Mom and Dad are here. You guys are here," I say in my defense.

"Yeah, and we were here for the eight years you played army soldier too, and we will still be here for you no matter where you physically are." When I don't reply, he continues, "Look around, Bobby. Where is this life you have here? You live in this barren apartment with no sign of a personality or even a picture on the wall. Hell, up until three days ago, you only had one mug. That is not the sign of a well-adjusted functioning person, Bobby."

"Do you even like being a deputy? Or did you fall into the first job that was wrapped up for you in a neat little bow? Did you take it because it offered you the routine and structure that you were accustomed to? Is breaking up bar fights and issuing jaywalking citations, and coming home to these sad, lifeless walls, really what you want to do with the rest of your life?" he questions, gesturing to my plain walls and bare bones living room.

"If you ask me, you've just been going through the motions, stuck in a holding pattern. I have seen you truly live for the first time in years this past week. Are you really going to throw it all away? For what?"

I look around my apartment. Really look at it, through his eyes as he described it, and he is fucking right. "What the fuck am I doing here?"

"That's what the fuck I'm saying!"

"Do me a favor?" I ask, digging through my wallet and throwing him my credit card. "Find me the first flight to Vegas." I grab my keys, but standing up too quickly still makes my head swim. I turn to him and toss him my keys too. "And drive me to the sheriff's office."

Leanne's desk sits empty, so I rapid fire tap the bell that says ring for service.

"Hold yer horses, I'm coming," says Jones, opening the door to the bullpen and stepping into the lobby. "Payne? Ain't your meeting tomorrow? Shit, is Anna okay?"

"Yes, it is, and no, she isn't, but I need to speak with Sheriff Dobbs. Is he in?" I need to be quick. I fly out of Charleston in two and a half hours, and it takes an hour to drive there.

"Yeah one sec." He disappears down the corridor, reemerging moments later with the sheriff in tow.

"Son, you aren't supposed to be here until tomorrow," the sheriff says with a sigh. He looks like he has aged ten years in a day. "I know that everything got all fouled up yesterday, but the terms of your suspension—"

"Are permanent," I interrupt. "Effective immediately, I resign."

"Now hold on a moment, if this is about how things were handled yesterday—"

"No. I mean, they were absolutely mishandled, but that isn't what this is about. I am moving. Well, hopefully. If I didn't fuck this all up."

"Moving where?"

"Wherever Anna wants to live. At the moment, Las Vegas." A look of understanding crosses his features and he nods.

"Well, alright, but what about your adjudication? You were going to be informed tomorrow of your terms. Eighty hours of community service to have your record expunged."

"Can we negotiate a buy-out of hours in place of the community service? The equivalent of eighty hours of my gross pay instead? I will cut you a check right now."

"That is almost two grand."

"It is one $1712 and eighty cents to be exact, but if it gets me out of here right now, I will round up."

"Let me get Judge Hershal on the line. If he agrees to it, then it's fine by me."

Luckily, the judge was available and agreeable. Before the ink is dry on the check, I am out the door and in my brother's truck, rushing towards the airport.

It has been twelve of the longest hours of my life since I held Anna in my arms, and now the GPS is saying I am ten minutes away from her apartment. I just hope I am not twelve hours too late. My palms are sweaty as I count out my taxi fare and tip the driver. I check my phone and make sure I have the right unit, do a quick breathing exercise to ground myself in this moment, then I climb the stairs two at a time and ring the buzzer at the door.

"We don't want any," Joanie's states, voice muffled through the door

"Joanie, listen, it's me, Bobby. I'm not selling anything."

"I know who you are, and I told you we don't want any. By that, I mean we don't want any man who would put my best friend on a cross-country flight *alone* after her whole understanding of the world was turned upside down. Go. Home."

She is making fair points, really, but she doesn't get it. Without Anna, I have no home. So, I try again. "Joanie, please just let me talk to her. I had a momentary lapse in sanity. I wasn't thinking straight. I thought I was doing right by her by not tying her to a place that'll just break her heart. I was trying to preserve it, I swear, not break it more. If after hearing me out, she wants me to leave, I'll go."

"Joanie let him in," comes the tired, timid voice of the woman I love, and I am not leaving here 'til she knows that I love her.

The door opens, and Joanie is staring daggers at me; if looks could kill, I'd be a dead man. But I can't blame her for protecting her sister, because blood or not, they are exactly that. "I'm watching you."

Exasperated Anna rounds the corner. "Leave him alone, Joanie. He didn't do anything wrong. He only did what I asked." She grabs my hand, leads me through a cozy-looking living room with way too many throw pillows, and into a hallway that spits at the end with three doors. Opening the one on the left, I get my first glimpse into a space that is all hers.

The walls are painted a sage green, and there are pictures of her, Joanie, and some others framed gallery-style on the wall opposite the bed. It is a shrine to the timeline of their friendship, starting in college and ending with a snapshot that had to be from earlier this year. On these four little walls, she has packed more personality than exists in my whole apartment back east.

She sits on her bed holding a pillow to her chest as if she needs a physical shield for this conversation, and that kills me a little inside. She had been so open and vulnerable with me this whole time, and to see her close up now is giving me anxiety.

I decide the only way out is through, and as she likes to say, I rip it off like a bandage and the words, "I love you," spill from my lips.

At the same time, she asks, "Why are you here?"

To avoid her asking me to repeat myself, I tell her again, this time stronger. "I love you. I am in love with you, and I thought momentarily that if I told you that it would be a burden to you, especially on the back of the news you just got."

She goes to speak, but I hold up my hand, wanting, *no, needing,* to get this all out in the open. "I haven't lived half the life I have in the past twelve years without you than I have in the last two weeks with you. I gave you my rock long before I even knew what it was to give. Like a penguin, we only have one rock to give, and mine is yours. I know that you can't build the life you planned back in West Virginia, and that's fine. We can build it here, or if you really are tired of Las Vegas, we can build it anywhere, because anywhere is home when I'm with you."

She smiles. It's small, but it is the first of hers I've seen in over twenty-four hours, and says, "I got lost a little there in the middle, but I love you too. I am in love with you, but I can't ask you to leave your family, your job, just to be with me."

"I already quit, and my family will be my family no matter where I live. They want me to be happy, and I am happiest when I am getting to make you happy."

"You would really move here? Or anywhere else I want to go?"

"Annastasia, I would live in a van if I got to wake up next to you every morning."

"Okay."

"Okay?" I ask, needing the clarification.

"I love you, Bobby Payne."

Spurred on by the words I thought I would never hear slip through her lips without a 'but' trailing behind them, I pick her up and spin her around. That raucous laughter, that sound that soothes my soul, bubbles out of her, effervescent and light. I vow to spend the rest of my life doing whatever I can to hear that sound forever.

Annastasia

As my feet touch the ground, I stare into the bloodshot eyes of the man I love. *He has been crying.* I know because my eyes must mirror his. When I left, I was so focused on my pain and what I needed in the moment. To put as many miles between me and Borementon as possible. I didn't stop to think what that could mean—would mean for us.

This wonderful man held me together as a tidal wave of grief swept me away, and never once thought to insert himself into the equation. He made it his mission to make me happy, even at his own expense. It wasn't until I was in the arms of my best friend, explaining the tempest of emotions I had been through in less than twenty-four hours, that it hit me. That my loss was compounded. My mother and Bobby, I thought, were lost to me forever in one devastating blow.

So, I did what I always do when grief over Bobby Payne consumes me. I read his letters, starting with the unopened one, I swiped from his room. It is sitting face up on my vanity now. If we are really going to do this, I don't want anything hanging over us anymore. All the ghosts are getting exorcised right now.

I sit him down on my bed, staring directly into the hazel eyes that star in all my favorite dreams and confess, "I have something you need to see before you choose to really stick it out with me."

"It's a little late for that now, Anna. Didn't you hear? I already gave you my rock."

"Yes, I did, and you'll have to explain that to me at some point, but I need you to see this." I grab the letter that until last week lived on a shelf in his childhood bedroom and hand it to him.

"Where did you get this?" he asks, confused.

I tell him about how I saw it in his room and couldn't leave it behind. Couldn't stand to leave it unread. Then I hand him the journal I was writing in right before he came knocking on my doorstep. His eyes scan the page, clarity seeping in with each word.

"You were answering my letter?"

I flip the pages of the notebook back and then lift the duvet up to grab a box from under my bed. I hand it to him. Opening it, he finds several more notebooks, each with letters sticking out of them like bookmarks.

"I answered all of your letters." I flip through the pages of one of the earlier notebooks and pick out the letter he sent me right before he left for bootcamp. "In this one, you asked me if I was mad at you for what you said about him." I can't bring myself to call that man my father, and Bobby doesn't need the clarification. "I wasn't. I couldn't be mad at you for telling the truth. I had a breakthrough that day. I hadn't spoken in months—the words would shrivel and die in my throat, but that day I needed to tell someone, even if I couldn't tell you how I felt about him. About what he did. So I spoke about it in a group. It was a real turning point in my healing."

"I already told you why I never wrote you back. I thought you would be better off without me, and you already told me why you joined the Army in the first place—because you didn't think you were good enough for me. We both do everything that we think will make the other happy, but we forget the most important thing."

"What's that?" he asks, stroking the words on the page like they are a puzzle piece he has been missing for years, unable to complete the full picture without them.

"We forget to ask. We forget to talk it out, to get on the same page, even if we have to fight it out." He sits there for a moment, allowing that to really sink in.

Grabbing my hand and rubbing soothing circles across my knuckles, he takes the first step and asks, "Annastasia, what would make you happy?"

My answer is immediate. "I want to build a life together with you. I love you, Bobby Payne."

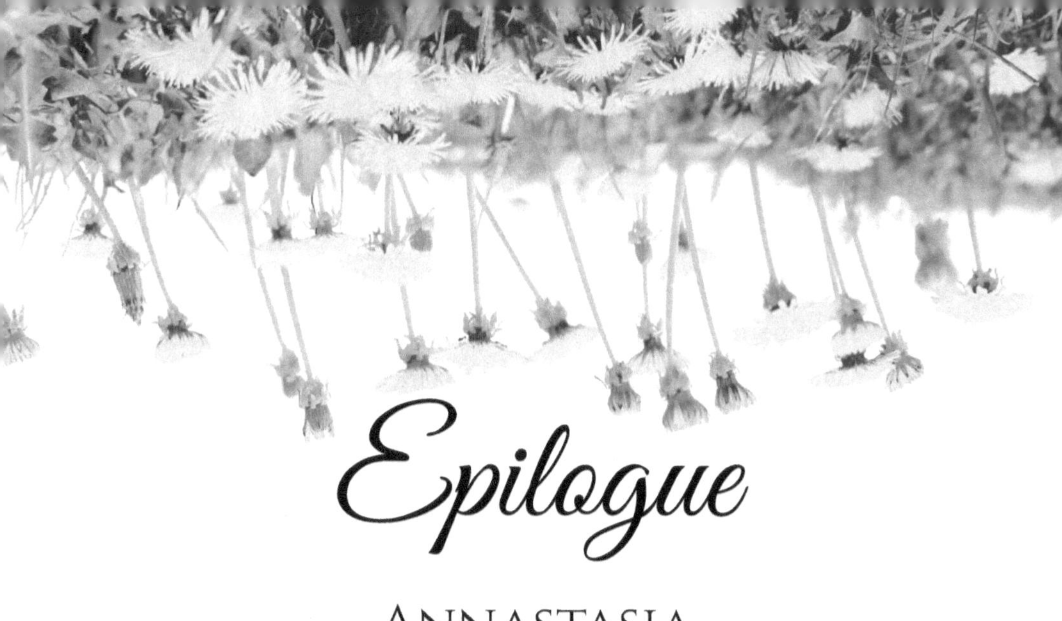

Epilogue

ANNASTASIA

(Ten months later...)

Ladies and gentlemen, it is my great honor as a representative of West Virginia Land Trust to call upon Annastasia Payne to cut the ceremonial ribbon marking the official opening of The Mary Monroe Memorial Wildlife Preserve, to be known going forward as Wolf Haven."

I am shaking, but a squeeze to my left hand, tracing our wedding band from my husband—*still getting used to that*—and one on my right hand from my best friend, *no, my sister,* grounds me in the moment. I take a deep breath of mountain air and walk to the temporary podium placed at the start of what used to be my driveway but is now the entrance to Wolf Haven. Taking the comically large shears from Jordan, the representative at West Virginia Land Trust that Diane connected me with months ago, I thank them. They have been an invaluable asset in this endeavor, and I don't know what I would have done with the land without their guidance.

Looking out at the gathered audience of familiar faces, including my family—*still getting used to that, too*—and friends who have come to support me, I feel at peace. This is an ending of sorts. My turbulent legacy with this land stops here. From this day forth, it will be the safe haven for wildlife that it could never be for me, and a preservation for the nature that makes this state 'Wild and Wonderful'. No machinations from any big-shot developer can change that now. It takes both hands to open the shears, and with a *snick* the ribbon falls to the ground. The audience bursts with raucous applause, with the occasional hoot or holler courtesy of my brothers-in-law.

We make our way up to where the house once stood. In its place, both a pavilion and playground made of reclaimed wood sit next to a man-made pond approved by West Virginia's rigorous conservation standards. It won't provide the woodland retreat I once had planned to run, but it will provide a recreational area for the town to use while the rest of the acreage is now officially posted land, safe from poachers of all sorts.

I leave the revelers to their reception as I make my way to the grotto. It sits in place of the shack that unknowingly marked my mother's grave for years. We had a plaque placed to enshrine her memory earlier today before half the town came to join in the fanfare. Only those I count closest, *and God, how that number has grown,* stood with me as I spread my mother's ashes in the butterfly garden I am now staring at. We planted it in her honor. Diane made sure that I was permitted to do so and that no red tape would stop me from doing this for my mother. The woman half the town scorned for over two decades as a horrible mother and a whore. She was neither of those things, and at least now they know.

A shadow blocks the sun, and I look up to find Joanie staring down at me before she takes a seat on my left. "Are you okay?"

Am I? I watch some butterflies dancing in the breeze among the wildflowers. I respond, "Yeah, I think I am. Are you sure you aren't coming back to Pennsylvania with us tomorrow?"

With the money from Bobby and my savings, added to Joanie's initial investment and another significant investment from Max, we found a property just outside of the Poconos in Pennsylvania that will make a great retreat. We are also looking into adding clinical staff to help run special retreats for people like me and Bobby who suffer with varying levels of PTSD, but we are a ways off from that. We broke ground last week and are living in a trailer until our adjacent farmhouse with a wrap-around porch is finished.

"What, and third wheel your literal honeymoon phase? No, thank you," she jokes.

Our lease in Vegas ended last month. As my last hurrah as a resident of Las Vegas, I shed the last connection I had with my father—my last name. Bobby and I were married by Elvis in front of our family and friends. Joanie stood as my maid of honor, and Caroline was my bridesmaid. Bobby's brothers played the most intense game of rock, paper, scissors I have ever witnessed to see who got to stand as best man, but they all took up at his side as groomsmen. Bobby's father walked me down the aisle, and I actually wore Lucy's dress. John, the usually jovial man, shed a tear when he saw me in it. It was perfect.

"Besides, it will be a year and a half at least until you are up and ready for events. What will I do with myself in Podunk, Pennsylvania until then?" she jests, but secretly, I think the small-town life is growing on her.

"Our lease is up, and we didn't renew it. Where are you going to stay 'til then?"

"Actually, I am only going back to put my stuff in storage. I wanted to wait until all this was settled to tell you, but I signed on with a cruise ship for the next year. While you build, I think it is time for my solo adventure, don't you?"

"I will always have room for you, Joanie. You know that, right?"

"Yes, I do, but I am taking a page out of your book and facing this new chapter alone, at least for a bit. I will be back in a year, ready to run your events, so everything is shipshape." I groan at her pun but accept that for whatever reason, she seems to need this, and I will support her. "And who knows? When I get back you may even have a niece or nephew on the way for me to focus my attention on."

"Let's not get ahead of ourselves. I am still getting used to being some-one's wife."

"Not someone's wife," the deep baritone of my husband joins the con-versation, and I can't help the sappy smile that comes to my face. "*My* wife." He leans down to place a kiss on top of my head.

Joanie groans, "With that, I am going to go see if Lucy has any more of that dandelion wine. If I am going to be subjected to something so sweet, it might as well come with a buzz." She leaves us alone with no one but the butterflies to witness the smacking kiss my husband pulls me into.

"She's sure about not staying with us until construction is complete?" he asks, watching her retreat as he releases me.

"She says she is. She is going to go on an adventure," I sigh.

"She is still adjusting to the new normal. Maybe she needs the change." I don't like that he is being practical, so I pout. He instantly flicks my lower lip with his calloused thumb, chuckling at my sour disposition. "She is always going to be your family, Anna, no matter how many miles separate you." I nod because I know he is right. "I spoke with Sheriff Dobbs. Still no solid leads on the case."

I shrug, not really caring either way. When the case was downgraded to theft, the scene of the crime shifted from my property to the university. As far as I am concerned, it is their problem now. With the only guilty party in my mother's case already long dead, the further investigation didn't tie up any of the work we were doing to convert the land to a preserve. That is the only interest I still hold in any of it whatsoever.

"So what's the plan? Are we staying with my parents, or is it too much? Do you want to go home?" It is about a seven-hour drive to our new living arrangement and he would make it if I said I wanted to; he is serious when it comes to whatever makes me happy.

I take his hand and kiss his palm and tell him, echoing his own words back to him, "Don't you know by now, Bobby Payne? Home is wherever I'm with you."

Acknowledgements

There are so many people who had a hand in the making of *Unearthed*. First and foremost, I would like to thank my mother who has always been my biggest cheerleader and well of encouragement. My only regret is that she will not be able to read this for herself, but I hope that I have made her proud.

I need to acknowledge my partner in crime and best friend, C.L. Leigh, who a little over a year ago, decided to go on this journey with me. She has been my sounding board and creative collaborator since day one. Any mentions of the fictional town of Aberville, Karlie's Konfectionery, and the fictional hockey team of the West Virginia Timberwolves are her intellectual property that she has allowed me to reference. She will be publishing her own series that shares a universe with *Unearthed*, and there will be some crossover.

Thank you to Westmoreland Writers Wolf Pack for helping to keep me accountable and on track with my word count and for offering endless support. I especially want to thank them for giving me a purpose when I felt lost. I am so glad to have found a group as supportive as you.

To the Wings and Words community, thank you for always supporting indie authors and being a place where readers can feel safe and accepted. The community that you have built is amazing. I am lucky to now count many of you as friends. Thank you to all in the community who volunteered to be my alpha and ARC Readers. Your time and feedback are priceless and appreciated. To Beth and Izzy, thank you for all you do for the community and for being so kind and generous with your time.

A special thank you to my editors, Wendy Miller-Norris and Rebecca|The Proof Fairy, who have helped me shape Unearthed into what you see today. Thank you for your support and expertise. I will forever sing your praises.

To all the indie authors that I love, it is you who inspired me to pursue this dream. Especially Chelsey Ann Tompkins, Ali Evers, and JJ Hynd. Thank you for being true inspirations and for all the time you have taken to provide advice and motivation. Thank you for blazing the trail and lighting the way for those who follow your example.

Thank you to my family and friends. Thank you for being there for me, especially this last year, as it has been one of my toughest. Thank you for the hugs and the texts, and for being listening ears on phone calls. Thank you for listening to me talk through my ideas and always asking me how my story is coming. I love you all and am forever grateful to have you in my life.

Finally, thank you, dear reader, for taking a chance on this story, and for taking a chance on me. Thank you for reading *Unearthed.*

About the author

Katie S. Scofield grew up in the Greater Pittsburgh area. Having graduated from college with a degree in Studio Arts, she has always found an escape through creative pursuits. Writing has always been a source of self-expression, and with the encouragement of those close to her, she has decided to share that passion with the world. She enjoys writing characters with complex backgrounds who, despite their flaws, find strength in a building community of found family. Katie dabbles in multi-genre fiction writing, and as a self-confessed mood reader, she is hard-pressed to be pinned to one genre.

Instagram: @katieandgroot

Tiktok: @katieandgroot

https://purplegiraffeprint.com/katie-s-scofield-author